ETHIC II

BY

ASHLEY ANTOINETTE

Ashley Antoinette Inc.
P.O. Box 181048
Utica, MI 48318

ISBN: 978-1-732-83130-8

Trade Paperback Printing October 2018
Printed in the United States of America

Distributed by Ashley Antoinette Inc.
Submit Wholesale Orders to:
owl.aac@gmail.com

DEDICATION

This book is dedicated to Margo Beverly White. My M-Go. I spent countless hours in your chair, as a young girl. Getting pressed, getting permed, getting game from you. You were the first one to read the first book JaQuavis and I ever wrote. You were the first one to tell me JaQuavis would be my husband. You styled my hair on my wedding day and gave me words of wisdom that have carried me through my darkest days. I will never forget you. I love you. May you rest in peace. Your name will forever live on in the pages of this book. I was blessed to have known you.

SPECIAL ACKNOWLEDGEMENTS

To Tanisha Hunt, a loyal fan of Ethic.
May you forever rest in peace.
-xoxo-
Ashley Antoinette

Thank you to Ashley Jackson for putting eyes on this series
before it was released. You allowed me to pick your brain
and ask you a million questions about my development
of these characters. Your test read helped me more
than you know. I appreciate you.
-xoxo-

LETTER TO THE FANS

My gosh! Ladies! Gentlemen! Hey, y'all! Who would have fucking thought little, old me would be 13 novels into this Ashley Antoinette thing? There would be no me without each and every one of you. When I created Ethic's character, I never could have imagined he would have this type of impact on women. He's so profound and I just enjoy giving him to all of you. As I pen his story, I feel this black man so potently I forget that he's not real. I have lived with Ethic in my head for 10 years and I'm so happy that you connect with my thoughts. This story just burns inside me; and just like you couldn't wait to read it, I was anxious to let it bleed out. Thank you so much for connecting to my work, for connecting to Ethic, and continuing to uplift, support, and encourage me. This is my art. This is my imprint on the world and no matter if it reaches one person or a million, as long as y'all feel it, I am satisfied. I'm so appreciative and honored that you trust me enough to allow me into your hearts, minds, and souls with this series. This one feels like more than just a book to me. I believe it feels like more than a book to you as well. It feels like a reflection of somebody's love somewhere in the world, and if there is no reality that looks like this, thank you for allowing me to create the fantasy. Now, y'all don't get on my head about n'annnnn 'nother book! I knocked this one out with superhuman speed just for y'all. I ignored my husband and was short-tempered with my child, just to give y'all what y'all asked for. Please, cut me a break after this one! LOL. I'll need it. I've given it my all. I hope it is enough.

-XOXO-
Ashley Antoinette

AUTHOR'S SUGGESTION TO THE FANS

If you are a member of the Ashley and JaQuavis Reading Club on Facebook, you know that music played a pivotal role in the writing of this book for me. I have attached a playlist of songs that helped me along this journey. I do suggest that to experience this book in the emotional way that I wrote it, you should listen to the suggested songs you see as you read along. Don't rush through this one. Savor it. Experience it. If you've been reading my work for a while, you know I like to evoke emotion. I want you to feel this one. If you are looking for something fun and lighthearted, this is not the book for you. This is HEAVY, this is dark, this is love and love comes with pain. To fall in love is to invite inevitable heartbreak. Grab a glass of wine and go there with me. Feel me. Happy reading!

ETHIC II PLAYLIST

H.E.R., Best Part
H.E.R., Changes
Ella Mai, 10,000 Hours
Ella Mai, Found
Ella Mai, Down
Jacquees, Trippin' Remix
Melanie Fiona, Wrong Side of a Love Song
Jagged Edge, Goodbye
Monica, Hurts the Most
Nivea, 25 Reasons
Brandy, Brokenhearted
Cardi B, Thru Your Phone
Cardi B, Money Bag
Blac Youngsta Remix, Booty

To the Ladies
...never settle for less than an Ezra "Ethic" Okafor.

ETHIC II

CHAPTER 1

I've been searchinggg for someone
But never looked before my eyesss
There you were to my surprise

Morgan hummed the words of the song, as she dipped her long, stiletto nails into the jar of coconut oil. She rubbed her almond-colored hands together, took one of Messiah's shoulder-length locs into her palm and rolled it. The smoke from the blunt he sparked rose into the air, dancing seductively from his lips, as he sat on the floor between her legs.

Monday - a friend of mine
Tuesday, we played a game
Wednesday, you went away
Thursday, things weren't the same on
Friday, you came back...
I wanted toooo...
kissss youuu on
Sattturday
Sunday - we make love
What are we gonna do

She dipped her finger into the jar, again, and greased the squared parts at the roots of his scalp, before moving on to the next. Her voice floated over the beat like she had written the song herself, as she hit the falsetto notes effortlessly. Music seemed to be her new obsession. After years of not knowing what it sounded like, she found enjoyment in closing her eyes and letting it take her mind to another place. It expressed things that she wouldn't dare be brave enough to say. Messiah turned his head to the side and planted a single kiss on the inside of her knee. The gesture was so simple, but Morgan quivered. The act required the complexity of intimacy; and for Messiah, that was foreign. He was new to trusting, new to loving, both giving and receiving. Morgan knew exposing his heart, even with something as unassuming as a kiss to the knee, took great effort for him.

She stared at the takeout boxes on her floor and their clothes that were strewn about carelessly. She couldn't believe Messiah was in her apartment, naked, between her legs. Their comfort level with one another was uncanny. Clothes were never a requirement. He had come by every night for weeks, since the day she moved in. She never had to call. She never had to wonder if he would fall through. The first night after he'd left, she had anxiously waited to hear from him, only for her heart to dip in disappointment when the next day passed her by and he hadn't called. She had gone to bed with a heavy heart, thinking he had no further interest once she had given him what he wanted. It wasn't until four o'clock in the morning when she heard the heavy knocks at her door. She had opened it to find him standing there, arms gripping the doorframe, Balenciaga sneakers on his feet, Fendi sweater laying over his muscular build, and dreads tied back by a red scarf. His eyes were low but hooded in need, and she could smell the blunt he had smoked on the drive up I-69. It mixed with the musk of his cologne, and instantly she caught a high…an euphoria that she only felt when he was around. He hadn't called, not for lack of wanting to, but because if he had let her creep into his thoughts even once, she would be the distraction that would get his head blown off. So, instead, he had pushed her out his mind as he trapped all day. As soon as he was done, he had come back to her. It had been the same routine ever since. School filled her days. The streets monopolized his, but their nights were reserved for one another. A secret love affair.

Morgan took another loc into her hand, sprayed it with rose water, slicked coconut oil in her palm, and twisted. He was comfortable. She could tell. He was more relaxed than she had ever seen him. Morgan wished she could be so tranquil. Her heart raced, and her stomach somersaulted every time he came around. Before, she had blamed it on attraction, but now that she had experienced the essence of Messiah, she knew it was so much more than that...it was addiction. He filled her, keeping her heart full, causing it to pump furiously. He kept her soul full, making her feel purpose-driven, like she was created to show him what true connection to another human being felt like. He kept her body full, penetrating her, turning her into a woman, driving into the apex of treasure between her thighs. Messiah fucked up her world; and while she was his peace, he was her storm. She just couldn't think straight around him. She had so many questions. They had crossed a line that they had been dancing dangerously close to for months.

What does this mean? Where do we go from here?

Messiah would always greet her at the door, earnestly, as if he had waited to taste her lips all day. She would hop onto him, wrap her legs around his waist as he carried her to the kitchen counter where he would fold her over and enter her from behind. After their lovemaking, they ate and he helped himself to her body again. They went from the kitchen... to the bed... to the shower... and sometimes, to the balcony.

God, I can't forget the balcony.

Messiah was insatiable, and the constant pulse she felt between her thighs told her that she couldn't get enough of him either. They were in a marathon of sexual bliss and the finish line was nowhere in sight, but Morgan was still unsure about her role in his life. Were they together? Were they just fucking? She didn't want to assume that sex meant love, although for her they were one in the same. He had told her she was special and that he loved her, but he had only said it the very first time. Sometimes, she wondered if the hours he spent away from her in Flint were spent with other women, because she knew she couldn't be the only one. She had seen the magnetism firsthand. He attracted women wherever he went. He was a god in their hometown and Morgan was out of sight, out of mind now that she was away at school. He could have a gang of women back home and she wouldn't even know.

Monday - a friend of mine
Tuesday, we played a game
Wednesday, you went away
Thursday, things weren't the same on
Friday, you came back...
I wanted toooo...
kissss youuu on
Sattturday
Sunday - we make love
What are we gonna do

"You've been into the music lately." Messiah noticed. "Dancing and singing all over your crib."

"I used to love to dance offbeat, now that I can finally hear it, I love it even more. I'm learning there is a song for every, single emotion I've ever felt. It's like I've got years of pent-up emotion to get out of my system," Morgan answered.

"This song is how you're feeling?" Messiah's voice was clouded by smoke, as he choked out the words. Morgan looked up, her singing suddenly stopping as if he had pressed mute on her voice. He looked up, craning his neck in discomfort to see her reaction.

"I don't know how I feel. Before this thing with you, I felt…" She shrugged, unable to fully put into words the type of loneliness being deaf had caused. Others simply couldn't relate to the struggles she had been through. Even with those who knew how to sign, she didn't feel like they ever truly knew how hard it was for her thoughts to not have a way out of her head.

"You felt what?" he pushed. He rested his head in her lap, eyes to the ceiling, as she placed her fingertips on his temple. She began to rub, clockwise, massaging every worry from his mind.

"Lonely," she said, forlorn. "I just don't want whatever we're doing to end and I'm back to that, you know? The loneliness."

"You know I was always there, right? Even before I knew what it was between us. If you ever needed me, I was on standby," Messiah said. "I done slapped the shit out of plenty mu'fuckas behind your little-ass." He smirked at the memory. He had always felt a nagging in his stomach, seeing Morgan game niggas on the scene. She hit the block at 15 years old, sneaking out to parlay in places she didn't belong. She was like fresh bait in a shark tank. Messiah hated it. Even before he was ever interested in her in any way. He had seen the streets corrupt plenty of good girls in his day.

Morgan smacked her lips. She hated when Messiah gamed her. "That's because of Ethic. You were loyal to him. I remember some days I would try so hard to impress you and you didn't even see me."

Messiah surrendered a lazy smile. She knew it was an effect of the blunt he was now bringing to his lips because he never smiled. He licked his full lips and took in a drag of the weed.

"Nah, I saw you," he choked out, as he exhaled a cloud of smoke. It floated out of him and into Morgan as she inhaled. "And it might have started out as loyalty, but after the night at the falls, every move I ever made was because of my loyalty to you. It was never you by yourself. You were never lonely, Mo. You're just a queen, shorty, and the queen sit on her throne dolo. You always got a general that's ready to ride for you. Always been here, always gon' be here."

"Until you get bored," Morgan mumbled. The uncertainty in her voice commanded his full attention. He snuffed out the blunt and laid his head back into her lap.

"I'm here every night with you, Mo," he said. "Do I look bored?"

"I don't want to apply pressure. I know you, Messiah. I don't want to expect too much. You know? Hurt my own feelings by putting a title on whatever this is," she said. Her eyes were filled with uncertainty, as he reached up with one hand and tangled his hand in her hair. He didn't care that he was destroying her silky hair. He always left money at the end of the night, so Morgan could visit a salon to re-press what he sweated out faithfully. He was grooming her to be high maintenance. He wouldn't give the next man any slack. If a man wanted to push up on Morgan, he would have big shoes to fill. He pulled her down to him, his natural aggression taking over as his tongue invaded her mouth. She could taste the ash flavor that the weed left behind.

"What you want it to be?" he asked.

"Real," she whispered, as she pulled back.

"That's what it is then," Messiah replied. "You want a boyfriend, I'll be your little boyfriend."

Morgan shook her head. "That's not funny. You're making me sound childish."

Messiah's eyes pierced hers and she saw them focus on her so raptly that she felt transparent.

"I'm dead-ass, Mo. I'm moving at your pace, shorty. You're young and I get it. You want to experience certain things. That boyfriend-girlfriend shit is important to you. You want that, I'll be that. No funny shit. It's whatever you want from me. That's what we on. It's all about you, Mo. *Whatever* you want. Anytime you want it. However you want it. You just got to let me know."

He reached up and lifted her from the bed, his strong arms making light work of her 150 pounds. He sat her down right on top of his face, sliding his tongue into her middle.

"Messiah, what are you doing? I'm going to suffocate you," she exclaimed. Her toes barely graced the carpet because all her weight was being held up by him, as he focused on her swollen clit.

"I'll die a happy man. As much shit as I've done, a nigga would be lucky to go out like this," he whispered, as he feasted on her. The song on her station changed and Messiah heard the heavy bass drop on the beat of the next track. "You say you like to dance. Dance on it, shorty."

Morgan gave him a subtle wind of her hips, as she twerked on his tongue.

"Ohhh!" The moan that escaped her made him chuckle, but he didn't stop and neither did she. He was nose deep in her in an attempt to seek a level of intimacy that would forever tattoo him on her soul. He didn't know how long they would last or if it was something that would burn out inevitably, but when she thought back on him, he wanted her to remember that he introduced her to pleasure. He wanted his memory to be the one she played inside her panties to because anybody after him just couldn't hit it right.

"You're the shit, Mo," he mumbled, never stopping…unable to stop. Here she was worried about him growing bored when he was silently hoping that she never reached a point where she realized she was out of his league. Ms. Morgan Atkins with her college girl vibe and invisible crown on her head was much too good for Messiah. Morgan's head fell back, and she rolled it from side to side. He couldn't keep doing this to her body. He was making her delirious. She had heard stories from her homegirls about older dudes who spoke cunnilingus, but to experience it with Messiah was other worldly. He was fluent.

"Hmm...Don't talk with your mouth full," she moaned.

He took pause to snicker, surprised at how quickly she was learning to master her sexuality. He had never been with a girl as young as Morgan because he didn't have the patience to deal with the clinginess and mediocre sex that came with inexperience. Morgan was the one exception; and although he was sure she would mature to a point of greatness that required her to elevate without him, he wanted her for as long as she would have him. Her inexperience intrigued Messiah, and every time he saw her, he made sure to bring her pleasure. She was learning her body through his touch, and as she leaned forward to release his manhood, he had to admit she was a quick study. Morgan was unselfish in her lovemaking. She took him into her mouth, relaxing her throat like he taught her, as she felt his tongue kiss her clit with pure passion. They were gluttons for one another, indulging in sex so erotic that they were developing an appetite that only the other could satisfy. Messiah split her with two, thick fingers but refused to surrender the pearl between his lips as he tackled both with expertise. So many sensations overcame Morgan that she cried out. Her back arched deeper in reaction.

"Mmm," was all she could get out because her mouth was full, but Morgan didn't mind pleasing Messiah because her heart was fuller. She wanted to satisfy his every need - sexual and otherwise. *I'll never leave room for another woman to replace me.* She didn't know that sex was the plus. She stimulated his heart, and for that she was already irreplaceable.

Messiah pulled her orgasm out of her, taking his time, reveling in the moment. He teased her, taking her to the edge only to pull back right before she could cum. He kept her at the edge but wasn't ready to let her jump. Morgan's effort tripled, as she chased her release, pressing her sex into his face, fervently, while deep-throating Messiah. The more he teased her, the better she performed. She could feel it building, she was so close...so anxious. She alternated between teasing his mushroom tip and deep-throating him while massaging his girth. From bow to stern, she waxed the boat. She stroked up, then down. Messiah plunged his fingers in and out, but when he applied pressure with his tongue and buried his nose in her wetness, Morgan's body bucked and released a sweet sap. Her legs shook, as Messiah held her ass in his hands like he was about to take a bite before spreading her wider, making her southern lips smile as he licked her clean.

"Shit, shorty, you...fuck!" He was stuck at how well she worked her tongue. His head spun, as the tip of him swelled. He couldn't form a complete sentence, as bliss stupefied him. He could feel the tingle in his loins and his toes curled. He tensed, pushing himself deeper into her mouth. "Mo, you can stop. Shorty, you don't have to..." Morgan hummed and made his entire length disappear into her mouth. The sight of her pretty lips stretched around him, the sound of her addicting moans in his ears, and the ridiculous amount of saliva in her throat was all she wrote. Messiah came hard and Morgan didn't stop until she milked him dry. He was limp when she arose from his lap.

"Yo, I swear this is something different. You're going to make a nigga crazy. What the fuck?" he whispered, in disbelief, breathing hard as he stared at the ceiling in confusion. He swiped his hands over his face. This type of emotion was foreign to Messiah. All he knew was hate and anger. The light Morgan brought to his life was blinding, it was almost painful to a man who had lived much of his life swallowed in darkness. He didn't know what to do with it. He was waiting for something to extinguish it, which is why he wanted to bask in it as much as possible before it was gone. His cold heart was in turmoil because he knew nothing about selflessness, nada about showing affection, zilch about love. He didn't want to ruin the only person who had ever tried to love him. Their demise was inevitable, but still he couldn't stay away. *God, please don't let me fuck this up. Please don't let her ever see me for the nigga I am without her. She can't love that. She won't love that.* Messiah's forehead creased because he couldn't even pray properly. He had never done it before her. He had never had anything worth praying over. It didn't even feel right, but to keep the blessing that was Morgan Atkins, he had to try. Morgan's face came into view, as she hovered over him, smiling.

"No, Siah, you've got it all wrong. I'm your sanity, baby. I'ma always keep your mind and your heart safe for you," she whispered, as she climbed on top of him and rested one cheek against his chest. There was no personal space with Morgan, and oddly, he didn't desire any. He would share the air in his lungs with her if she wanted him to. "I'm home."

"Home, huh?" he pondered the notion. He had plenty roofs over his head. Violent ones. Leaky ones. Barely ones. Lonely ones. Never had they been homes though.

Morgan's eyes closed and burned with tears from the uncertainty she heard in Messiah's voice. She didn't know his entire story. She hadn't pried into his past yet and he hadn't divulged the details, but she knew he had never had a place to call home. She could feel his heart quickening beneath her, as he anxiously awaited her answer. She tucked her arms underneath his body, strengthening her hold on him and a tear slipped when she felt his arms wrap around her back tightly. She wished she could put a lock around those arms, so she could secure them forever.

"You can always come home," she whispered.

The buzzing of his cell phone burst their intimate bubble and Morgan sighed. There was always a phone ringing, a text buzzing. He was a busy man…a real man, indeed, so his time was limited. She appreciated what he allotted for her, but she would be lying if she said she didn't want more.

"I'm not ready for you to leave," she said. "I don't want to let the world back in yet. Don't answer."

Messiah kissed the top of her head, as he rubbed her back. He didn't move. Whoever was calling could wait, and if they couldn't, fuck 'em. He would put the entire world on pause for this here. He soothed her, until he felt her body relax and she slid off to seek the comfort of her mattress. Only then did he move. He checked the clock. It was close to 4:00 a.m. Hustling hours. He rolled out of bed and headed to Morgan's bathroom to shower. Dread filled his heavy footsteps. She was balance. It was getting harder and harder to leave her at night. Messiah wanted Morgan to be his, all the time, day and night. Ethic wasn't the only obstacle stopping him from doing so. His involvement in the streets was another reason why Morgan only saw him at night. He couldn't wear his heart on his sleeves. There could be no social media posts. No public displays of affection. Morgan was safer when she was disconnected from him. He didn't need their relationship ringing through the grapevine because she would instantly be on the hood's radar. Old hoes would come out the wood work to hate. Niggas would want her just because he had her first. Enemies would realize his weakness. He couldn't have any of that. Messiah also didn't want to take away Morgan's independence. She was just figuring out her place in the world. He knew she would drop everything if he asked her to, but he didn't want that for her. He didn't want her to be a ride or die. What was that anyway? Women reducing themselves to make a man feel whole? Women sticking out lies and infidelity just to say she had a piece of a man? Nah, Messiah had no intentions of her riding or dying for him. He wanted her to live. He wanted her to teach him to live because with her he felt like he could breathe deeply. She didn't have to play the role that so many other hood chicks coveted…wifey… baby mama… the main. Morgan was above that. She deserved more than that. The pedestal he had her on was so high he could barely reach it. So, to avoid distracting her from the life she was building for herself, he made himself scarce during the day, despite the craving for her presence that tugged at him when he was out of her bounds.

He stepped under the hot stream of water and put his palms on the wall in front of him, bowing his head, rinsing her scent off him. The potency of what he felt for her made his chest tight, as the beads of water cleansed his muscular frame. He hated for her scent to even run down the drain. It seemed like a waste to wash off something so lovely. He grabbed the bottle of soap, the men's soap that Morgan had insisted on buying for him to use while at her place, and cleansed his body before stepping out. It was the little things, like buying toiletries and ordering organic coconut oil for his locs that opened his soul wider and wider to her. She wanted to take care of him. She thought of him when no one else in the world ever had. He remembered a time he used to have to steal soap because no one under any of those 'roofs' gave him shit for free. So, yes, Morgan buying soap for him was a sentiment he appreciated. He dried and dressed as he admired Morgan, naked on the bed, sleeping with a look of contentment on her face. He knew she was cold from the tautness of her nipples. He fought the urge to take one of them into his mouth and his dick jumped in protest. Instead, he grabbed the cover from the end of the bed and pulled it over her before he left, locking the door behind him with the key she had gifted him.

He grabbed the Ducati helmet off the back of his bike and mounted it. Placing it on his head, he revved his engine, before kicking off the stand and taking off into the early morning.

CHAPTER 2

Alani pinched her eyes closed, as she sat on the edge of her bathtub, locked behind the privacy of the door, her phone in her hand. Her thumb hovered over Ethic's name. Her loyalties were split in half, right down the middle. Ethic on one side; Cream on the other. He had just left her home with his lies, and his deception, and his treason.

He's a murderer. He deserves whatever the fuck he gets.

Still, a part of her wanted to warn him. The part of her that had given herself to him the night before needed him to avoid an ambush. He was a part of her now. Inside her. Connected. As soon as she gave her body to him, she had soaked him up like a spiritual sponge. She couldn't eradicate him from her soul if she wanted to. She hated him, but if he died, would a part of her die too? Alani brought her thumb to her mouth and bit her fingernail, a nervous tick.

KNOCK! KNOCK!

The wooden door rattled and caused her to jump. She hit the home button on her phone.

"Just give me a minute," she called, barely able to contain the crack in her voice. Her stomach twisted in angst. She tried to will away her tears, but her eyes just kept burning and they just kept falling and…*Godddd. He came into my home and sat at my kitchen table like he had never been here before. What kind of person can stomach that? He touched my body. His hands. All over me. In my hair.* Visions of him fisting her hair as she rode him the night before filled her mind and Alani shook her head. *He's all over me.* She pulled open the drawer in the bathroom and grabbed the pair of scissors she kept there. She was hysterical, as she began cutting.

SNIP

A chunk of curly hair came out in her hand.

SNIP

Another handful fell into the sink.

Again, and again, she cut until she stood, sobbing, in front of the vanity, her head bowed in disgrace.

KNOCK! KNOCK!

"La, open this muthafucking door," Cream shouted. "Whose fucking truck is that sitting out front?"

Alani gripped the scissors in her hand, as she contemplated ending it all. This was too much pain for one person to endure. What she had thought had been her light in the darkness was only lightning in a storm. How she had fallen so hard for Ethic, so quickly, she would never understand. He had penetrated the fortress it had taken her years to build around her heart. He had disarmed her with ease and she had allowed him to infiltrate her life, to witness her vulnerabilities...only for it all to be a ruse of the worst kind. She wanted to jab those scissors into her neck. That would be less painful than what she was enduring.

And Nannie knew. She recognized him.

"Alani!"

She took zombie steps over to the door. Her feet barely lifted from the ground, she was in such a daze. She was like the Living Dead. Moving, but her heart no longer beat. It would never beat the same after this. There were some pains you just couldn't heal from. Some things were so damaging that you just never reverted back to the person you used to be before they occurred. This was that life-altering pain. She had thought it was her daughter's death, but she realized that hadn't been it. Ethic had been able to love her back to health after that. No one, not a man, not a woman, not God, not a friend could make life feel livable after this. She pulled open the door and the bewilderment on Cream's face told her the hack job she had done on her hair was a gruesome sight. It matched the hack job Ethic had put on her soul.

"What did you do?" Cream asked. He seized her wrist and removed the scissors from her grasp.

"I fucked up," she whispered. "I fucked up so bad. I have to tell you something."

"The only thing you got to tell me is whose fucking truck you whipping?" Cream's hazel-tinted lenses turned dark and Alani recognized the spark of jealousy that flashed in his eyes.

He gripped her chin, lifting it, examining her. Alani slapped his hand away so forcefully that she stunned him.

"The day you had a bitch coming to my door to confront me about some community dick was the day your privilege of asking me questions ended," she snapped. Alani had a rage in her that Cream hadn't been acquainted with. It was a fire that burned boldly, a hatred that Ethic had ignited. Cream was the recipient based on proximity alone. He was there so he was feeling her wrath. He recovered from the shock of her brazen reaction in a split second.

"Have you lost your fucking mind?"

His massive hand wrapped around her throat with ease, as he pinned her against the wall, his body against her body. He was threatening, all gangster, but Alani had never backed down from a fight. Today was the wrong day to try her. They were like oil and water, but she remembered a time when they had been the best of friends. Once upon a time, the good outweighed the bad, but with a dead child between them, she couldn't ever see them getting back to a happy place. His face matched her child's. It was hard to even look at him. They had been through so many bad days while he was locked up. So much time had passed without even communicating that Alani now considered him an adversary. He was a mistake from her past, but he was Kenzie's father. She owed him answers. The ones he sought would feel so inconsequential once he discovered the truth. "Now, answer my question, La."

Alani's eyes filled with emotion. She pushed him, again, barely moving him as he stood firm, looking down at her in confusion. She hit him, her fist jabbing his chest in frustration but causing no injury. He grabbed her wrists, hemming her against the wall.

"Whoa, whoa! What the fuck is wrong with you?" Cream dwarfed her with his six-foot height, bending in concern. Alani sobbed. "Calm your ass down!"

"I trusted him," she whispered. She leaned her head against the wall. Drained. *How. Could. I. Be. So. Stupid?* Her head knocked on the wall between every word. She shook it, before melting onto the floor, her face an ugly mess as it contorted to display her sorrow.

"Who? I can't help you if you don't talk, La. Who?" Cream asked, yelling in frustration, as he kneeled in front of her.

Alani marked him with remorseful eyes. The bags that rested beneath them told a story of a woman burdened. She had cried a million tears and felt a million heartbreaks in mere hours. Nothing had ever ruined her like this. Ethic had broken her, like a mirror, splintering her into so many pieces that she couldn't put herself back together without being cut. She would be stepping on pieces of her glass soul for the rest of her life, because there was no way she could clean it all up. "He killed my baby," Alani sobbed. Her face sought retreat in her hands, as she pulled her knees to her chest. "And then I..." She was destroyed, unable to complete whole sentences, unable to shake Ethic from her thoughts. His consciousness had become hers. They shared an energy that she could sense all the way across town. Alani still felt him. She remembered why she hated having sex before going somewhere important. She didn't dry easily. She would be wet all day. Uncomfortable and insecure all day because she felt like other people knew she had just been intimate. With Ethic, she would be wet for the rest of her life. The things he had done to her the night before...ways she hadn't even known a man could please a woman...the depths he had convinced her to explore...the ways in which he stretched her. The places he had put his tongue. The taste of him in her mouth. The way he had whispered her name while spilling into her. She could still feel a tender ache between her thighs where he had been. She hadn't thought twice. She had never questioned his motives. He had not only snuck inside her body, but her heart...her soul...he had left his DNA inside her. There was no cleansing that.

God, nooooo. Alani's hands were at the sides of her face, balled into fists, beating herself, trying to figure out how she hadn't seen this coming. How had he deceived her so? What happened to the gift of a woman? She had felt no reserves about falling in love at first sight. Her intuition had failed her.

"You what? What did you do?" Cream asked, frustrated.

Alani's eyes were void, as if she had nothing left, as if she had checked out. Ethic had sucked the life out of her. "I slept with the man that killed Kenzie."

"What the fuck you just say to me?"

Cream went from concerned to deadly in the blink of an eye. The odium he felt forced his hands around her neck. It was pure instinct. Blind rage. "You fucking who?" He demanded. Alani couldn't answer. She had no air. His hold was too tight, and she felt a wetness on the back of her head. Cream's face blurred, as he pushed her, repeatedly, with all his might, slamming her head against the wall so hard that the plaster behind her crumbled. His forehead creased in bewilderment, as he connected his actions to his consciousness. Cream released her and staggered backward, retreating to the opposite wall of the hallway. With his back against the wall and intertwined fingertips balled in praying fashion, his eyes burned as he stared at her. He was stuck between disbelief and betrayal. He reached for her.

"La, I'm sor…"

Disoriented, she held out one hand to keep him away as she used the other one to grab the ledge above her head. She barely found the strength in her legs to scramble for the bathroom. She closed him out, right before he was able to follow her, but not even the click of the lock made her feel safe.

"Alani!"

She watched the handle jiggle, as a dizzy fog snatched the strength from her legs. The toilet became her seat and she covered her ears while shutting her eyes to drown out Cream's heavy hand against the door.

"You running from me but you fucking the nigga that murdered my baby?!" That notion made him furious. The thought muddled her. "Dirty-ass bitch! Open this fucking door!"

He had never laid a hand on her before, not even during their worst fight, but this was different, the stakes were higher…and she had done the unforgivable. She deserved this. His rage was warranted.

"I didn't know!" she shouted at the door, hysterically. A blinding throb rattled her brain and Alani brought a shaky hand to the back of her skull. When she pulled back bloody fingertips, she gasped. She didn't fault him, but her fear was real, and she prayed that he didn't get his hands on her again.

BOOM! BOOM! BOOM!

Cream was rabid, kicking the door, shouting, calling her out her name. Pure hurt. What Ethic had made Alani feel, she had passed onto Cream. She was not who he thought she was. She wasn't even close. She knew that pain. She wanted to open the door to let him take out his anger because she knew it so well.

"You muthafucking bitch!"

She sobbed, as she stood to put her weight against the door, just in case the lock gave. If he got through that door he would make her a memory. Alani couldn't help but think, perhaps, that would be best. Someone had to atone for the death of her baby girl. *Why not me?* Heavy footsteps echoed off the walls in her home, as they descended the stairs before the front door slammed shut.

Bella's hands shook, as she dressed for school. Her light skin, long hair, freshly-pressed uniform, and Gucci backpack hid her bothered soul well. There was a lump in her throat.

"You made me love the person who murdered my daughter!"

She heard the words as clear as day, as if the argument between her father and Alani was still taking place downstairs. They echoed off the walls in their massive home long after they had been spoken.

Why did he keep saying he was sorry? If he didn't do it, he wouldn't have kept saying it over and over again. I'm sorry…I'm sorry.

Bella's heart was in turmoil. Her father, her hero. A murderer? *He wouldn't do that.*

Bella wished Morgan was home. If she had heard the argument, then Bella would be able to ask for help. Morgan would be able to explain away what Bella had overheard. The argument was so horrible that Bella didn't dare repeat it. She felt like she had been let in on a secret, one too painful for her to forget. She tried to remember a time when her father had ever displayed aggression. He had never even yelled at her too loudly. He was patient and considerate, even when he was angry. Even when she disappointed him or disobeyed him, his reaction was never fueled with fury. She couldn't fathom him being anything less than gentle. She didn't know Ethic the gangster. She only saw her father and she felt defensive from the accusation Alani tossed around. What confused her was Ethic's apology. She hadn't heard the inciting admission of guilt Ethic had offered. He had whispered it so softly that it had barely reached Alani's ears. Bella had only heard Alani's reaction. Alani's dismay. That had been loud, and fear-filled. As she sat at the top of the stairs with wide eyes and a racing heart, she hadn't missed a detail. Bella had wanted to run down those stairs and defend her father. She had wanted to tell Alani to leave with her lies, but how could she defend what Ethic had not?

It must be true. Is it?

Bella had been desperate for answers, but Alani had left, and her father had retreated to the basement right after. She knew not to interrupt his time down there. When Lily had arrived for her shift, Ethic had left, and he hadn't returned all night. She knew because she had waited up.

The knock at her door terrified her because she knew it was her daddy. Lily's fists on the door were lighter. Eazy didn't knock at all and Morgan was gone. It was Ethic. He was on the other side of her door with one knuckle curled, knocking in a cadence he had used since she was old enough to request privacy. Bella's stomach hollowed, and her breath skipped a beat. She hadn't felt this way since the 5th grade, when the school bully threatened to beat her up for being stuck-up. It was fear. She was afraid of her father because he hadn't denied Alani's accusations. She knew if it hadn't been true he would have said so. Ethic had taught her, "Your name is your name. Integrity is everything. Never let anyone taint your name. Stand in your truth, always, Bella."

It was one of many lessons he had preached over the years. Alani was tainting his name...where was the protest? Why wasn't he up in arms over the things she had said?

Knock Knock

"B?"

"C...come in." How she had found her voice was beyond her. Ethic entered, and Bella's throat dried and constricted. Fear. She turned to the door and she could see the guilt all over him. His posture had changed, and worry had taken residence in the wrinkles in his forehead. His eyes were red. The love of her life, her father, who had kissed her boo-boos when she was a baby girl and had stayed up all night with her when she was sick…was a killer.

"Did you do it, Daddy?"

Ethic steeled. The only thing that could have been worse than Alani finding out about his actions was Bella's discovery of them. He faltered. He didn't know how to answer this. He had always been honest with her, but she was only 12 years old. This was his baby girl, his first born. Omission. It was the lesser of the evils.

"Did I do what, baby girl?" he asked. A stalling technique because they both knew what she spoke of.

Bella's eyes betrayed her and watered. She recognized deflection because he had taught her that as well. "A man will answer you straight up. Truth is truth. It doesn't require time to manufacture and it never changes," he had said. Bella never thought she would be using the things he had taught her to analyze fact from fiction with him. She knew he was about to lie before she asked the question.

"What did you do to Alani?" She was unable to bring herself to accuse him outright. He was her daddy. He received the benefit of the doubt off general principle alone.

Ethic knew then, in that moment, that bringing Alani into his life had been a mistake. His love for her…his *need* for her, didn't outweigh his responsibility to his children. This look in Bella's eyes. This doubt. He had walked it right through the front door the moment he brought Alani home.

Is my baby shaking?

Ethic was crushed. He had to sit. He pulled out her computer chair and brought praying hands to his nose. He had allowed his street life and his home life to intersect. It was a drastic mistake. He had worked hard over the years to keep the darkness away from the light, but somehow it had all blended to make gray. A storm was brewing in his heart. If Alani's disappointed eyes hadn't

24

been enough to break him, Bella's certainly had done the job. The throne they held him up on was so high that falling off had incapacitated him. He hadn't felt this empty in a long time… since the day Raven died. How could he answer this question without destroying his daughter's perception of him? How could he lie without erasing trust? A father was supposed to protect his children from the darkest parts of people, not expose them to it. He didn't even want Bella to live in a world where murder was a possibility…where it was a solution to a problem. He had raised her in a bubble, putting all his energy into blowing it up around her, only allowing security and happiness to fill her life. This would deflate her perception of not only him, but of the world she lived in. Just overhearing him fighting with a woman had changed her a bit. He could see it.

Why is she shaking?

Ethic sniffed away emotion, as he stared out her window.

"You did it, didn't you?" she asked. Bella backpedaled to the door.

"Bella," he started. He paused. That pause was all she needed, all it took to charge him of the crime. "Things between Alani and I…" Another pause and he was convicted. Her father…the killer.

"The truth needs no time to manufacture…" she whispered. "You did it?" With bewildered eyes, she turned and ran.

"Bella!" Ethic shouted after her, but she was already down the stairs.

She bumped Lily and Eazy in her frenzy on her way down.

"Bella?" Lily tried to stop a distraught Bella, but she was like a tornado, blowing everything down that was in her path.

Bella's feet flew down each step, one after another, as she darted for the front door.

She didn't know why she was running or where she was going, but she just couldn't look at him. He was her hero. How did men who read bedtime stories turn into murderers? Even still, at 12 years old, he would sit up with her when she couldn't sleep. Ethic at one end of her bed, her at the other, reading the same book... Harry Potter had been the latest, and discussing the ends of each chapter before moving on to the next. How had that man done this? That man raised kids, by himself, like Superman...he didn't kill them.

Bella knew he would be coming after her, but she didn't want to face him. She tossed her backpack over the gated fence of one of their neighbors and then hopped to the other side. She ducked down behind a bush, peeking between the wrought iron until she saw Ethic's Tesla drive by at a snail's pace. His eyes scoured the block for her. Those worried eyes, the frantic bellowing of her name almost made her turn back...almost. She waited until he pulled further up the block before she stood. Instead of going back onto the street, she went through the backyard and hopped another gate onto the next street. Destination unknown, all Bella knew was that she wasn't ready to go back home because in the blink of an eye her daddy had become someone she didn't recognize. She would remember this day forever because it signified the first time a man broke her heart.

CHAPTER 3

"**H**i, Mr. Williams, welcome back. Your guests are waiting. We've cleared the sauna for you." The high yellow beauty greeted him as soon as he stepped foot inside the luxury spa.

Messiah stepped up to the counter and placed his Louis backpack on the countertop. He unzipped it and pulled out his wallet to retrieve his black card. Ethic had let him ride his corporate accounts at not only the trucking distribution company, but his funeral home, and auto repair shop. "Drug dealers carry cash, businessmen carry credit," Ethic had schooled. Messiah had listened. He had A-1 credit, so whenever he was ready to make his exit from the streets, he could switch over without much effort at all. He handed over the plastic Amex, and checked his watch as she checked him in. He wasn't that late. An hour. In fact, he wasn't late at all. His team was just operating on Eastern Standard. Messiah, on the other hand, was on Morgan Atkins' time. It was the new standard. They would just have to get used to it.

"The cameras?" he asked.

"What cameras, sir?" the yellow-skinned girl asked, with a seductive bite of her lip. He paid a hefty sum to ensure that his actions in and outside of the spa were not recorded.

"Good girl," he answered, writing $1,000 on the tip line.

"I feel like I should earn that money. I can put in work, outside of here, you know," she said. "I'm good at a few things I think you'd like."

Messiah lifted his eyes to meet hers and his jaw chiseled. Even if he didn't have Morgan, he wouldn't knock this girl down. Business was business, personal was personal. She had already spent up too much of his time trying to intermingle the two. He didn't speak one word to get his point across. She diverted her gaze and handed him his card.

"Lucky girl," the girl whispered, as he zipped up his bag.

"Nah, lucky boy," he stated, as he stepped away.

"If she ever fuck up..."

Messiah didn't stick around long enough to hear the rest. He walked into the men's changing room before she could even finish shooting her shot.

"About time, G," Isa said. He sat in a waffle print, white robe with Gucci slides on his feet.

"Quit bitching, nigga," Messiah said, as he removed his gun from his shoulder holster and placed it in a locker.

"Little Morgan got you slipping," Isa snickered.

Messiah turned, eyebrow raised. Was he that transparent? "Fuck you talking about?"

Messiah hadn't discussed Morgan with anyone. They were trying to keep things low.

"I know you, mu'fucka," Isa stated. "The nigga teeth in the stands at the hoop game, moving her up to State, every time we hit you, you coming from an hour away. It ain't rocket science, G. You in that."

Messiah didn't respond, as he stashed his belongings in the locker.

"You sure that's a good idea?" Isa pushed.

"Nah, but it is what it is at this point," Messiah spoke, his voice holding a bit of repentance.

"You know you can change the play, right? If Morgan is a factor," Isa said.

"Nothing's changed. That's the one thing Mo don't change. The play is the same," Messiah said. "Where's Meek?"

"He already in there. He exfoliating and shit. Pretty-boy-ass nigga." Isa smirked.

"He might as well enjoy the shit. We pay them enough to use the place, we could damn near buy it," Messiah stated. He paused. "As a matter-of-fact. Put the wheels in motion to do that."

"Buy this bitch?" Isa asked.

Messiah nodded.

"Say no more," Isa said.

"I'll be in there, though. Give me a minute, bro'," Messiah said. Isa disappeared into the steam room. When he was alone, Messiah slid into the robe and locked up his belongings before entering the steam room. The scent of eucalyptus mints filled the air, as billows of mist rose from the floor. He could barely see through the clouds.

"So, you trying to run a spa?" Ahmeek's voice cut through the room, while Messiah took a seat on the tiled ledge. Sweat instantly formed all over his body.

"I'm trying to run the city," Messiah said. "We buy this shit, run the street money through the spa, all of a sudden we making legit money, filing taxes, establishing something on paper."

"You already own the car wash. What you buying next? Park Place?" Ahmeek asked. "You playing Monopoly with real money, G."

"I'm buying up the block. I ain't in this for forever," Messiah said. "Now, let's lay down the blue print. What's coming up 75?"

Messiah only spoke business in the sauna because it was a requirement to strip naked. It was hard to hide a wire in a steam room. The humidity alone would disrupt the feed. He took every precaution when it came to his freedom, and although he trusted Ahmeek and Isa with his life, boss talk with them was no exception.

"Xanies, Percs, and Oxy on the first truck. Codeine, Fentanyl, and Adderall on the second one," Ahmeek ran down.

Messiah put a towel over his head and leaned onto his knees. He moved everything. From cocaine, to heroin, to lean to pills. The black market in the city belonged to him. Pills were new money and most of the young boys had transitioned to that hustle, but crackheads weren't going to stop being crackheads, so Messiah never gave up the powder. Instead, he monopolized it all. Pills were manufactured by corporations, so acquiring them was much riskier, but the diversity of the clientele made it more profitable. His team sold to everyone from college students wanting to stay up and study, rappers looking for lean, white moms who liked to take pain pills to dull their existence, to dirty doctors looking to stock their pharmacies under the table. Every dollar was welcomed.

"Two trucks mean we got to split up. Seems risky," Messiah stated.

"Yup, but we don't have a choice, unless you want to promote one of the pups. A semi coming East on 69 and the other running up 75. Depending on how often the drivers stop, the window is somewhere between one and three in the morning," Ahmeek stated, as he gave the details on the particular highway routes.

Messiah's mind flashed to Morgan. The night shift was their time, but money was money and no way could he miss this load. "Tonight?" he asked.

"Tonight," Isa confirmed.

"Bet."

"And that other thing?" Ahmeek asked. "I know you knocking little Morgan down now..."

"You don't know shit," Messiah retorted, calmly. He knew Meek meant no harm...Isa either. They jargoned with one another about women in the past, but Morgan wasn't just any conquest. Her name on their tongues was unacceptable. There would be no inquiry of the usual fashion. No asking if *it* was good, and although *it* was…extremely, in fact, Messiah didn't feel the urge to brag. In fact, he wanted to keep that shit a secret. He didn't want Morgan on any other man's mind but his; so, hell no, there would be no talk about the ways she performed. No Yelp reviews on her pussy. Make no mistake about it, Morgan was a star but bullshit banter amongst his crew was restricted and advice on how he should proceed was unwanted.

"Let me be clear with you, G," Messiah stated. "You too," he said, pointing to Isa. "She's not up for discussion. I know what I got to work out. I know what all this eventually leads to. In the meantime, don't speak her name."

"You got it, bro'," Ahmeek said, falling back.

"I've got it under control."

Why won't it stop?

There was a pounding in her head that just wouldn't go away, and the ache was so great that Alani wondered if she should call for help. She had showered and tried to clean the wound to the back of her head, but blood just kept rinsing down her drain. She had bandaged it and wrapped a scarf around her head to hold it all in place, but her bed had been the furthest she could make it, before the blinding ache forced her into bed. She had slipped into a trauma-induced sleep, but the pounding had returned, and it was loud, louder than before. She sat up and grimaced, as she reached for the back of her head. Relief filled her when she realized blood hadn't soaked through her scarf. The bleeding had stopped, but that damn pounding…

BAM! BAM! BAM!

Alani's eyes shot to her closed bedroom door, as the fog cleared from her mind. The noise was real. It was the sound her old, aluminum screen door made when someone knocked. She knew it couldn't have been Cream. He had found his way inside her home before. If he returned, he wouldn't knock first. He would probably come back shooting, he had been so angry.

Ethic? She went to the window, rushing so clumsily that she stubbed her toe on the leg of the bed.

"Shit!" she yelled in pain, as she pulled down the slits of her blinds and peered outside. The truck that she had borrowed was gone. *Did he come get it?* She thought. There was no car in sight.

BAM! BAM! BAM!

Alani's head turned once more, and she tightened her robe before her feet rushed across the carpet. The knock was urgent, persistent.

Alani put her face to the peephole and without hesitation pulled open the door.

"Bella?" Alani stepped out onto the porch and looked left, and then right.

"He's not with me. I came by myself," Bella whispered. "I didn't know where else to go."

Alani opened her mouth to speak but the shock of Bella's presence stole her words. She shook her head from side to side.

"Is it true? Did he kill your daughter?" Bella asked.

Alani lost air. Bella sucked it right from her lungs with her question. Alani hadn't considered Bella and Eazy when she was yelling and screaming in Ethic's home. She had just reacted, and a twinge of remorse sprouted inside her, as she saw the repercussions to that standing in front of her.

"You can't be here, Bella. Does your father know you're here?" she asked.

Deflection. Bella recognized it instantly, but for some reason she didn't anger with Alani the way she had with her father.

Bella shook her head.

"Can I come in? I can't go home," Bella said.

Alani's mind flashed to Cream. "I don't think that's a good idea," Alani whispered. Alani feathered her sore neck and Bella's eyes followed her fingers there. Bella's eyes widened in dismay.

"Did my dad do that to your neck?" she asked, her voice cracking.

Alani frowned. She stepped back into the entryway to her home and turned to the mirror that hung there. She gasped. Bruises that resembled hand prints were butterflied on both sides of her neck. She thanked God that the head scarf covered her hair and the wound, but the bruises were enough to reveal the fight she had endured.

Alani pulled the collar of her robe up and pinched it in the front, covering the injury.

"No, he would never," Alani said, but she halted, realizing that she couldn't speak on what Ethic would or would not do. She had never thought he would be capable of murder, or even simpler, lying. She couldn't speak to his credibility at all, so she simply corrected. "No. He didn't do this."

"I just don't know. I don't know anything anymore. I just want the truth," Bella whispered.

Me too, sweetheart, Alani thought, as she stepped to the side. "Come in."

She felt a cocktail of emotions intoxicating her. Resentment swirled in her chest with a splash of anger, garnished with hatred on top. It seemed to be the emotional special of her life. Like men could just pull a seat up at her table and order it off the menu.

A lesser woman would seek revenge. An evil woman would feed Bella to Cream for retribution. An eye for an eye, or in this case, a child for a child. Fair exchange wasn't robbery. Alani was none of those things and Bella wasn't her father. She had no role to play in Alani's hurt.

"You said I could talk to you," Bella paused, as she hooked her thumbs onto the sides of her backpack. Her voice was so small that she appeared younger than her 12 years. Her eyes were filled with confusion as she stood under Alani's scrutiny. Her long, feather light hair was swept into a ponytail on top of her head. A green and red ribbon, Gucci, if Alani was to assume that Ethic had provided it…because, well, he just provided the very best of everything. Extraordinary shit for an extraordinary man. No beauty supply bow would do for his little girl. No Honda for her… just straight to a Benz. Straight to the best. Yet, he turned out to be counterfeit. A misrepresentation of a real man. A knockoff version of a king. A fraud. Which meant this premature bond with his child had to be contrived too.

Then why does it feel so real?

"You said we were friends," Bella said.

"Of course, we're friends," Alani whispered. What else could she say? Just because Ethic had broken her didn't give her the right to mishandle Bella. An urge to, yes; the right to, never. Nobody had the right to shatter an individual despite many who take the liberty to do so every, single day. Alani wouldn't spread hurt. It wasn't in her nature, especially where a child was concerned. "But how did you get here, Bella? Aren't you supposed to be in school? I'm sure you have a lot of people worried about you."

"I took the bus," Bella said. "I remembered the street from the night at the movies. The house with the cardboard in the window."

Alani closed her eyes, wetness from her tears lined her lashes like glue, sealing them shut. Her daughter had broken that window while playing baseball with the neighborhood kids. The cardboard was supposed to be temporary and then Kenzie died…and everything became permanent. The window, Kenzie's room, the blood-stained pajamas that the hospital had cut off her baby's body…it was all still the same. They were things she didn't dare change. Symbolic shrines that she hadn't dreamt of those years of motherhood. Alani's lip quivered, and she reached down for the arm of the La-Z-Boy, the one she had saved up to purchase because Nannie couldn't get up the stairs too good. Lucas had put it together wrong, so it didn't recline, but it was still comfortable. Alani sat, consumed by thoughts of the people she had lost at the hands of a man she loved. She was so alone.

"What did my daddy do to you?" Bella asked.

Alani drew in a sharp breath. She couldn't tell her. Wouldn't tell her. No sense in breaking two hearts on this day.

"He just wasn't who I thought he was," Alani sighed. It was the PG version of the truth.

"But I heard you. You said he…" Bella sucked in a breath. "Is he a killer?"

Alani shook her head and put some moxie behind her frame, tightening her stomach to stop herself from folding in half from anguish. Ethic had killed her daughter, and Alani could kill his; right now, in this moment, she could destroy her. *The truth hurts.* She looked into Bella's eyes.

"No, he isn't, Bella. He's many things, but I don't believe he's that."

Bella frowned. *She paused. She hesitated, but she's telling the truth?* Bella thought.

Alani's words were meant to come out as a lie. They were spoken to spare Bella's feelings, but they reverberated through her entire body like gospel. Yes, he had killed. No, he wasn't a killer. How did those two things match? How could she be the one speaking them?

"I was scared of him this morning. I was mad, and I was scared," Bella admitted.

"Oh, Bella," Alani whispered. She leaned forward and reached across the coffee table to where Bella sat on the couch. She grabbed her hands. "I'm sorry for coming to your house and disrupting your peace. He's your father. You don't ever have to be afraid of him. How he handles people in the world will always be different than the way he handles you. He loves you."

Bella's tear-drops were so heavy they didn't hit her cheeks. They just fell onto Alani's hands, as Bella nodded in understanding.

"He loves you too," Bella cried. "Like, a lot. Whatever he did, I know he's sorry." Alani's chest spasmed. Her pulse quickened. This beautiful girl, not quite a baby, not quite a young woman, but right in the middle where innocence was still present, was pleading on her father's behalf.

Alani rounded the table, sat beside Bella, and pulled her into a hug. "That's not for you to worry about," she said, as she rubbed the back of Bella's head. "I think you should call your father."

Bella looked down and twiddled her fingers, nervously.

"He's probably mad," she whispered.

Alani lifted Bella's chin with one finger.

"He's probably worried out of his mind. Let's just ease it a little, okay?"

Bella sniffed away her distress and nodded.

"I'll be right back. I'm going to get my phone," Alani said. She stood and raced up the stairs.

The thought of seeing him terrified Alani, but what could she do? His child was on her doorstep, seeking friendship, looking for help to answers she shouldn't be addressing. She entered her room, rushing, feeling panicked as she tossed the covers from her bed. She had no idea where Cream was or when he was coming back. She needed Bella gone by the time he got there. He wouldn't even think twice before taking his rage out on her.

"Where is it?" she said, through gritted teeth. Her heart galloped out of her chest. "Damn it!" She flipped pillows to the floor, and then got on all fours to look under the bed. *The bathroom.*

She rushed down the hall and into the bathroom. Relief flooded her when she saw it lying on the edge of the sink. She snatched it up and headed downstairs.

"Bella, I—"

Her words caught in her throat when she saw Cream coming through the front door. He stepped heavy, tattered Timberlands over the threshold and rolled his head from the couch where Bella sat, to the staircase where Alani stood. She was like a deer in headlights, just waiting for the collision.

"Who the fuck is this?" he asked. The slur. She caught it. He wasn't sloppy drunk, but he had indulged in something to take the sting off the cut she had delivered.

"She's from the church, Cream. I mentor her," Alani rushed out. It was the first thing she could think of. Bring God into it. Remind him that God was watching and maybe he would come down off that murderous ledge she could see him flirting with in his mind. It wasn't the entire truth, but it wasn't a lie either, which is why Alani was able to deliver it with such finesse. "She was just leaving." Alani tried to bypass Cream, but he put up a yielding arm, pressing it to the wall and blocking her path.

"They let deadbeat bitches mentor kids? What you gon' teach her, La? What you gon' do for her when you couldn't keep your own kid safe?" Cream sneered, as he gripped Alani's chin. His words stung, because despite their distance, she cared what he thought about how she had reared their child. Alani had tried to be the best mother she knew how. To nurture, to provide, to teach, to soothe, to educate. She had given a thousand percent because one hundred simply wasn't enough. A mother was expected to pour her all into her child, often until she was empty, retaining nothing for herself. Alani had done that, alone, without complaint and many days through absolute exhaustion. How dare he call *her* the deadbeat? Where was he? Why did his total lack of accountability get overlooked while the blame landed on her? Alani wanted to say something to defend herself, but with Bella there, her only focus was getting her out the house unharmed.

"Cream, please," she whispered. She could see Bella tuned in, half on, half off the couch, as if she was trying to decide if she should run or not.

"Get her the fuck out of here. We've got unsettled business," Cream spat. His eyes spoke his intentions. Every, single fiber of agony that he felt would be taken out on her. Better her than Bella, because if he knew whose daughter she was, it would end deadly.

"Fucking mentor," Cream sneered, as he sauntered into the kitchen.

Alani rushed over to Bella and pulled her from the couch. She planted her cell phone in her hand. Placing her hands on Bella's shoulders, she looked her square in the eyes. Alani's watered a bit and Bella's forehead frowned in confusion. Bella looked from Alani to Cream, who was moving around in the kitchen behind Alani's shoulder.

"Take my phone and call your father, Bella. Leave now. Don't turn around no matter what you hear. There's a corner store three blocks to your left. Wait for him there," she ordered, in a hushed tone. A tear fell, and Alani swiped it away.

Bella nodded, and Alani recognized that her fear had returned. Alani ushered her to the door and closed it.

She hated to send her out in the middle of the hood, because Bella hadn't been bred there, but it was safer than being near Cream.

"Now, come sit your ass down so you can tell me how you fucked the nigga that killed my daughter..."

"She was mine too," Alani interrupted. "You don't think I..."

Cream came up behind her and pushed her head into the door, before she could finish. Alani's face hit the wood like a pinball and Alani saw white flash behind her lids. It was blinding. Like lightning. This wasn't the Cream she knew but still she didn't blame him, didn't judge him. He was only acting out the way she was feeling inside.

He pushed her toward the kitchen table.

"Sit down," Cream gritted.

Alani stumbled to the wooden chair and sat down. Cream sat across from her. Her opponent. Her child's father. On the other side of the table. She didn't know how it had happened. How had she carried his seed and ended up his enemy? How had they shared a bed once upon a time and let destiny lead them here? Adversaries. It was the saddest tragedy. Mommy against Daddy; Kenzie's parents at a standoff. "I want to know everything there is to know about this nigga. Niggas think just because you're gone you're forgotten. I can pull up on any block in this city and get love. It ain't always about the bread. My name is heavy out here. Niggas used to eat with me and they respect me. They owe favors. There's a code. No kids. No fucking kids!" He said, pointing a stern finger into the table. Three times for emphasis. *No! Fucking! Kids!* "So, when I put word out that I wanted to see this muthafucka, niggas put their ears to the streets. Problem is, every place he usually move in and out of is suddenly a ghost town. He ain't nowhere to be found. You know what I think?" he asked, as he pointed the accusation at her, shaping his fingers in the shape of a gun, as if he wished he could fire bullets from them. He looked at her in disgust.

"I think you warned that nigga," Cream alleged. He stood and walked around the table. He placed both hands on her shoulders and Alani tensed. He was so angry that it made her forget that she shared in the emotion. She was too busy dreading his next move to focus on her pain. Defending herself from his devastation had distracted her. He leaned down into her ear. "Where is he, La? I had one person in this world..." Cream's voice fractured, and a sob escaped him. "She was all I had, La. She was all the good that I had to give." Cream's grip loosened, and Alani felt him wrap his arms around her. This time, with no intention of inflicting harm. She closed her eyes and felt her tears come. He was back; out of the rage. He had bypassed that emotion...that stage of grief, and now he needed her to comfort him. It was what she did. It was what was always expected of her, to take care of everything and everyone before herself. There was an encumbrance of anguish in the room. It was suffocating. They were the sum of one bad decision after another and neither knew how to rectify their actions. Their baby was in the ground and they were standing on two, opposite sides of her grave, divided, and it hurt.

"I didn't know. I didn't know," she whispered, as she leaned into her hands and broke down. "Not until it was too late. I'm so sorry." He kissed the top of her head and then lifted from her, heading for the backdoor.

"Cream, please, don't..."

He pulled open the screen and paused. "Don't what, La? I'm her father!" The way he said it...the word father...it was like the word bled from his lips with conviction. Years of neglect and half-parenting had made Alani feel like he was less than one, barely one, but here in her kitchen, she realized he loved their daughter with his entirety. "There's only one way to make this right. You know me. This will weigh on me. I need someone to blame and I'm out of control right now. When I look at you, I see that nigga, Messiah, killing my daughter then fucking you," Cream said.

Who? Alani looked up in shock. *He doesn't know it was Ethic.* Alani wanted to speak, but she was afraid to. Would the revelation that he had it all wrong be better or worse? Would he beat her again? Would his hurt lessen or magnify? She didn't know who Messiah was, but correcting Cream felt dangerous, so she said nothing.

"My intentions ain't good for you right now, La. Somebody's going to die behind this, and if you don't want it to be you, then I got to go."

CHAPTER 4

The black, .38 revolver sat at her fingertips atop of the kitchen table fully loaded. Alani just didn't feel safe. She needed protection. From Cream. From Ethic. From life. She had once hated the idea of having it in the house, but Nannie played no games.

"I wish one of those little knucklehead negroes would step foot over this threshold. I'll blow 'em to kingdom come!" she had yelled, when she first purchased it from the pawn shop. It was a summer ago, when a few brazen junkies had been breaking into the surrounding homes on her block. Her home had remained untouched, thank God, so the gun had just sat in a closet. Until now. She knew the heavy knocks at the door would come. She had sat there for nearly an hour, anticipating them, but when they came, she still startled. She hated that her heart skipped a beat.

Alani picked up the gun. It hung in despair at her side, as she went to the front door.

She reached for the knob but paused. She couldn't open it because the energy coming from the other side told her it was him. He needed no announcement. *Him*... would always refer to Ethic. He would be her *him* for the rest of her life.

"Lenika..."

She cringed because what he had said at his house was true.

After he admitted his sins, they had gone back to being strangers, even down to the name he called her; the name she gave to people she didn't know well…to those she didn't trust, and he was calling her that. How absolutely absurd after the things he had done to her? Nobody had become better acquainted than him, and yet, she had become Lenika.

"I'm going to need you to open the door," Ethic said.

Alani closed her eyes and rested her weary head against the door.

"I'm fine," she called out. "Please, leave." Her voice was laced in fear and he could tell she was trying to dress it up in strength to give him the illusion that she had everything under control. Story of a black woman's life…faking like everything was okay, when really, they were just epitomes of struggle disguised as strength… all burdened by something that a man had put on her heart. He had put a load on Alani, one he was sure she was incapable of carrying alone.

"Bella said there's a man inside. She said there were marks on your neck," Ethic said. "So, I can't leave. Not until I know you're safe."

"And that's with you?" The response was so automatic she didn't have time to filter it. It was a knee-jerk reaction…a black girl reaction…pop off first and think later. He heard her resentment and it ate away at his manhood like moths to an old, hanging suit. He wasn't leaving, however. Not after the terror he had heard in Bella's voice. It was enough for him to take the extra time to drop her off at home first before coming back to Alani's. He took a seat on the top step of her porch and leaned over onto his knees, as he surveyed the block. It was a cold place with abandoned homes all around, graffiti-marked aluminum siding, and chain-link fences. It was the ghetto and in the middle of it was his rose. He didn't even know how these streets had produced someone like her.

"I've got all day," he called out. "I'm not leaving until I see your face."

He noticed his truck was gone and his assumptions of whom the man was inside her house were confirmed. Only a man who had entitlement to a woman would run off with her car…well… his car.

Her baby father's home.

It angered him to know Bella had been so close to harm. It warmed him to know that Alani had prevented it. It meant there was still hope.

Ethic slid his phone from his pocket and prepared to send a text to Messiah, but when he heard the door creak open, he halted.

Alani was barely a shadow through the tiny slit in the door. He dusted himself off, as he stood and approached the door. He pushed his palm to the wood, but the security chain stopped it from opening further.

Alani looked down, trying to hide her face.

"Hey," he said, to jar her attention.

Her eyes lifted, and when they met his, he felt a wrench in his loins. *This woman,* he thought, mesmerized at the pull she had over him. It was natural, not manipulative in the slightest… ordained.

"Open."

One word. A command. She followed. She always followed because he was a man fit to lead, at least he used to be.

The heaviest sigh he had ever heard fell from her lips and the door closed. Alani slid the chain off the top of the door, before swinging it open fully.

Ethic felt like he had been punched in the gut when he saw the damage. He knew better than to touch her. She wouldn't want that, but his urge to was overwhelming. Her eye was beginning to blacken. The bruises on her neck were even worse. He wasn't even privy to the knot on the back of her head because of the scarf, but he felt that something else was wrong. It was like they shared the headache…like it was splintering through his brain as well.

Ethic took in everything about her and the house in a millisecond. His jaw locked, as Alani stood before him trembling.

"You tell the nigga goodbye before he left?" Ethic asked.

Alani shook her head, as she struggled to breathe under his scrutiny. She was holding onto the biggest tears in her life. They weighed down her eyes and blurred her vision, but she couldn't blink. She was frozen.

"You should have. He won't be coming back," Ethic said, calmly. It wasn't a soothing calm, however. It was a deadly one, a malicious one. Like he had a button he pressed when he needed to access the darkness inside him. "Can I touch you, baby?"

No longer able to hold back the flood, she blinked. He took a step forward and she put up a defensive arm, stepping back. She shook her head.

Ethic sniffed away the sting of rejection.

"Just leave," she muttered, weakly.

Ethic took a moment to breathe her air a little longer. He loved this woman. Walking away from her was agonizing.

"Get out of my house," she said. She turned, and he noticed a piece of bandage showing from the bottom of the headscarf. *Fuck permission.* He caught her wrist.

"What are you doing?" she was stricken with terror, as she noticed his disposition. His body language screamed anger and she wondered how she had never noticed how terrifying he was before.

"What's under the scarf?" he asked.

Her fingers finessed the knot at the front in insecurity.

"Ethic…he didn't mean…"

Before she could finish her sentence, his hands were unraveling the knot in the center of her scarf.

"He didn't do this...I just...it looks worse than...you..."

"I'm putting the nigga in the dirt," Ethic said. There was no bravado. No grandstanding. He said it so casually, as if he were talking about the weather. It was 70 degrees with a 100% chance of murder. She recognized his gangster. She had been blinded before, but she saw it clearly now.

"I cut my hair," she blurted. She swallowed down the lump in her throat, as a tear trailed down the tip of her nose, itching it before it fell. She was shaking so badly. She was losing it. Again. Right in front of him. "Your hands were in my hair last night. I didn't want it anymore," she whispered, in embarrassment. It sounded insane, even to her, but it was the truth.

He swiped a hand down his mouth. "Lenika," he whispered. His face twitched, as distress broke through his chiseled jawline and he cupped her face. His fingers squeezing her head made her wince. He frowned, and then turned her around, swiftly. He removed the bandage from her head to find a two-inch cut on the back of her skull, matted with blood. Fire seared him, as she turned around, unable to look him in the eyes. She opted for his feet.

"If you're even a fraction of who you pretended to be, you'll stay out of it," she whispered.

"Niggas die every day. Today just happens to be his day," Ethic said.

"She was his daughter, Ethic!" That one wasn't fabricated. She had found her strength. Defending the actions of her baby's father. "He ain't right, but you are worse. I don't want to bury anyone else. Just stay out of my life. Just get out." She sounded exhausted.

Ethic already had his plans for the evening lined up in his mind. That forecast was accurate. Her pleas made him no never mind.

He would never be cognizant of someone disrespecting her and not act on it. He could see his presence was upsetting her. He pulled her cell phone from his pocket and placed it on the hutch near the door before he retreated. He stepped over the threshold of her home as she slammed the door.

Ethic rested a fist against it in angst, as he placed his forehead on top of it. He had lost a good one, but he'd be damned if he let Cream or anyone else lay hands on her. He wouldn't come back again. He respected her decision to walk away, but he couldn't leave without making sure she was covered first. He would always protect those he held dear; and whether she wanted to or not, she occupied his heart.

CHAPTER 5

MORGAN
*If I told you I wanted to wake up to you every day and go
to bed next to you every night, what would you say?*

Morgan stared at her text messages, resting a balled fist against her cheek, as her elbow leaned onto the classroom desk. It had been eight minutes since she had sent it. Four hundred and eighty agonizing seconds and counting. He always responded to her texts immediately. Messiah never left her with time to worry about anything, but as the minutes ticked by, Morgan couldn't help but wonder where he was.

Her phone vibrated but disappointment filled her when she discovered it wasn't him.

BESTIE
So, you acting funny now, college girl?

Morgan frowned at the random text. She hadn't heard from Nish since leaving for school. In truth, she had been relieved to leave it all behind. The embarrassment, the drama...things were going smoothly at State. She hadn't made many friends yet, but between classes and Messiah, she didn't have much room for any either. Speaking of. *Where is he?*

"Ms. Atkins, are you with us?"

Morgan looked up from her phone and realized the entire class was staring in her direction. The teaching assistant stared at Morgan, curiously. "You're in outer space."

"I'm sorry, I'm here," Morgan answered, as she slid her phone off the desk and into her handbag.

"You here with me?" he asked. It wasn't what he said, but how he said it that made butterflies form in her stomach. She looked up into the eyes of the light-skinned teaching assistant in front of her. He stared, intently, with one leg propped up on the chair in front of her desk, as he leaned his elbows onto his knee.

"I'm paying attention," she said, making sure to answer him appropriately. *Is he flirting with me?*

He was her teacher, but she had to admit he was attractive.

How is he even old enough to teach this course? And why is he looking at me like that?

"Why don't you tell us your perspective on love, since Aristotle's doesn't interest you."

"Love is…" she paused, as she thought of Messiah. She blushed, as if he were in the room, waiting to hear her answer. "Love isn't an explanation. It's a feeling. It can't be learned in a book or presented in front of a class. It's not meant for everyone to understand," she said.

"Well said, Ms. Atkins," he said. His eyes lingered a moment longer than necessary before he stood. "Assignments for Thursday. Read Plato's theory on love. Chapters 5-10."

The sound of chairs scraping the ground erupted, as the class was dismissed. Morgan grabbed her phone and her books, moving slowly. She opened her texts. No Messiah. Just more Nish. Morgan rolled her eyes.

BESTIE

*Seriously, Mo. I miss you. We used to text every day. Now,
it's radio silence. What's the move this weekend? I want
to come visit you at State. You busy this weekend? I heard
it's lit up there. If I come down, can I crash with you?*

Morgan sat there as the classroom emptied, her fingers
lingering over the screen in thought. Nish was her only friend.
It had been that way for years, but she held insecurities about
Nish and Messiah. Messiah claimed his time with Nish had been
nothing, Nish claimed it had been everything...somewhere in
between lied the truth. There was a time where Morgan would
have trusted her lengthy friendship over her short bond with
Messiah, but her gut told her to roll the dice on him. He had
done nothing but protect her, whereas Nish had inflicted hurt on
Morgan repeatedly. Morgan's feelings were soft and easily bruised.
She would be lying if she said the wedge in their friendship didn't
hurt her. She remembered Nish standing by her side throughout
grade school and high school, defending her. She had stuck by her
despite how different she was. It was those memories that made
Morgan not want to let Nish fall to the wayside.

MORGAN

*I'm not really trying to go out, but we do need to talk.
I don't want to get into it over text. I'd rather do it in
person. I don't have class tomorrow, anyway. You can
come down.*

BESTIE

*Bitch, I know I've been the worst type of friend. You're
going to check my ass and then we're going out!*

Morgan smirked and shook her head. Nish was still Nish. She sent her the address. She wasn't sure if their friendship was repairable, but it was at least worth a conversation, if not for anything more than closure.

"Must be an interesting conversation for you to ignore my entire lecture."

Morgan turned toward the teaching assistant.

"It's not, actually," she said. "I'm sorry. It won't happen again." She gathered her things.

"It's cool," he said. "With a face like that I can only imagine the things you get away with."

Morgan popped her eyes up in surprise. Flabbergasted, she jerked her neck back, as she placed the books inside her designer tote. "You...um...isn't there some kind of rule against flirting with your students," she said, finally gathering her thoughts and able to convey a complete sentence.

"Sure. No professors and students. I'm just a grad student who's fulfilling a requirement by being a teaching assistant for a semester," he said, with a smile. He was rugged, like he was trying to rough up his light skin, with a beard and an even-cut fade. His smile pulled her in and she had to look away, down at her phone, which reminded her of Messiah.

Where is he?

"So, I'm free to ask you for a cup of coffee with a clear conscious," he said. "Ms. Atkins."

"Means you're free to stop calling me that, too. It's Morgan. Just Morgan, and I can't. I'm seeing someone."

He nodded and placed a hand over his heart.

"Of course you are," he surmised. "Well, I'm perfectly fine with waiting in the friend zone. You know you can call me when he's messing up and I can wait with baited breath for my opportunity to snatch you."

"And that's not thirsty at all." Morgan's sarcasm caused them to share a laugh. "This conversation has already gone too far. See you next class."

Morgan was halfway to the hallway when he shouted, "Sebastian. My friends call me Bash."

"I don't call you anything," she said, as she closed the door on her way out.

Morgan stood staring at herself in the 360-degree mirrors that covered every wall in the dance studio. Her denim shorts crept up her thighs so high that the lining of her pockets hung from the bottom. The Nike, cropped hoodie she wore had her belly ring on display. A small M shined in her navel. Most would think it stood for Morgan. Morgan knew it stood for Messiah. The high-heeled, open toe booties she wore on her feet made her feel sexy, as she waited patiently for the beat to drop. Messiah wasn't answering her calls or texts and it caused anxiety to build inside her. *Maybe I'm moving too fast. He doesn't want to live with me and doesn't know how to say it.* The unknown and the silence scared her. She wasn't ready to go home, so she opted for the next best thing… to dance. She hadn't been out dancing since the night of her rape. Before that night, it was her favorite pastime, to get cute and fuck shit up on the dance floor. Finding a dude and putting on a show had been her thing. It had made her feel powerful and seductive to have all eyes on her. It made her feel wanted to feel a guy rise in his jeans behind her, as she put her body to work against him. Morgan's body was slim, but her behind and hips were not to be denied. She worked them like no other, dancing, choreographing, to nothing but the feel of the bass in the music and what she imagined it would sound like in her head. Since her rape, she hadn't wanted to be touched. She hadn't wanted to feel the arousal of a strange man or the roughness of strange hands on her body. So, she hadn't gone out. She only danced in the privacy of her own home, but today she felt the urge to express herself...to purge her system of the nervous energy Messiah's silence produced. The rain was pouring outside, night was falling, and her heart was heavy because her man was MIA. She needed to sweat Messiah out her system because she should be able to function when he wasn't around. She needed to work her body, and if she couldn't do it underneath him, she would work it out on her own. Thank God for the recreation center on campus. This studio was hers for the taking. For some reason she was nervous. She had never danced in front of a room full of mirrors and she wondered if she would look awkward. She didn't quite catch the beats of music like other people; still, she loved it just as much.

Twerk
Girl, I wanna see you twerk
I'll throw a li'l money if you twerk
I don't really think you can twerk
If you broke go to work
Make that big booty twerk

She started bopping, discreetly, moving her chest up and down to the trap beat. She was amazed at how just the sound of the drums made her pulse race. It excited her, geeking her up in a way that music never had before. It was something about those mirrors that stimulated her. She couldn't quite match the beat with precision. She was a half-step behind the tempo, which gave her a unique interpretation of dance that looked intentional to anyone who didn't know she was born deaf. Slowly, she added a roll to her stomach and her top lip curled, as if there was a distasteful smell in the room. Morgan's thighs butterflied, while her hands met her knees and she dipped low. She worked her middle.

POP! POP! POP!

Fast, then she slowed it down, letting her ass gyrate in between each dramatic arch of her back before adding one final POP! She brought her fists in front of her body, palms facing her as she beat them together while twerking hard. She lowered onto both knees and rolled her body, putting her hands in her hair, pulling at the sides like she was going crazy. Her abs rolled, as she opened her thick thighs, knees sliding outward, her pussy lowering to the floor. Up and down like Messiah was nestled beneath her, riding, hard. She stuck one arm out like she was grabbing those dreads she loved so much and tucked the other fist under her armpit, working her middle. Up and down, using her muscles to make each cheek of her nicely-shaped behind work individually. She leaned forward on her elbows and then slithered onto her chest like a snake, as she kept that arch tooted high, ass on full display. She moved it side to side. The music did something to her. Having it flow through her body made her appreciate the gift of hearing in a new way. She was in her element. Sweat accumulated on her forehead and the *Blac Youngsta* remix told her to TWERK.

Yeah, smack it up, flip it, rub it down, BBD
Yeah, I know you heard the news about that BBC

Morgan came up on her elbows and slowly let her legs slide into a full split, as she captured one wrist behind her back with the other hand. She bounced up and down in that split, using only the strength of her thighs. She smirked, Messiah had taught her well. She gritted her teeth, her face scrunched arrogantly, and she stuck her tongue out, biting it in seduction. Morgan rolled her body to the side, swinging one leg in a windmill until she was standing smoothly.

BOOM! BOOOM! BOOOOM! BOOOOOM!

With every 808, she swung her hair before bending over, legs straight as she made it shake before strutting off, ending her routine with a sexy walk-off. The music faded, and Morgan smiled as she scoffed in disbelief. She felt incredible. Hearing felt incredible. She didn't think she would ever truly get used to it. Music was becoming her addiction. She couldn't believe she had gone her entire life without it. The way her body reacted to it, you would think she had been dancing and singing forever.

CLAP! CLAP! CLAP!

"Shit!" Morgan jumped out of her skin when she heard the slow, dramatic, round of applause, and she turned to the door as a figure stepped out of the shadows of the darkened hallway. Morgan had never seen someone drenched in skin so sultry. It was dark like granite and rich, almost sparkling it was so magnificent. She was beautiful.

"That was fucking fire," the girl complimented.

Morgan leaned down to grab her bag, Beats pill, and cell phone. Her eyes glanced at it. Still, no Messiah. Rustling her hair, she blew out a breath of exhaustion. She had worked out all her anxiety in that dance.

"Sorry. I didn't know anybody had reserved the room," Morgan said. She threw the Gucci tote bag on her shoulder and headed for the door.

"Hey! You're super dope," the girl complimented.

"Thanks. It's just for fun, nothing serious," Morgan replied.

"Looks serious to me," the girl complimented. "I'm Aria."

"Morgan," she replied.

"Why haven't I seen you around?" Aria asked.

"I just got here. I came in mid-semester," Morgan answered.

"Well, maybe I'll see you around," Aria said.

"Maybe," Mo returned. She pushed open the door.

"Hey!" Aria called out. "Hold up." Morgan watched her go into her duffle bag. She retrieved a flyer and hurried across the wooden floor to deliver it to Morgan.

"Auditions? What's this?" Morgan asked, staring at the details.

"Stiletto Gang?" Aria replied. "It's like a hip-hop dance group, but less corny than it sounds."

Morgan smiled.

"It's like a school thing, like a team or something?" Morgan asked.

"Nah, it's something I put together a few years back. I'm a film major, dance minor. It's dope though. We perform at Retro Night Club every Saturday. There's a class on Wednesday nights where we hit choreo. We upload routines from the class to YouTube. We have a pretty big following. A few artists have picked up dancers from our group for tours and shows. We've done backup at the BET awards a few times. I don't just ask anybody to come through, but you're good. You should just come check it out. See if it's something you'd be interested in," Aria invited.

Morgan placed the flyer in her bag and shrugged. "Yeah, maybe," she said. "See you around."

CHAPTER 6

The sun burned orange in the sky as it began its descent in the distance. The tranquility of the upscale neighborhood was the perfect stage. It was a lovely night to die. Cream sat inside the Range Rover, leaned low, as he parked curbside at the apartment building. He watched the block. It was quiet. He expected nothing less in this quiet, college town. A .45 automatic pistol sat in his lap. He stretched his right arm out, gripping the back side of the passenger seat, anxiety filled him. His head was all over the place. Learning of Alani's disloyalty had sent him over the edge. He hadn't meant to lay a finger on her, but something inside him snapped. The worst thoughts ran through his mind. Alani had never given him a reason to question her character before, but suddenly everything she had ever told him seemed sketchy. Had Alani played a role in hurting his daughter? Had she set the whole thing up? Did she collect insurance after his baby's death? Was it for the money? She had told him there was no insurance, but how was his baby's funeral so elaborate? It was these thoughts that made him want to wring her neck, but her screams had been so potent that he had to retreat. Her hurt was recognizable. It matched his own. That was the only thing that talked him down, because after hearing what she had done, he was prepared to do the unthinkable. He hoped the information he had gotten was accurate.

Bitch-ass nigga hiding out all the way up here, the pussy must be official.

He noticed the honey-colored girl climb out of her car with a duffel bag hanging from her shoulder. He squeezed the gun in his palm. He wanted to pull the trigger so badly he could already see her body hitting the pavement. His thirst for blood was real. In a world where men didn't care about knocking off babies, he had no problems retaliating.

He was caught between wanting slow revenge and quick justice. He knew it would hurt more if he took everyone away from Messiah, one by one before putting a bullet in him too. The only problem was, word on the street was Messiah only had one that he coveted. "Some bad bitch he spazzed over at a basketball game a while ago," his mans had informed.

"Bad bitch indeed," Cream commented, as his eyes followed the ass of young light skin walking up the walkway, struggling with her bags. Cream flipped the hood to his jacket over his head and opened the car door. He stood to tuck his pistol in his waistline, before heading up the walkway behind her. He kept a fair distance, waiting until she was at her door with the key inserted before he strolled casually behind her. It wasn't until she had the door open did he bum-rush his way inside. He gripped the back of her neck and forced her to the ground, as he pointed the gun point blank range to her head.

"I'ma ask you one fucking time, where is that nigga, Messiah?"

Seven toes became six and she screamed against the duct tape over her mouth. Nothing had ever felt this painful and she shook in sheer terror. This was supposed to be a college town. It was supposed to be safe. How had she survived 18 years in a city like Flint to be caught up in Lansing, MI? Why wasn't help coming. Someone had to hear her muffled screams, right? She jerked against the chair she was tied to. The zip ties Cream had brought with him told her that he was prepared to kill her. Whatever Messiah had done had warranted this cruel retribution and she was in the crosshairs from affiliation alone. What she had once coveted, she regretted. She didn't want any connection to him at all in this excruciating moment. Cream picked up a piece of mail from the living room table.

"Morgan Atkins," he read.

She shook her head, as she sobbed, her eyes pleading with him. Cream looked at her, bleeding, crying, and he felt no sympathy. All he saw was his little girl.

"Where is he?" Cream pulled the tape from her mouth.

"I don't know! Please! He won't answer for me!" she shouted. Cream put the tape back over her mouth.

Cream pulled out her cell phone that he had retrieved from her bag and clicked on Messiah's name again. He put the phone on speaker.

"The voicemail pick up again and that's another toe, bitch," Cream said, again.

"AGHHH!" Muffled screams made the hair on the back of his neck stand. He was cutting through her flesh with kitchen knives, so it was painful and slow. He pulled it off and held it up in front of her face, getting so close that she had to crane her neck back to see him. She was woozy, and vomit tickled the back of her throat, but she couldn't let it come up. It had nowhere to go.

Cream looked at the time. He had been there for hours, waiting, lurking, torturing. Messiah had yet to arrive and he was beginning to think he wouldn't show. He would leave his mark, however. Tired of the games, Cream stood and pulled the silencer out of his back pocket. Tears leaked out of her eyes, as she shook her head back and forth. This was how her life would end. She was only 18. She had seen more dark days than good. She had thought she had her entire life ahead of her to experience a little good…to find a little love…but her expiration had come. She closed her eyes, as Cream pressed the gun to her nose. He pulled the trigger three times. Another moth. Another flame. Her affiliation with a bad boy had caused her own demise.

Messiah sat in the shadows of the underpass, leaned up against the wall as he waited for the semi. The vibration in his pocket surprised him. He lifted the simple phone from his pocket. No numbers were stored but he recognized it instantly. If Ethic was calling, it wasn't something that could wait. He answered.

"Big homie, I'm kind of in the middle of something right now." Messiah was waiting at the underpass on I-75. The truck was due within a 15-minute window and he could afford no distractions. He was surprised Ethic had even called this line. It was the one he used for business, a burner that couldn't be traced back to him; one that he used for communication with Ahmeek and Isa only. Messiah didn't even carry his iPhone when he was doing dirt. Too much monitoring, microphones, and GPS. He was like an 80's gangster in the way he moved. The authorities would have to put surveillance on him to catch him up. He wouldn't make it easy for them by being stupid. He had never minded being disconnected from the rush of the world, prior to Morgan, but today he had been filled with a nagging need to contact her. Business came first, however, so he'd resisted. *Get the money for her, get back to her.*

"I need you to cut that short and get to State. Morgan isn't answering her phone. I need you to bring her home for the weekend. I need all my kids in the same place for a few days." Ethic's voice was serious. It was only this way when he was about to do one thing...commit murder.

Messiah checked the Rolex on his wrist. *Fuck.* All he needed was another hour to pull of this robbery. It would set his team up for months, but his gut was telling him to go now...to get to Morgan right fucking now. He hadn't spoken to her all day, hadn't heard her voice, and it hadn't been a concern at first, but now with Ethic on his line he second-guessed everything.

"Everything good? I need to come off the bench?" Messiah asked. "Niggas ain't wanted smoke with you ever. Somebody done lost their mind or something?"

"Cash rules everything around me. Bring her home. I'll handle the rest," Ethic stated.

C.R.E.A.M

Messiah decoded the hidden message, instantly, and hung up the phone. No hesitation. He kicked off his stand and gripped his throttle, as he pulled out into the flow of traffic. If Cream was out of prison, he was a problem. The rules of an eye for an eye would apply. Ethic had taken a kid, Cream would take a kid. The easiest target would be Morgan. His temperament bubbled, as a combination of unease and fury rumbled in the pit of him. *I'ma fucking kill this nigga*, he thought, as weaved in and out of cars on the road. The wind whistled around him, he was going so fast, maxing out his speedometer. If he made one mistake at that speed, it would be over, but he didn't care. All he could think of was her. Any cop that pulled him over would be a memory before he could even ask for his license and registration. He wouldn't think twice about blowing a nigga head off to get to her. The possibility of Morgan's safety being in jeopardy put Messiah in a dangerous state of mind. He clenched his jaw and squeezed his throttle tighter. The horse power of his custom engine lunged him forward.

"Fuck, fuck, fuck!" he whispered.

Why didn't I just call her?

He had to reach under his helmet to wipe the condensation from his vision. He couldn't understand why the outside of his helmet wasn't wet. It was raining, right? It had to be, because he could barely see. He looked down. His bike was dry. His eyes were wet. He was crying. Effortless worry spilled from his eyes, leaking like that annoying drop that dripped from his bathroom sink all night. If he had any doubt about how he felt about Morgan before, it was erased. Love scared him, but loss scared him more. If Cream thought Ethic was callous for killing his daughter, he didn't want any parts of what Messiah would inflict if anything happened to Morgan. He would erase his entire lineage…his mama, grandmama, the baby mama and the brat he had on the other side of town…Cream would have to line up caskets in a parade by the time Messiah was done. Messiah was too emotional to plan it out. If Morgan's smile was even diminished by Cream. If any detail about her was disturbed, Messiah was committing murder tonight and going to jail in the morning. Niggas would know that a man named Messiah had loved a girl named Morgan, once upon a time. The thought of her being vulnerable, exposed and open to attack, broke him down. Shorty Doo-Wop had gotten under his skin like no one before her.

It took him 25 minutes to close the 60-mile gap between them, and when he got off at the exit, his heart stopped.

There were red, white and blue lights in the distance. He ran every red light until he was on the scene. The crowd of residents and students surrounding Morgan's building put a sickness in him and it was spreading with every step he took. A firetruck was there, an ambulance, and multiple police cars. People stood around with their hands covering their mouths in disbelief. Messiah didn't even park his bike. He slowed, hopped off, tossing it to the ground on its side. A $60,000 motorcycle disregarded like the little Huffy he had stolen from the corner store as a kid. Nothing mattered but her.

Messiah broke through the crowd. "Where is she?" he shouted. He pushed his way to the front and his worst fears were confirmed. He lunged for the men rolling the body out of Morgan's apartment beneath a white sheet. An officer restrained him.

"Whoa! Whoa!"

Messiah pushed him.

"Get the fuck off me!" he shouted. He was pushing past this officer with ease, like he wasn't a black man that the cops were just waiting to gun down. It would be better now, anyway. That cop would be dubbed a hero if he killed Messiah right now, before he got on his shit, because he was with all the shits after seeing that white tarp. The cop was looking at a murder suspect and didn't even know it.

"Kid! You don't wanna see her like this," the officer shouted, as he blocked Messiah from passing. Messiah kept pushing, kept fighting to get to that white sheet. It took three officers to bring Messiah to his knees. He was so out of control they were forced to cuff him.

"Look, Kid! I don't want to take you in, but you've got to calm down."

The officer standing in front of him was black and Messiah looked him in the eyes, but he felt his strength wavering. He was about to breakdown. He couldn't even look himself in the mirror and cry, so letting another man see him weak wasn't an option, but damn his insides were so tender, and his eyes were so full. He lowered his head, locs hanging in his vision, as he bit his lower lip in turmoil. He sniffed away his emotions because the only one he wanted to feel was rage. Morgan had turned him on and not just in a sexual way. She had gotten his mind and his heart and his soul to work, like all he was missing was a battery to function like a human being and she possessed the right size. That's where this emotion was coming from. It was residual goodness from her. He needed to turn all those parts of him off, so he could go back to savagery. He was a barbarian, and now that she was gone, he was about to remind niggas. He lifted his head.

"Does she have any distinguishing marks that you can identify besides her face?" The officer asked.

The question gutted Messiah. Cream had destroyed her face. That face. The one he decided in that moment to put on his back. That walking piece of art.

"Her wrist." He barely got it out. "There's a tattoo there. A moth. On the inside of her left wrist."

The officer walked over to the body and pulled out the identifying arm. Messiah fell to his knees when he saw the cop's reaction. With his hands behind his back, he leaned forward, planting his head in the dirt as he screamed at the top of his lungs.

CHAPTER 7

Black heart. Lost soul. Messiah rode shotgun in Meek's whip, staring out the window as the ghost town of Flint passed him by. The gun on his hip was burning a hole there. He needed to pull triggers tonight. The only sound was the low vibes of Kendrick Lamar, pumping from the subwoofers. Ahmeek and Isa knew better than to encourage or interrupt the murderous thoughts going through his mind. On the other hand, they offered no protest either. If he was rocking, they were rolling. When Messiah decided it was time for a nigga to meet his maker, not one but three grim reapers showed up for the pomp and circumstance. Sure, Ethic had said to kill alone, but this was war. Messiah didn't know whom Cream had on his team, but any and everyone involved in the demise of Morgan Atkins was a dead man walking. All he knew was that he used to be heavy in the streets before going to prison. Messiah wasn't coming unprepared. Isa and Ahmeek didn't even need an explanation, but for this one, they had received the worst type. Morgan Atkins' murder couldn't go without retribution. Messiah didn't even take the time to run it by Ethic. This time, her honor would be his to defend. He was headed to Alani's house. He knew she would know where Cream was. Messiah would get the information out of her one way or another. Nothing was off limits. The car rolled to a stop a house down from Alani's.

"Yo, this might just be the dumbest nigga on the planet. Is that him?"

Cream stood on the porch, arguing with Alani, trying to force his way into her home.

Messiah wasn't the type to take three-point shots. He preferred the lay-up. It was closer, less room for error and he never missed. He hopped out the car but felt the overwhelming urge to get his hands dirty on this one. He ran up on Cream, without warning.

"No!" Alani shouted. Standing in the doorway, she saw him coming, but Cream was slow to turn. Messiah yoked Cream up by the back of the neck and tossed him down Alani's porch stairs. Cream hit the pavement hard, the back of his skull bounced off it like a basketball, as Messiah descended the steps, pulling up his pants slightly.

Cream reached for his gun, but before he could even aim it, Messiah sent a vicious kick to Cream's face.

"No! No! Wait! Please!" Alani yelled, as Cream rolled on the ground, grimacing and groaning, blood pouring from his mouth. Messiah gripped the back of his jacket and forced him over. He grabbed one of the flower pots that lined the walkway. He gripped it with one hand and grabbed Cream's collar with the other, slamming that flower pot again and again into Cream's face until it crumbled in his hands.

"Stop!" Alani shouted, as she stood horrified on the porch, her hands covering her face. She shook her head back and forth. This was too much violence, too much torture. She didn't know what he had done, but she didn't know if it warranted this. Messiah took heavy boots to Cream. Breaking ribs and knocking out teeth, as he stomped him out, uncaring where his thick soles landed.

The lights to the house next door flickered on from the commotion but Messiah didn't care. He wasn't stopping until Cream ceased to exist.

"Bro', the neighbors," Isa warned.

Messiah heard nothing. He was in a zone, checked out of reality, as he punched Cream again and again. Again, and again. Messiah was sure his hand was broken from the impact, but the pain felt good, the pain felt like justice. Her face flashed in his mind with every blow and he went harder. He was like a wild animal.

"This nigga," Ahmeek whispered, as he looked around and saw more neighbors emerging from their homes. Someone was going to call the police. Messiah would gladly go to jail, as long as he committed this murder first. Cream never had time to defend himself, Messiah was all over him. Messiah heaved as his locs hung in his face. He swept them to the back, and when he looked up he saw the bat, propped against the side of the porch. He licked his lips, sneering as he snatched it up.

CRACK!

The wood splintered over Cream's skull. The crushing of bone was audible.

"Bro', chill, nigga, all these mu'fuckas out here," Isa said, as he grabbed Messiah's arm. Messiah shrugged him off.

"Touch me again and I'll kill you, nigga," Messiah said to his friend. They had never seen Messiah this wild. He was reckless and uncalculating, operating on pure emotion. No one had ever broken his heart, this...Morgan's murder...visions of her under that white sheet...it destroyed him.

Alani was hysterical, crying on the porch, and when she saw Ethic's truck pull up she felt relief. He would stop this. It was madness. He would at least do that.

"Messiah. Let the nigga live," Ethic stated, calmly, as he rolled up his sleeves.

Messiah wasn't in the mood for taking orders, he was executing this man tonight. Messiah brought the bat down again, this time crushing ribs.

Ethic grabbed Messiah's arm and seeing red Messiah drew his pistol and put it to Ethic's head. Messiah sneered, gritting his teeth. Tears filled his eyes. Ethic didn't flinch. He stayed ready. It wasn't even a thought to come underneath with his pistol simultaneously, resting it under Messiah's chin. He was his soldier, but he would send him to his maker if it came to that. Ethic was level-headed, while Messiah's mind was clouded with emotion. He was stuck in a rage where he saw everything in red. Ethic's gaze was void of sentiment, as if he were working on logic alone. As if he was following a set of instructions where pulling the trigger came next and he could do that then go home and eat dinner, as if nothing had even occurred. There wasn't a doubt in Ethic's mind that Messiah loved Morgan the best he knew how and with all he had. It resonated in the young bull's eyes fiercely. Ethic knew a love like that. He had experienced it a couple times, but Messiah was a live wire. The same passion he would love Morgan with, he would mishandle her with if things went wrong. He was all G with no finesse. He hadn't learned restraint, yet. Ethic would never bless a union like that, not where Morgan was concerned.

"This is why you're no good for her," Ethic stated. "When I say let a nigga walk, you let him walk." Ethic was speaking through gritted teeth, as he nudged Messiah's chin higher with his pistol and zeroed in on his eyes. The intensity of the stare down silenced everyone. No one knew what could occur. If the wind blew the wrong way, either man could end up circled in chalk. Ethic dared Messiah to pull the trigger.

"Messiah!"

Messiah's world crashed when he heard her voice. He would

have thought it was in his head, if he didn't see Morgan's car pulling up recklessly to the curb. She hopped out and stood with worried eyes as she placed a hand on the roof of her car. "Messiah, stop!" Like she had some type of mind control, Messiah lowered his gun and clicked on the safety. She had pressed his off switch. Just the sound of her voice snapped him out of his fit of rage. His stomach caved. How was she *here*? When she had been *there*? Under the white sheet with the tattoo on her arm? He gripped his gun and placed hands on top of his head, as he backpedaled. He couldn't breathe. She was alive. She was breathing. Had she borrowed his air because suddenly there wasn't enough left for him?

Fuck.

Messiah delivered a final kick to Cream's head for good measure.

"Messiah!" His name. Her tongue. He was spellbound. Messiah lifted grateful eyes to her. He wanted to touch her to make sure she was real, but with Ethic watching his every move, he couldn't. His logic had returned, and although he was willing to say fuck Ethic and everyone else looking on, he knew Morgan would not.

Everyone was on edge, everyone except Ethic because while Messiah was a beast, Ethic had trained him. Alani stood deathly still on her porch, as she looked from the pulp that was left of her child's father to Ethic. Ethic motioned for Ahmeek and Isa.

"Pull him to his feet," he said, calmly. Cream was barely conscious and groaned in agony.

"Ethic," Alani whispered. "Please."

Ethic raised a finger to silence her, as Ahmeek and Isa did as they were told.

"I heard you were looking for me," Ethic stated. "You put hands on her, as punishment for fucking with me."

Cream's entire face was beaten in and swollen, he staggered against Ahmeek and Isa.

"I killed your daughter," Ethic said. "Although, if you were a man and you were here to protect her, to provide for her and the woman that carried her, I suspect she would have never been there to begin with. That's neither here nor there. Her death is still on me. A horrible accident that I'll never atone for, but still, her blood is on my hands. Now, I'm right here in front of you, nigga. What we going to do about it?"

"Ethic." Alani took a step down off her porch.

Again, with the finger, halting her like she was an impatient child trying to interrupt the grown folks while they talked.

"Now me, I'm an everyday-type-of-father, not a come-in-and-out-type but I guess a father is a father. I understand how it's laying because, just off GP, I should put a bullet in your brain for the shit you pulled tonight. But, I understand what you're feeling. I get it. You want my head." Ethic nodded. "But I don't play no games about mine and her," he pointed to Morgan who was still looking on in distress, eyes wide, watering, nervous. Then, he pointed to Alani. "And her." He saw her breath catch in surprise.

Cream looked up at Alani who stood, braced with her arms in front of her, like she was trying to keep her balance. "Nah, that ain't you no more," Ethic said, answering the question that was in Cream's swollen eyes. He had gone to jail with Alani as an option. He had come home, and she was a priority to another man. Life was like that. It was that trash and treasure thing. One man's something was another man's something else. It was all about how a man perceived the value of a woman. "She don't got to fuck with me another day of her life and that'll still be me. The wind blow a tress of her hair the wrong way and I'ma think you got too rough with her. Keep your hands to yourself before I take 'em. You got me?"

Cream spit out blood and nodded, snickering a bit.

Ain't that a bitch?

Ethic knew the thought before it even flashed in Cream's simple mind. Challenge lived in Cream's eyes. Alani hadn't chosen a baby father with no heart. Ethic recognized that much. Cream would be a problem one day, but he didn't want Alani to see him take his life. To know he could kill was one thing, but to witness it was a completely different story. It wasn't prettied up like in the movies or books. In real life, it was haunting. It rotted your soul and the smell of blood never left you.

"Walk away while it's still an option," Ethic said. His tone stilled the air and Alani quivered. His demeanor was noxious, and Alani stood in disbelief. He was like a different person standing in front of her. There was something sinister inside a man that could admit to killing a child without flinching. He looked at her and only then did his demeanor soften. With Cream he was one way, with her he was another. Like a double-sided illusion, and Alani was struggling to discern which one was the real him. He didn't speak to her again, but his eyes held an apology in them. When he turned his back and headed to the car, Alani's legs folded. She sat on her top step, as she watched him leave.

Morgan met him at the curb and buried her head in his shoulders. "What are you doing here?" he asked.

"Your locations," she whispered. "And his locations. They were in the same place. I thought there might be trouble," she whispered, trying hard not to let on that she had come here for her man.

"Go home," he instructed. He kissed the top of her head.

Her eyes glanced at Messiah. Every part of her wanted to run to him, but she couldn't, not with Ethic present. She nodded and got into her car before pulling away.

"Bring the Range back to the house. We need to talk," he ordered, as he passed Messiah.

He didn't even acknowledge Meek and Isa, before he pulled away from the scene.

She makes me out of control. I can't have something that I care about losing. Shit ain't safe for nobody.

Messiah stood in Ethic's office, hands folded across his body, chin up.

"Leaving him alive was a mistake," Messiah said. "The nigga dropped a body at Morgan's apartment. I thought it was her under that sheet."

"And that makes a difference to you. Whether it was her life or someone else's?" Ethic gauged.

"I said I'd let her go live her life, she's doing that. I'm in Flint doing me. She's at college doing her. The distance is there," Messiah said, trying hard to speak without lying because he felt like liars were only liars because they feared something. Messiah feared nothing, not even Ethic, so he didn't want to lie; but for Morgan's sake, he danced finely between the lie of fact and fiction. "Can't change what I can't change, though. Can't 'un-feel' what I feel for her. I thought it was her and for that I offer no apologies," Messiah said.

"And if it had been her?" Ethic asked.

"It would be a lot of bodies dropping tonight," Messiah stated.

"Next time you pull a gun on me..." Ethic stopped himself. "Get your temper under control and get your fucking hand looked at." Ethic left it there. He wasn't angry at Messiah. Ethic knew he had been blinded by a feeling so unfamiliar that he didn't know how to respond.

I've got to put the brakes on that. Under no circumstances would Ethic allow Messiah to steer Morgan astray. He had no idea the type of energy and connection he was trying to deter. Messiah exited the office, and when he stepped outside, Morgan was sitting on the porch, waiting anxiously.

"It was Nish," she whispered. She was such a pure soul that she still cried for her fallen friend, the same friend who had done her dirty, time and time again. "Campus security sent out an update to all the students. They identified her by the tattoo." She held up her wrist. "We got them together in 11th grade." Morgan looked up at Messiah who stood, staring straight ahead, his hands tucked in the pockets of his sweat pants. "You thought it was me."

She stood and rushed into his arms. He held her so tightly that it felt like they were one.

"My head is all fucked up, Mo," he whispered into her ear.

"I'm right here, baby," she whispered back. "I'm right here."

His hand was in her hair, fucking up her silk press like always, and he wished he could just merge their bodies, tuck her inside his, so he could ensure her safety. He had always intended on offing Nish for the shit she had pulled with Morgan. He wouldn't lose sleep over her death, but the fact that it had come so close to Morgan shook him.

"Where were you, shorty?" he asked. "I thought it was you under that sheet." He grimaced, tightening his face to stop himself from folding. It was so hard for him to remain just that…hard.

"I was dancing at the rec. You weren't responding to my texts. You hadn't called. I was thinking stupid thoughts, overthinking, wondering if you were with someone else…" She noticed his swollen and bloodied knuckles. She reached for it in concern.

"I thought it was you," he repeated.

Messiah took a step back.

"I need a break from this. From you," Messiah said. The

realization of what could have been made him realize Ethic's logic. Good girls and gangsters. Oil and water. They didn't belong together. The risk was greater than just distraction. He wasn't willing to risk her life. He had to love her enough to know that he wasn't the man for her, despite how much he revered her.

"Messiah, I'm fine," she whispered, reaching for his cheek. He swiped her hand away, as he moved his face out of the way.

"But you could have..." He stopped speaking and shook his head. If Morgan was going to move on and heal, he had to make a clean break. It was something he should have never started anyway because he had his own reasons why they would never work. Safety was one of many. Then, there was that other one. "Nah. This is a wrap. I'm off it."

He was restoring a guard with her, blocking her out, and Morgan felt like her heart was a piece of paper being torn straight down the middle.

"Messiah!" she hissed.

He was walking away.

She wanted to scream his name and make a scene, but it would only lure Ethic out the house. He was taking his attention from her; and after it being given so freely, she would die without it. Messiah turned and walked back over to her. He pulled her into his body and gripped her chin as he stared down at her.

"I'ma come home one day, shorty. Just... right now, this ain't for us," he said.

Her eyes welled with tears, as she choked on her sobs. He kissed her lips, not giving a damn if Ethic was inside. He took her entire tongue into his mouth, sucking on her lips with so much intensity that her nipples pebbled. His phone buzzed on his hip and he knew his people were up the block, waiting.

"That's Meek. I got to go." He pulled away, nudging her chin before leaving her standing alone.

The glow illuminating the crack under Bella's door caught Ethic's attention, as he headed to his bedroom. It was almost four o'clock in the morning. If she was still awake it was because she was afraid to go to sleep. He had tried his best to soothe her, but the things she had experienced today had matured her. He had seen an instant transformation in the things she processed in her mind. He had sugarcoated it as best as he could without lying, but he knew there would be more questions to come because Bella was growing up. He stopped and knocked. Not knocking would have been an invasion of privacy. Her words, not his. Ones that told him his baby girl was slowly beginning to erase the baby from her title. She was a girl, a beautiful girl, who was dipping a toe into her teen years, checking the temperature of those deep waters and Ethic was terrified.

"Come in," she called, softly, and Ethic opened the door to peek inside.

"It's late, B," Ethic whispered, as he crossed the carpet and took a seat on the edge of her bed.

"I keep thinking about her. Do you think she's okay? I've never heard somebody sound like that when they were crying...like it hurt so bad, Daddy," Bella said.

Ethic hung his head and nodded. He knew the sound she was speaking of. It was still echoing in his mind. He imagined it would for a while.

"It does hurt, B. Alani is..." He paused. What could he say? Not one thing.

"What about the man that hit her?" Bella pushed. "We have to do something. We have to help her."

"She's safe from him, Bella. I took care of that part."

"Did you kill him?"

Ethic was gutted. Her perception of him was changed. She now knew there was a possibility that he would kill and that alone made Ethic want to cry. He had taken away her naïveté . It was like the moment your child didn't believe in Santa anymore, or the Easter bunny. When you saw reality creeping into their consciousness and you wanted to stop it because the real world was cold. She saw him for the man he was, and it took strength to appear unmoved by it.

"No," Ethic answered. He rubbed his hands together as he leaned forward. "Being a man is hard, Bella. Being a black man is harder. It's my job to protect my children. At times, I've done things I'm not proud of to make sure you, your brother, and Mo are safe. I love you more than I love myself. If I ever have to make the choice between your life and someone else's life, I'm obligated to choose you, Bella...the three of you. Sometimes, that makes me the bad guy. To Alani, I'm the bad guy. I'm no good for her."

"But how can you be bad if you love her?" Bella asked.

He looked at his daughter.

"Love isn't enough, sometimes," Ethic answered.

"I'm sorry I ran from you," Bella offered.

He nodded and sniffed, as his brows furrowed in distress. He never wanted his daughter to apologize for feeling something.

"I hope you know that I would never ever hurt you," Ethic stated, pained.

"I know, Daddy. Alani told me," she said.

He scoffed, in disbelief. He had underestimated her greatness. Even in Alani's darkest hour she had somehow scraped up enough light for him. A fucking phenomenal woman. He could never comprehend how black women managed the type of strength they possessed. He had seen a lot of things in his lifetime that had made him question God's existence, but the strength of melanin-drenched women had to be divine. There was no other explanation for it.

"Get some sleep," he whispered. He planted a kiss on her forehead and then lifted from her bed. It was time to call it a night. Some problems just couldn't be resolved within the span of a day; and as he carried himself to his room, he knew that the ones he had created would linger for a while. Shit, they would linger for a lifetime.

CHAPTER 8

One Week Later

A sadness had taken residence in the Okafor household, and as Ethic sat at the head of the table, eating breakfast with Mo, Eazy, and Bella, he felt like a failure. He questioned so many choices he had made over the years. He had moved his family from St. Louis to Flint years ago. He thought it only fair for Morgan to be near her parents' gravesites and he had an overwhelming urge to be near Raven's. But Flint was a volatile place. It seemed no matter how hard he tried to protect his family, the streets reached in and touched them. He sat with Morgan to his left and his two youngest to his right and an empty chair across the table. He wondered if perhaps he should have placed Dolce in that seat. He didn't love her, but she was consistent. She had moved her entire life to Flint to follow him there. He hadn't asked but she had done it and he hadn't stopped her. Perhaps, he could have learned to love her, instead of looking for something organic. One thing he knew was that Dolce didn't have the power to wound him the way he was now. There would have been no extreme highs of love or lows of despair, just a consistent, constant body to fill the empty space. That empty chair plagued his brain. The vacancy killed him because he could visualize Alani there. He could practically smell her. He was an empty man just letting the time clock on his life waste away. He wanted to love Alani, but after the parts of himself he had exposed, he would be lucky to ever lay eyes on her again. He knew she was hurting, and he wouldn't be Ethic if he didn't want to fix everything that ailed her, but he knew some wounds would only get infected when touched. This one was too deep. The only thing he could do was leave it alone and let time do its job. Thinking about it put a lump in his throat and more weight on his chest than he preferred. He looked at his babies. Despite Morgan's newfound independence, she still qualified as such. Even their faces were drawn tight. Everyone, except Eazy's and he thanked God for him. The girls were high maintenance and drew from him emotionally. Eazy was the well he filled up from after Bella and Morgan depleted him. His big man. His very best friend.

"Have you heard from Alani?" Bella asked. He could tell it had been heavy on her mind. She had come into his room every night for the past week and crawled under the covers at the end of his bed. She only did that when something was bothering her. She had simply seen and heard too much, lately. He would have to put some work into reversing the damage.

"Fuck her," Morgan whispered.

"Yo, Mo," Ethic stated, as he shot her a warning glare. He was much like a father in that way. All it took was one look. She conceded. Her attitude had been unbearable lately as well, but she too was going through a storm. With Nish's murder and funeral, that she had opted not to attend, Ethic knew she was hurting. He wasn't privy to the heartbreak Messiah had left her with, but he knew her mood matched her circumstance.

"No. I haven't, B. She's going through a lot," Ethic explained. "But she's safe."

"What about the debutante pageant?" Bella asked. "Do you think she will still do that with me?"

Ethic sighed. "I don't suppose she'll be better by then, B. Maybe Mo can participate with you?"

"Mo's not my mother," Bella snapped.

"Alani ain't either. She's not family at all," Morgan spat back.

Two temperamental girls. Ethic rubbed circles over his head.

"What's with this Alani chick, anyway? She doesn't belong here. She's *his* sister," Mo said, as she looked at Ethic with challenging eyes.

"She won't be around anymore, anyway, Mo. Nothing for you to worry about," he said, rising from the table. He stopped behind her chair and kissed the top of Mo's head. Then rounded the table and kissed Eazy's head. When he got to Bella, he leaned into her ear. "Daddy will walk you down that aisle myself, if I got to, a'ight?"

Bella nodded, and he kissed her cheek.

"The bus will be here any minute," Ethic stated. "Let's hustle." He clapped his hands together loudly and roused them from their seats. Mo stayed seated but Eazy and Bella climbed up to gather their things before rushing out the door.

"Bye, Mo Money!" Eazy yelled, on his way out the door, hitting some kind of half jump, half kick, to mark his exit. Morgan laughed.

"Bye, Mo," Bella added, less than enthused and holding a grudge about their petty spat. Bella was growing up and she was growing into her identity. Her opinions mattered, even if no one took heed yet.

"B?" Morgan called after her. Bella turned, gripping the straps of her backpack with her thumbs.

"I love you," Morgan said.

Bella's icy demeanor melted slightly, and she gave a small smile. "Love you," she replied. "Love you, Daddy!" When his youngest two were out the door, Ethic focused on Morgan.

"You sure you trying to go back to school right away? I don't know how comfortable I am with that," Ethic admitted.

"The school is willing to place me in an on-campus apartment. I'll be fine, and I'll keep my locations on, so you'll be able to find me whenever," she said. "I just feel like I can't miss too much time there. I already started mid-semester. I've missed a week already. If I miss any more classes, it'll just put me further behind."

"And how you feeling about Nish?" Ethic asked.

Morgan shrugged, as she looked down into her tea cup. "I don't know," she whispered. "I just want to get back, so I don't have to think about it, you know?"

Ethic nodded. "Yeah, I know," he answered. She stood and grabbed her handbag. She walked over to Ethic and he wrapped her in his arms, holding on tightly as he rested his chin against the top of her head.

"Raven would be proud. Benny and Justine too," he said. "*I'm* proud, Mo. You're just as much my daughter as Bella and I love you. I hope you know."

She pulled back and looked up at Ethic before going in for a second hug.

"I love you too," she said.

Ethic eased from her hold because he felt himself buckling. It was the emptiness of his home when his children departed that got to him. It was supposed to be the time he spent with the one he loved. Hours they would have spent in the throes of passion, moments they would have collected laughing and watching movies, or doing yoga because yoga with him led to other things. Whatever the fuck they wanted to do. Whatever *she* wanted to do. He watched Morgan walk out the door and then picked up his phone. Morgan was crazy if he thought he was going to send her back to campus unprotected. He had tried the unsupervised thing and it had gone horribly wrong. He was going back to overprotective and only offering the illusion of independence until he was sure Cream was gone for good. He put six, private, retired police officers on payroll before Morgan could even wake up. There would be one in each building she entered for her four courses and two manning her new apartment building. He could have put goons on her. He had a gang of young ones who were dying to get close to him, but Ethic wanted her removed from the street life. He needed to do it legitimately; that way, if they ever had to come off their hips to protect Morgan, it would all be legal. Her belongings were already moved into the new spot. Within a week's time, Ethic had worked magic to erase the tragic events that had taken place as best he could. If only money could erase the ills that burdened him as easily.

It wasn't the things that happened to Alani that devastated her most. It was the aftermath. It was the struggle it took to pick herself up off the floor and put the pieces of her life back together. She didn't know where to start. So many things needed mending. She had slept with her bedroom door locked, with a dresser pushed in front of it and a gun at her side for good measure. She wasn't sure if she was protecting herself from Cream or Ethic... all she knew was she couldn't shake the lack of security that consumed her. She felt unsafe. She felt uncovered, like she had gotten caught out in an unexpected rainstorm...her life was storming, and she was getting soaked. She had let the sun rise and fall seven times without leaving her house. The only time she left her bed was to pee. She didn't want to be awake. Facing reality was torture, so she swallowed NyQuil pills to knock herself out. It was the only time she didn't hurt because she was living in glorious, self-induced dreams with her daughter. Her pillow was stiff from the tears wetting the pillow case and drying repeatedly.

The kind of crying Alani had done had strained her eyes and made her head hurt. It came from the pit of her and she couldn't stop. She needed to cry him out. Why couldn't she cry him out? He was still there and now her eyes were so swollen, her gut so empty that she couldn't squeeze another drop from her soul. The feeling was still there, however. The weakness. It ate away at the lining of her stomach and made her feel nauseous. So nauseous, like even if she sprinted she wouldn't make it to the bathroom in time. She peeled herself from the bed linens and stood to her feet. Her legs were weak. Maybe from not using them much the past few days. Probably, from lack of food. She hadn't eaten one thing in a week. If it weren't for the water bottles she kept stored in her bathroom, she would have no water to sustain her this long. She sat and licked her crusted lips. Her throat was so dry it felt like she was sick, like she was developing the makings of a cold. Or maybe she was. Maybe she had caught a bug called love and it was the trickiest of all to get rid of. Alani had never neglected herself to this magnitude. It was scary. It was unhealthy, and she didn't care. Who was she living for anyway? Nobody needed her. Nobody would miss her, if she took that gun and pulled the hair trigger. Her weary legs carried her to the bathroom and she stood in front of the covered vanity. She pulled down the scarf she had used to block her reflection and what she saw made her eyes water. The black eye had turned green and her hair was matted to her scalp. She looked like she had been pulled in off the streets. She looked like her mother, rundown, like she had been drinking and smoking her life away. Like the streets had chewed her up and spit her back out; but no, this wasn't that. Love had done the chewing up and spitting out. It had destroyed her. Her lip quivered, and she closed her eyes. She turned to her bathtub and looked at the stack of bottled waters that sat beside it. She began pouring them one after another into the bath tub. Such a tedious task. Such a third world thing to do. Ethic had just had her in his palace, showering with clean water, now she was back in the hood, like the clock had struck midnight and her carriage had turned back into a pumpkin. She went to the kitchen and filled up three large stock pots and placed them on the stove to boil. She didn't know why this struggle felt different today. It was like she had less patience; like she was less accepting of it because she had experienced a moment of something different with Ethic. She carried the boiling water up the stairs to her bathroom, one by one, and emptied the hot water into the tub, mixing it with the water from the bottles. Then she submerged her tired body. So much effort for such little reward; but in this moment, her little bath tub was a five-star spa. It soothed her aches and she exhaled a troubled breath.

She leaned into the water and stayed there until the water chilled, forcing her to wash her body and climb out. The bath did little to put strength back into her. She took one of the room temperature water bottles and guzzled an entire one before grabbing another. That one she would use to brush her teeth with. Alani fingered the war zone that was her scalp and sighed.

"What the hell were you thinking?" she whispered.

The first thing she would have to do is go to the salon to see if they could salvage what was left of her hair. At least then she wouldn't look as bad as she felt.

She was stunned when she stepped outside. As soon as her foot crossed the threshold, she kicked a set of keys. She bent to pick them up. Her white Mercedes sat in the driveway. She wondered when he had brought it. Had she been that out of it? She hesitated. Was it wrong to drive it? It was a gift from the devil. It was either that or walk. If she drove it did it mean she was disrespecting her daughter's memory? Was it a pay off? A bribe to keep her mouth shut? Alani powered on her phone and she was surprised when she found no missed calls or texts from Ethic. She had expected them, but there were none. She had fallen off the face of the planet for days and no one had missed her. No one had needed her. *So, what's the point?* Alani walked over to the car and unlocked the door. It was ridiculous for her to own it. She was bathing with water bottles but driving a luxury car. She didn't want it anyway. Just the sight reminded her of Ethic. It made her feel cheap. Like she was for sale and Ethic had scooped her off the clearance rack. She didn't know why her self-worth fluctuated with every relationship she had with men. This was the most reduced she had ever been, probably because he had inflated her so much before dropping the ball. She had plummeted when he let her down - straight to the bottom. Crashed and burned. She made her way across town and pulled into her old salon. She hadn't been in so long because things had been tight before him. She was barely making ends meet, so getting her hair done was a rarity. When she pulled into *Margo's,* she knew she would be in good hands. Margo was one of the most knowledgeable stylists in the entire city. She was a heavyset, older woman, with chocolate skin, and a smile that warmed her clients at first sight. Alani used to love to sit in her chair when she was a teenager. She hadn't been in a while, but she was the only person Alani trusted to fix the mess she had made. Margo had a way of healing raggedy heads and raggedy hearts. Alani climbed out of the car and walked inside.

"Now I know that ain't my girl?!"

Margo recognized her instantly and Alani gave a gracious smile. This was the woman who had groomed her hair as a child and young girl. Alani didn't realize how much she missed her until Margo came from her chair and wrapped Alani in her warm arms. The woman pulled back and gripped both of Alani's hands. "I'm real sorry to hear about your baby, La La," Margo said. She was the only person who ever called her *La La*, and hearing the nickname brought back happier times…easier times.

Alani nodded and teared, unable to find words.

"Shaniece get your ass up out my chair. My girl is here! She came to visit an old lady! Trina gon' finish you up," Margo said, jovially, as she hustled the girl from her chair and spun it around to Alani. The girl didn't take offense. Everyone loved Margo. She was just good people like that. "Let me see what you hiding up under that scarf. You done messed up all that curly, pretty hair it took me years to tame?"

Alani sat in the leather swivel chair and Margo began to unravel the scarf. Alani felt the pause when she saw what lied beneath.

"Come on, baby. We'll go to the private booth in the back," Margo said, as she gave her a pat on the shoulder. Hairstylists were to black girls what therapists were to mental patients. Privacy and confidentiality were needed for the secrets Alani had the potential to expose.

Alani lifted and followed her to the back where a single station was inside its own private room. It was for the prestigious clients who came into town and required a private experience. Alani was being dubbed important today and it felt like she had someone who cared.

"Got to have a space I can come when these young hoes get on my nerves," she said, with a robust chuckle. Alani knew Margo didn't need the relief. She was gamed up. She could run circles around any spring chickens that walked into the shop. She wanted to save Alani the embarrassment of styling her hair in front of the gossiping women up front.

Margo pointed to the shampoo bowl and Alani sat as Margo wrapped a towel around her neck before leaning her back. Her fingertips to Alani's scalp was curing. Alani closed her eyes.

"People always say the craziest things...a woman who cuts her hair is about to change her life. They got it backwards, though. In all my years of doing hair, I've come to learn that a woman cuts her hair when life gets so heavy you can't even stand the weight of your own strands on your head. You want all that shit gone; and after what happened to you, I can't blame you, baby. Cut it all off. You want to talk about it?"

Alani let the pause linger until the wash and condition was over because she wasn't sure if she wanted to share the details. Nannie would normally be her sounding board and moral compass, but now she had no one. She knew that Margo's ears were probably the most sealed vault in the city. She was free to speak here without it being repeated and without judgement. Just good, old-fashioned love and advice. She would throw in a hug, if her client really needed it, or if she had good energy, because you couldn't just go around hugging anybody. Hug the wrong person and you could invite their demons. *Did I take on some of his?* Alani thought.

"I met a man," Alani whispered, as Margo put a cape around her.

"Well, is he a good man?" Margo asked, as she began to blow dry Alani's hair. Alani felt a tear fall and she pressed a hand to her face to trap it before wiping it away. He had felt like one. He was like the leather jacket you purchased on the street that felt 100% authentic. It came with tags and a garment bag and everything, but after trying it on a couple times it ripped. Pleather. That's what Ethic was, a pleather-ass nigga. Fake.

"No, I don't think he was," Alani answered. "But it felt so good and I thought it was healing...You know, the type of man that touches you and you just feel good all over? You feel brave and you feel confident...and you feel beautiful." Alani shook her head and she felt the pop of the comb against her scalp.

"Man must have been some type of good, he has you moving that damn head while I work," Margo fussed.

Alani straightened and took a deep breath as she released a chuckle.

"It was all a façade," Alani whispered. Margo pulled out the pressing comb and Alani didn't even flinch. Margo was skilled with that pressing comb. She wouldn't have one burn. She wouldn't even feel the sizzle of the comb as it moved through her scalp.

"Well, what was the façade? He must have been bad in bed. Lawd! Did you have to give that man back because he wasn't breaking you off right, La La?" she asked.

"He was amazing. The best I've ever had. So unselfish," Alani whispered.

"He must have laid in the wet spot! Hmm, hmm, hmm! You get a man that will lay in that wet spot and put you on the dry side of the bed and you got a winner," Margo bragged, while sticking out her tongue. "So, what was the problem?"

"He killed my daughter," Alani barely uttered those words and Margo stopped styling.

Margo shook her head. "Hold up, La La," she said. She went to the door and closed it, and then closed the blinds in the room, so no one could see in. She turned her chair around, so they were facing one another. "Alani. I thought your baby was hit by accident over some street stuff Lucas was into."

Alan nodded. "That's what he said. That's what he tried to say, but he didn't tell me. He let me fall for him. He let me lower my guard. He let me allow him to touch me. He knew the entire time that it would break me, and he let me fall with no intentions of catching me," she whispered. "And now my baby's gone, he's gone, and I'm empty."

Margo stood upright and began styling.

"How did you find out it was him?" Margo asked.

"He told me. He took me to his home, made love to me all

night, and then confessed in the morning. How sick is that?" She closed her eyes.

"So, he loves you," Margo assumed.

"That's not love," Alani rejected.

"He gave you the power to ruin his whole life. He put his freedom on the line to be honest with you. Can you imagine how difficult that had to be for *him*? To know he was about to tell you something that would make him a new slave and destroy you at the same time? All so he could be honest? Most men would have loved you their whole lives and took that secret to the grave. That sounds like love, La La," Margo said. "What was Lucas into?"

"Lucas hurt his daughter, raped her. His adopted daughter. Morgan..."

"What's his name?" Margo asked.

"Ezra..."

"Alani, you talking about Ethic?" Margo had to stop to sit in the chair across from Alani.

Alani's eyes widened in recognition, but she didn't want to place his name.

"Ethic is the one who shot Lucas?" Margo asked.

Again, Alani didn't respond. Margo stood and resumed her work.

"Morgan Atkins is royalty in this city. She's the only living member of Benny Atkins' family. His youngest daughter. I remember Justine used to bring Raven and Morgan in here twice a week and Ethic would be out there, guarding them like he was Kevin Costner, baby. He loved that Raven. I could see it in his eyes, but he never made a move. He was a respectable young man, had some manners about himself, loyal. First time I met him he strolled in here with Raven's spoiled-ass, sat in here with her for three hours without complaining. Then, when it was time to go, do you know this boy...and I say boy because he was maybe in his

20's back then…he held out her coat for her and slipped it on her shoulders. I ain't seen a gentleman his age ever! Held open that girl's door, walked her to the passenger side of his car. This whole shop was up in arms when that boy walked up out of here. Pussy dripping everywhere," Margo bragged, laughing at the memory. "He took Morgan in after her whole family was murdered. Ethic ain't no baby killer, La La. If he says it was an accident, you can take that to the bank. It sounds like your brother broke rule number one. Be careful who you offend. Lucas didn't know who he was fucking with when he hurt that girl and his karma came back on your baby," Margo said. She left Alani with an earful to think about. By the time she was done speaking, she spun Alani to the mirror.

"Gave you a little Kyla Pratt cut. It looks good on you, La La," Margo complimented. Alani pushed out a breath, as she feathered the cut. She went into her purse to pay, but Margo waved her off.

"Next time," Margo said. "You think about what I told you."

Margo wrapped her in another hug and Alani whispered, "Thank you, Margo." She walked out the shop the same way she had walked in – burdened - only now she didn't look it as well.

Morgan walked into the studio wearing a pair of Versace stilettos and adidas tights with an adidas sports bra to match. She had a red and black checkered shirt tied around her waist to cover her behind. It was crowded. Over 30 dancers filled the room. Her heart pounded. She didn't do stuff like this...try new things… meet new people. New people had always judged her, so she had stuck to the old, even when they didn't treat her the best. She would rather deal with the devils she knew than the ones she had yet to discover. Morgan was trying to find herself. She had known who deaf Morgan was. She knew her limitations, she knew what deaf Morgan preferred. She didn't know herself now. She thought she did, when she had Messiah, but since he had left she had been lost. She missed him terribly, but he hadn't reached out one time. Refusing to be the one to call first, she suffered in silence. That part, she was good at. She had suffered silently for years. Her Louis Vuitton duffel hung over her shoulder, as she made her way through the crowd. Aria was at the front of the class. Morgan waved, and she was sure she looked awkward.

"Hey! You came!" Aria greeted, stepping away from the group she was talking too.

"This is a lot of people," Morgan said, as she looked around.

"Yeah, it's kind of a big deal. Everybody isn't affiliated, though. Some people just come to learn choreo, some come because it beats the treadmill," Aria explained. She shrugged. "You ready to dance?"

"I might just watch," Morgan said.

"Girl. After what I saw you do at the rec?" Aria countered with a wave of the hand. "Come on. You up here with me. I teach the count first and then we perform it in groups. You want to snap this? Give me your phone, I'll have my camera guy do it while he's doing mine."

Morgan handed over her iPhone and sat her bag down against the mirror. Her hands were sweating, and she wiped them on her leggings as she stood nervously. She looked in the mirror. She looked the part. Nobody would be able to tell that she was an amateur. Her long hair was blown out but not flat ironed, so it was big and fluffy in the mirror.

"All right, y'all! Find a spot," Aria yelled. "I'm about to go through the first eight count."

The beat dropped, and Cardi B's voice filled the room.

I do the Maybach on Monday
Ferrari Friday
This is Sweet Pussy Saturday
That's just what Plies say

"Okay, so we got one, two, three, four," Aria started, going through a series of dance moves. Morgan concentrated on the count, not the beat, because she heard the beat differently. She mimicked the first four counts. "Now five, six, seven, eight."

Morgan zoned in and performed the moves without error, keeping the count in her head. The music made her come alive, as she stared at herself in the mirror. The entire room was in unison as they learned the entire song. Morgan's body rolled to the beat, a slight sweat made her clothes stick to her skin. Aria was dancing just as hard and the two were directly in front. The people in the back followed their lead. Aria stopped dancing.

"Keep going!"

She came up on the side of Morgan and clapped her hands in excitement, urging her to go harder. "Aye!!! Okay!!"

"Clear the floor. It's her eight count. Freestyle," she shouted. "Line 'em up to follow her count. Get in pairs."

Morgan was heaving from adrenaline.

"What do I do?" she asked.

"Whatever you want to do. They gone follow your lead," Aria said.

Money bag
Money bag
Money bag

The beat dropped, again, and Morgan danced.

"Yo, she's cold," Morgan heard a girl to the side say. "What beat she catching? I can't hear it. It's like she dancing to half counts," a guy said.

"You better go OFF!" Aria geeked. "Do it again." Aria joined in the second eight count, mimicking Morgan's movements, proving that she was a quick learner. "Two more!" Aria called out. Two by two, the dancers joined in, mastering the eight count Morgan had created. Morgan had never felt so empowered.

By the end of the class, Morgan was exhausted.

"Stick around for a while?" Aria asked.

Morgan nodded, as she leaned over onto her knees to catch her breath. Morgan walked over to her bag and sat beside it, leaning her back against the mirror. She pulled her wild hair up into a pony tail.

Aria cleared the studio and then walked back over to Morgan. She held out Morgan's phone.

"Thanks," Morgan whispered.

"Look at yourself," Aria said, holding up her own video of the session. "Looks serious to me. What you think?" Aria asked, cocking an eyebrow in challenge.

Morgan watched the video play back. She couldn't believe it was her in the video.

"It's already got five thousand likes on YouTube. And that's in an hour. You're fire. It's like you interpret the music differently. I couldn't put those eight counts together like that if I wanted to... and I'm the best," Aria said, confidently.

"I was born deaf," Morgan shared. "I hear something different than you do. I'm always behind. A little awkward with the music."

"Wow," Aria commented in shock. "Deaf? How do you even..."

"I had a surgery that restored my hearing. It's not 100 percent but I get by. I wouldn't be able to keep up with all this." Morgan motioned to the room.

"Keep up? Dancing like that, we need to keep up with you.

Artists pay good money for choreography like that. Nobody's looking for the same, old two steps. Just think about it."

Morgan nodded.

Aria glanced down at Morgan's phone.

"See, you got followers already," she said, as she pointed to the screen. The amount of views had gone up in minutes. Morgan wondered if she could handle the challenge, plus keep up with her classes. Her head was all over the place, lately, with Messiah's absence. This was the first time she had felt relief all week from the agony of him walking away.

"We'll do your choreography the fourth Saturday this month. Come if you feel like it and hop on stage with us. If not, I'll know your answer."

The scent of marijuana filled the air, as Messiah sat at the table with different denominations of bills flipping through his fingertips. Fives, tens, twenties, fifties, few hundreds, but they were there. He was obsessed with his paper being neat, so he put them all in the same direction and stacked them up. Isa sat across from him doing the same.

"Make sure that shit neat, bruh," Messiah instructed.

"Your OCD-ass," Isa snapped, but he already knew the routine. They had done it many times before. Ahmeek came through the door carrying two more duffel bags. He placed one on the floor and unzipped the second, emptying out more bills onto the table.

"This pill business is a different beast. It moves itself," Ahmeek said.

"That's because we live in a fucked-up world. Mu'fuckas sick and can't afford to go to the doctor, can't afford insurance, so they just guessing, just self-medicating," Messiah stated. He looked up at Ahmeek who had suddenly gone quiet and was standing above them, thumbing through his phone.

"Nigga, you gon' help sort through all this paper or what?" Isa asked.

Messiah snickered. "You ain't know, that's Facebook Meek? The nigga famous in his head. All those friends got the nigga walking around thinking he a celebrity," Messiah jargoned.

"Fuck you talking about? This where the hoes at!" Meek defended. "I can order up pussy like pizza, my G. They deliver that shit straight to a nigga inbox." The trio laughed. All the wisecracking was always in good fun. "If you were on social media, you would be able to see what your girl up to."

Meek passed Messiah the phone and Messiah frowned before taking it.

Morgan's face made his stomach hollow. The days that were passing by without her felt like detox. It felt brutal and he was uncomfortable with how much need she filled him with. He almost wished he had never known what she felt like at all, because without her he was a shell. Getting back to his money kept him distracted. He had robbed every semi-truck coming up the highway over the past seven days, just to keep his mind off her. Still, in moments of stillness, she invaded his thoughts. He smirked at the video, as he watched Morgan dance. It was raw, pained even, and exotic. He slid Ahmeek's phone across the table and pulled out his own. He wasn't on social media. He never understood the need to broadcast his every move. He was too busy trying to conceal his moves to stay off the radar. He signed up for an account. The entire time feeling childish but needing this bridge to stay connected to Morgan, despite his inability to do so in real life. Suddenly, social media felt genius…not stalker-ish at all…not intrusive like he had originally thought. If it gave him a glimpse of her, he was appreciative. He went to her page and couldn't stop himself before his thumb scrolled down her history. Moments during him and before filled his screen.

Pretty-ass.

He knew better than to hit like, but the visual did things to him. He went to the video of her dancing. Niggas on top of niggas filled the comments.

Peaches and heart eyes and shit.

Messiah felt the spark that could ignite a jealousy so bold it would send him up the highway and have him at her doorstep. He doused it quickly and put the phone away.

Live, shorty.

The thought was followed by a bite to his lip because she put a hunger in him.

"Fuck you following her for anyway, nigga?" Messiah asked, at second thought. "Hit that unfollow button, mu'fucka."

He chuckled and dragged his hands down his face in distress. He was going to have to get under someone else to erase the yearning he felt for Morgan. New pussy distracted from old pussy, right? Maybe, but when the connection was deeper than sexual, new pussy could come wrapped in a bow and a man would still have his mind occupied with thoughts of that old thang. Oh, how desperately he wanted that old thing back, but it just wasn't in the cards for them. It wasn't right for so many reasons. Reasons he couldn't explain aloud.

CHAPTER 9

Ethic closed the hood to the 1985 Buick Regal and
reached for the mechanic's rag that sat on the tool
bench beside him. He was dirty as hell. His defined
arms and white wife beater were covered in oil and
grime. The mechanic's coverall only covered his bottom half.
The top was rolled down around his waist to fight the heat
inside the shop. He had remodeled the entire car, piece by
piece. What was supposed to be a project he worked on in
his spare time had become an obsession. To fix something.
To restore something. To make that which was ugly beautiful
again. He desperately wanted to do that. He sat back and
looked at the marvel before him and wished he could piece
the rest of his life back so simply. He had worked day and
night for a month to restore the classic car. It was striking.
He had put only the best of the best parts inside, leaving out
everything that was cheap and avoiding what would weather
over time. He wanted something lasting, needed something
that could withstand the test of time. He thought of *her*. She
lived behind that deep-set scowl. She had been squatting in his
mind, refusing to give up residency since the day he met her.
Nothing he did could evict her from his head.

"That's a hell of a machine, boss," Redneck Larry said, as he whistled at the impressive red candy paint. "You got the tint on their so deep you can't even see through it."

Ethic tossed the keys up into the air and Larry snatched them up.

"I can take her for a spin?" he asked, turning crimson in excitement.

Ethic chuckled. "You can have it," Ethic stated. "For all the work you do around here. Consider it a bonus."

Ethic didn't have a need for an old-school car. It was a young, drug dealer's, but his tastes were more refined. Now that it was restored, he had no need for it.

"Really?" Larry asked.

Ethic nodded.

"Wow, boss, thanks," Larry said. Ethic held out his hand and Larry shook it firmly. "You mind if I test her out? Take her up the block and back? I'm almost done on Ms. Lewis' car."

"Enjoy, man," Ethic said. "I test drove it last night before I put the shocks on it and it still drove like a champ."

"Ha, ha! Shirley ain't going to believe it when I pull up in this!" The man guffawed.

Ethic watched Larry pull out of the last bay and headed to the office to grab the keys to his Tesla.

RAT TAT TAT TAT TAT

The sound of gunfire caused everyone in the shop to duck for cover. Ethic reached for the gun he kept in the desk and rushed to the front door. He slipped his head out. The Regal, with Larry inside, was being riddled with bullets. Cream hung out of the passenger window of a car, letting loose on the tinted vehicle. Ethic emerged from the building firing, with a marksman's aim that sent a bullet through the window of the windshield, hitting the driver instantly. Ethic saw Cream's eyes widen in surprise when he realized Ethic wasn't the one behind the tinted windows but was advancing on him in the parking lot. The split second when recognition froze Cream, Ethic could have ended him, he should have ended him. Instead, he thought of her. Alani. She would be the one they would call to identify him. She would be responsible for the body; death knocking at her door, again, because of him. Another black man dead because of him. Something weighed on Ethic that made him fire without the intention of killing. Warning shots, which he was sure would make Cream underestimate his gangster. Cream scrambled over the front seat and propped open the driver's door, pushing the body of his comrade onto the pavement before pulling off, recklessly, down the block.

"Call 911!" Ethic ordered to one of his workers huddled inside, as he rushed to the bullet-ridden car. He pulled open the driver's door and it was like déjà vu. Redneck Larry came spilling out into his arms, but all Ethic saw was Raven. That day, so long ago, at Mott Park, haunted him in this moment. He staggered back, horrified. Her face was as clear as day. He put his hands on top of his head, closing his eyes in grief. When he opened them again, she was gone, and Redneck Larry's dead eyes stared up into the sky. Such a vacant gaze…one that he had seen many times before. He would be a man forever haunted…a man that would never be able to move past his sins because, somehow, they seemed to follow him.

"Okay, mothers, line up down the left aisle. Daughters, down the right aisle."

Bella stepped into her place and as she looked across the church pews to the other side of the room she felt a hole inside. She was last because Mo couldn't make it and she had no escort. *I hate this stupid pageant.*

"Ladies, shoulders back," the director, Ms. White, stood at the front of the sanctuary where the aisles merged. "Step heel to toe, eyes forward, smile big but relaxed."

Bella rolled her eyes and blew out a breath of exasperation, following the directions. "No stomping. This isn't marching band, ladies."

Bella didn't know why she felt embarrassed about not having a mother. She knew it was out of her control, but it seemed like a flaw. Everyone around her was being taught things that she had to figure out herself. She had her father, but she was even timid about asking him certain things. Her body was changing, as were her thoughts and the way she viewed the world around her, but nobody was there to guide her through the confusion. She was always the motherless child. People looked at her with sympathy, like she was the ugly dog at the pound that no one wanted to adopt. She had so many questions. Her breasts hurt when she handled them too roughly, or she bumped into things. The girls at school told her she had white girl hair and told her she was shaped like a boy. Then, there was a boy that made her feel sick to her stomach every time he smiled at her. She couldn't talk about these things with her father, and Mo was too busy, lately. She kept it all locked inside. Resentment was building in her by the day because she just wanted what everyone else had - a mother. She didn't care, any mother would do. She heard the girls at school complaining about theirs. Some drank too much, others were strict, others were mean…Bella would take any of those because having no one to look up to, no one that understood, made Bella feel empty. She stepped forward toward the front of the church.

"Now, when it is your turn to present your daughter in front of the audience, daughters will curtsy while holding their candles. Mothers, you will light them. Then, the pastor will add the candle to the chalice under the pulpit. He will pray over the pair, and then mother and daughter will walk back up center aisle together hand in hand."

Each girl went through the motions, and when it was Bella's turn, she stepped up with her candle only there was nothing but empty space on the other side. "Umm, Bella, baby, I'll stand in for your sister today," Ms. White offered. She gave her a smile and Bella cringed on the inside. It was the same smile everyone gave her. The one that people plastered on their faces when they thought she was pathetic and wondered why she would even try to participate in something that required a mother in the first place. Bella felt out of place. She had wanted to call Alani to beg her to still participate with her. She had even snuck into her father's phone to retrieve the number, but something always stopped her. Bringing up Alani's name seemed to put Ethic in a mood. His eyes changed whenever she was mentioned, and Bella almost wanted to cry every time she saw his face transform in that way. It was like someone had died and her father was fighting a memory when he heard Alani's name, but Bella needed her. *I'm messing up the entire pageant.*

She hurried through the motions and hurried up the aisle to get it over as quickly as possible.

"Very good, ladies. Our next meeting, we will go over proper table etiquette to prepare for the banquet portion of the evening."

Bella stood and walked out of the sanctuary, as soon as they were dismissed. She just wanted to get home, behind the safety of her closed bedroom door, so she could cry. Lily was parked in front of the door, waiting for her and Bella hopped inside, slamming the door. She felt the ache in her chest and her eyes went wet. She didn't even make it out of the parking lot. The back seat of the car would have to do because her tears had a mind of their own.

The days were flying by and Morgan had found her stride at Michigan State. She had friends. She and Aria met at the rec to go over choreography almost every day. Somehow, through music, a former deaf girl had found people whom she could relate to. She was grateful for Aria's energy. It made the breakup with Messiah bearable. The fact that he hadn't called wounded her. She had thought what they shared meant more to him, and the reality that he could go without her made her want to let him. Despite the tears that wet her pillow at night, Morgan was trying her hardest to move on. She sat in the cafeteria, going over notes for her philosophy class. It was her favorite subject. She enjoyed debating basic human nature with basic humans. There was no right or wrong answer in the subject, just perspective, and she loved it.

"This seat taken?"

Morgan looked up and smiled.

She motioned her hand for him to sit.

"I was actually just studying for your class," she admitted. She shifted the books into a stack and moved them aside.

"I didn't think pretty girls studied. I thought you all just showed up and enchanted your way to an A," Bash said.

"What's pretty about me? My hair? My face? My body? You stay throwing compliments, but I've heard all of that before. It just sounds like game," she said. "And you, sir, look like you play games well."

He held up his hands in defense. "No games."

"Yeah, okay. You probably sleep with a different freshman every semester. Some vulnerable, pretty girl, straight out of high school that falls for all this dreamy-eyed, good boy charm," Morgan said, twirling her spoon at him as she sized him up.

"I'm really not that guy," Bash answered, with a chuckle and a shake of his head.

"Okay then, tell me something I haven't heard before. Why the constant interest in me? The flirtatious smiles, the stares when you don't think I'm looking. What do you see when you look at me?"

"Insecurities," he answered. He said it so quick and succinct, like he had sat up at night thinking about it. His response made Morgan sit back in her seat. She thought she hid herself better than that. She tried hard to build herself up and reinforce the things that Messiah had told her when he was around. She had no idea she was so transparent without him. "You've been different this past month. Like something hurt you and you're trying to pretend like it didn't."

Morgan's stomach soured, and she sat down her yogurt. She lowered her eyes into her lap.

"I'm trying to start over here. I'm trying to be different here," she said.

"How about you just be yourself," Bash said. "It's okay to let the bad stuff show too. That way you know who really riding for you and who just around for the good. If you never show the bad, how will you be able to tell the real from the fake?"

"The bad is just really bad, you know?" she said.

She thought of her entire history in seconds. A drug dealer's daughter, deaf, a drug dealer's girlfriend, a dead best friend, dead parents, dead sister, a drug dealer for an adopted father. It seemed like her destiny was already written. Death or destruction. Who would even understand what she had been through here? State was filled with privilege. Children of alumni who had trusts and college funds. They would never be able to understand who she was and where she came from. Her last name carried a different type of privilege. No, she didn't have a legacy of scholars in her family, but she damn sure had a legacy of gangsters. She could never reveal that side.

"Yeah, well, if you ever want to talk about it, or just kick back and not talk about anything at all. I'd very much like to oblige," he said.

He stood and rounded her chair. He leaned down into her ear. "Oh yeah, and all that other stuff you mentioned. The face, the hair, the body…"

Morgan tensed, as his cologne invaded her space. She hadn't been this close to any other man except Messiah, since her rape. Her throat constricted, as her heart raced in anxiety. She was unsure of what she was feeling. A part of her reacted in intrigue but a very small part that she kept tucked in the deepest part of her heart felt fear.

"Perfection," he stated.

She exhaled when he walked away and a bit of guilt overcame her. She had been friendly, open even, to the conversation of possibility with him. She wasn't over Messiah, by far, but he had left her with a hole to fill. A girl like Morgan who was starved for attention didn't do well when she was forced to go without it. She didn't know if she was justified in feeling guilty. Was she right or wrong? What was Messiah doing during their break. *Clearly, he isn't thinking about you. He ended things. He didn't want you. He doesn't even check up on you.*

She turned in her seat. "Hey, Bash?"

He was clear across the quad and she had to yell to get his attention. He turned to her. She stood and walked over to him, scrunching her face, as she held up a hand to shield the sun from her eyes. She looked up at him. He was handsome, an obvious catch to anyone who was in the market, but he didn't light a fire in her the way Messiah had. She remembered overhearing her mother give advice to her older sister when she was young. "Run away from the boy that gives you butterflies. He's going to break your heart. Marry the one who makes you feel solid. He feels boring and predictable, but he's safe and he knows he's lucky to have you, so he'll never mess it up."

Bash was boring. Messiah was butterflies.

"I'm dancing Saturday with Stiletto Gang at Retro. Maybe I'll see you there?"

"You're Stiletto Gang?" he asked.

She shrugged, and he looked on in astonishment.

He put praying hands in front of his mouth and tucked his lips inside his mouth as he bowed to her. "I'm on your time. If that's the only way I can get a little bit of it, I'll take it."

"Maybe breakfast, Sunday," she added, hesitantly. She pulled out her phone. "What's your number?"

He recited it and she sent him a text.

"Call me," she said, before she turned and walked away. She couldn't be with the one she wanted, so she would have to settle for the one who wanted her.

When Messiah and his crew stepped into the club they seemed to part the dense crowd like the Red Sea. They entered, dripping in jewelry. Messiah was in rare form, on his flashy shit, mobbing through, wearing four diamond chains, a Rolex on his wrist, and a Baroque Versace blazer over black, fitted slacks. Red Bottom, suede loafers graced his feet. He looked like money and his crew filled up the vault in similar attire. Messiah wasn't with the college scene, but he was trying to be supportive. He didn't want to pull Morgan out of her world completely, but he could no longer just stare at her pictures on an iPhone screen. He needed to see the real thing. She had blossomed in his absence and he wanted her to continue to do so, but he had to just see her...had to be there for her first performance. If this was important to her, it was important to him. No matter how things were laying between them, he wanted her to know he would always come through for her. The little niggas in Foot Locker, white t-shirts and sneakers, not even dope ones at that, were blowing his high. His eyes gravitated toward her without effort, picking her out of the crowd with ease. Morgan just emitted light. She shined where ever she went. She gave off an energy that he craved and whenever in her proximity he was drawn to her. The million-watt smile on her face normally intoxicated him. Today, it infuriated him. The 6'2, light-skinned, pretty boy in her face sparked a flame inside Messiah that he couldn't control. Messiah sized him up in seconds. He was older than Morgan, considerably, and Messiah didn't like it, despite that he, himself, was her senior.

"We got action?" Isa asked, ready to detonate shit for the smallest of reasons. Even he knew that Morgan was the best reason to make things go boom.

"Stop hyping this nigga up, G," Ahmeek added. "This a college town. We don't want no smoke up here."

Messiah was tight about the kid that was in Morgan's space. He didn't know Morgan's smile could be manipulated by someone other than him and it burned him. "I'm good," Messiah said. He chose not to beeline for Morgan and instead made his way to a booth. The waitress came through and Messiah beckoned her with two fingers.

"I need bottles, five for now, Henny VSOP, Patrón, and whatever these niggas want. Run a tab," he instructed, as he slid her his Amex. She smiled and then scurried off as he and the crew got comfortable.

"All right!" Messiah watched as a dark-skinned girl hopped on the stage and took the microphone. "Y'all ready for Stiletto Gang?"

The crowd amped up the volume but Messiah sat in the shadows of the darkened booth, surveying the scene. His eyes drifted to her against his will.

"She just talking, G," Ahmeek settled. "Take a drink, bro'. You gon' go crazy in this mu'fucka." Meek chuckled, as he handed Messiah a glass. Messiah held it in two hands, as he leaned forward and shook his head, smirking before taking a sip. Why was she doing so much smiling? Why was she standing so close to him? She was beautiful and every subtle touch she placed to the dude's arm made Messiah cringe.

"Yo, who the fuck is that?" Isa asked, eyes glued to the raven beauty on the microphone. "Shorty strapped." He pulled at the brim of his hat, attention captivated. Aria was a stunner and her body was lethal. She simply shined in any room. Much like Morgan. No wonder their videos got hundreds of thousands of likes.

"I'm going to bring my girls up here with me and we're going to do a little something for y'all! That's cool?"

Again, the crowd responded. "Show us some love, y'all!"

Six girls walked onto the stage. Each one had their own vibe, dressed differently, hair styled differently...the only thing that was the same was the stilettos on their feet. Morgan had an Aaliyah vibe going on. Baggy, Tommy Hilfiger jeans with exposed boxers, and a tube top that Messiah prayed she didn't pop out of. Red Bottoms graced her feet.

I put my feelings on safety
So I don't go shooting where your heart be
Cuz you'd take the bullet trying to save me
Then I'm left to deal with making you bleed

Ella Mai's voice filled the club and the crowd went crazy, as they performed. Messiah was amazed at Morgan's confidence. She was blooming right before him. For a girl who had been afraid to speak only months ago, he didn't see an ounce of fear in her. The whole group was dope, but Morgan and Aria were stars. They were front and center. Their harmony with each other made it appear as if they had been dancing with one another for years.

My bad, my bad for trippin' on you
My bad, my bad for trippin' on you

Messiah shook his head in disbelief because Morgan was fucking shit up. The dance, the crowd, his mind. If she kept moving her body like that he would be fucking something up later. He hadn't come for all that, but shit happens.

"Yo, I thought this shit was gon' be corny as fuck, but they're dope," Meek complimented.

Suddenly, a line of frat guys came stepping in a line through the crowd. They made their way all the way to the stage and aligned themselves behind the girls. The beat changed, and the flow went from easy to raw, as the DJ mixed some Future track into the beat. The merger was dope, but erotic and Messiah's stomach clenched. Morgan was putting on a show, and apparently, she and her dance partner had quite the chemistry. The rest of the dancers backed up, giving Morgan room to work. She didn't disappoint, and the dude was all over her, hands in her hair, pulling it, rolling her neck, licking his lips.

You know your love is big enough, make me trip up on you
Yeah, it's big enough, got me trippin' on you

Morgan's ass and hips rolled into him and the song became more erotic, the dance following suit. He was sure the lyrics were "tripping" but in his crazed mind he heard "dripping" and his eyes saw her dripping, what was supposed to be his, all over the next nigga.

Yeah, it's big enough, got me DRIPPING on you

Morgan turned her back to the crowd, and when she twerked, he pictured her naked. She was moving that shit like she was dancing for dollars and Messiah's blood boiled. He felt like snatching her off the stage. He was sick, like need a thermometer, might throw up, sick. He had seen enough.

"Yo, we up," Messiah said, tapping Isa's leg.

Already knowing what time it was, Meek and Isa stood. His sudden movement toward the exit drew Morgan's attention his way.

Messiah?

She didn't even finish the song. She hopped off the stage and bypassed Bash who was waiting for her. "I'm sorry. Give me a minute," she said, as Bash grabbed her arm. "Messiah!" Her voice was drowned out over the music and she inched through the dense crowd, trying desperately to get to him.

Morgan ran after Messiah, her heart racing as she burst out of the heavy metal door, her eyes bouncing around the parking lot in search of him.

"Messiah!" she called, as she spotted him. Her stilettos snapped against the concrete, rapidly. There was urgency in her step. It matched the worry in her heart, coordinating with the tension on his face as he turned toward her.

Isa and Meek already knew to keep walking. The discussion to be had was a private one.

"What are you doing here? I didn't even know you were here," she said, head cocked to the side as she stared up at him, trying to infiltrate his thoughts. "You were going to leave without speaking to me?"

"I got to shoot a move, shorty. I'ma check for you." His tone was casual, but Morgan felt an energy shift. She frowned, searching for answers in his nonchalance. They hadn't seen each other in weeks. It had been unbearable for her. Why was he acting like he had been perfectly fine without her? He turned and walked away, and Morgan felt a gnawing in her gut. Like she had done something wrong. Like there was hurt underneath his cool exterior. She didn't know if she was reading too much into his departure or if she was spot on.

"Check for me? What does that mean?" she yelled at his back. She wasn't used to him looking forward to leaving. She stalked after him and pulled his arm, forcing him to face her.

"It means let me break out before I take a nigga head off," he stated. There it was. His aggression. Messiah was like a Pit Bull, loving and loyal to his owner, but deadly to a stranger.

"We were only dancing, Messiah. He's just a guy I met at school. He's one of the fraternity guys," she dismissed, with a wave of her hand. "They join our routines when we need guys. He likes the way I ride the beat. He's not into me like that. It's

114

just about the choreography," she explained.

"Ride the beat," Messiah scoffed. He ran both hands down his face, blowing out a sharp breath. He nodded. He could feel something bubbling in his chest. He didn't know if it was disdain, jealousy, or rage. He had a feeling it was a recipe that combined the three. He couldn't pin point if he was angry at her, college boy, or himself.

And who the fuck was the light-skinned nigga you were showing all 32 for?

The thought had him ready to reach for his strap. All he knew was that if he didn't leave soon there would be problems in the parking lot of this night club. His eyes narrowed, but he didn't look her in the face. That face. It could calm the storm in his heart. No, Messiah looked over her head at the crowd of goofy-ass niggas filtering out the club. Was that her type? Clean-cut, arrogant, and corny? Nah, he knew better, but the problem was Morgan was every man's type. Any man with red blood in his veins had a taste for a young girl like Morgan. This streak of insecurity mystified Messiah. Never had he fucking ever been afraid of a woman choosing to move around him. He was intimidated because, truth was, college boy was better suited for Morgan. Messiah was a street legend in the making. He was her opposite.

"Yo, Mo!" A guy behind her shouted.

"Your people need you," Messiah said, as he backpedaled and lifted his hands in surrender. "Don't ride that beat too hard. Somebody might get hurt."

"Messiah," she pleaded in a low tone. She didn't want to make a scene. She didn't want to fight at all, but somehow, she found herself in the middle of turmoil.

"I'ma fall back tonight. Have fun, Shorty Doo-Wop," he said.

Morgan stood in the middle of the parking lot, heart on the

pavement, as Messiah climbed into his car and drove away.

Messiah was a block up the road when he turned around in the middle of traffic, causing cars to blare their horns and narrowly causing an accident.

"Yo, nigga! You tripping!" Isa said, as he placed a firm hand on the dash board.

"Nigga going to get his bitch before another nigga fix what he breaking," Ahmeek stated from the backseat.

Messiah was silent, as he stopped at the light before the club.

"Looks like it's too late," Isa commented.

Messiah landed eyes on Morgan who stood in the middle of the parking lot, her lips on another man's.

He had never felt disappointment like what filled him in that moment. He thought of all the ways he could react. He was ill. Physically, mentally, emotionally. He couldn't even take a breath. The light turned green and Messiah didn't even pull into the parking lot. He simply kept driving and turned up his radio, as he tried his very hardest not to show how badly it hurt.

Morgan pulled away from Bash wearing shocked eyes.

"Bash," she whispered, as she feathered her lips. "I'm…"

"I overstepped. My bad," he said, as he took a step back.

"It's just…"

She paused. What was she being loyal to? Messiah had left her. He always left her. Morgan wanted to say fuck him and let this man in front of her explore his interests, but she was struggling. "Can we just slow this down? Like, hit the brakes. I just got out of something. I don't even know if I'm out of it, actually. It's complicated and I just don't want to start something with you before getting out of that. I'm trying to be honest…"

"I respect it," Bash answered. "I'll slow down. Your rules. Your pace."

She nodded. It sounded similar to what Messiah had promised her in the beginning, but he had lied because she wanted to move fast, and he was pulling away.

"Mo! Come on!" Aria called from the entrance of the club. "Time to get lit!"

"I'll see you inside?" she asked.

Bash nodded. "Nah, I'll pass. I've got to go home and line my clothes up for tomorrow. You know, lay out the shirt and the pants and the shoes, make sure it's all crispy."

She laughed and remembered why she liked him. He was uncomplicated. Easy.

"Big day tomorrow, huh? Sounds like the first day of elementary school."

"I got a girl to impress in the morning," he said, with a wink, before backpedaling to his car.

Messiah's head was all cloudy. He kept seeing it. Her lips connected to someone else's. *What the fuck did you expect? You sent her into the wild,* he thought. It had taken every bit of restraint he could muster to not react. He knew where his temper would take him. He would cut off college boy's lips and feed them to him for touching Morgan, but he couldn't. He had asked her to grow. He wanted her to live. This was a part of the experience. It gnawed at him with fury, however, so much so that he had fallen into the bed of a random groupie, who now lay beneath him. Messiah was propped up in the hotel room bed, one knee raised, the other leg straight, one hand behind his head, as the beauty beneath him breathed easy under his shoulder, tucked in Morgan's spot. It felt like the ultimate betrayal. The girl had given her very best performance. He was a man, so he had enjoyed it, but there was something missing. It didn't satisfy his soul. When Morgan kissed him, she tasted more than his exterior. She kissed his heart and soothed something that hadn't functioned quite right before. The substitute wasn't as fulfilling. It was like when he would be forced to pour PET milk in his cereal in the mornings as a child because they had run out of the real thing. It would do but it wasn't the same. He had tried to force it. Instead of leaving directly after sex, he did what he did with Morgan. He showered, ordered room service, tried to scratch at the surface of a decent conversation, searching for a spark, for that feeling that Mo gave him, but it wasn't there.

It was close to one o'clock in the morning when he heard the vibration of his phone in his pants pocket on the floor. He slid from the bed and picked up his clothes, sliding into them before pulling the phone from his pocket. He put his chains back on his neck and placed his Rolex on his wrist. Before he could button his shirt, his phone buzzed again.

Who the fuck blowing me up?

When he saw her name on his lock screen his heart skipped a beat. Even that natural reaction bothered him. That was bitch shit, hearts and the skipping of beats and shit. He didn't like the control Morgan had...the way she could puppeteer his mood. Send him from zero to a trillion with behavior he was sure wasn't even ill-intended. Morgan had sent a voice memo. He pressed play.

"Messiah, he's here. I need you."

The second text was a picture. Messiah clicked on the picture and although a little grainy, Messiah recognized the face instantly. He had been searching high and low for that face since the day Ethic had handled Lucas. The second rapist. He had never spoken of his hunt because he didn't want Morgan to worry. Apparently, the kid had fled to the college town after realizing how Lucas had paid the ultimate cost.

Messiah could hear the absolute fear in her voice. It wasn't fabricated. and he took off for the door. He dialed her number and the voicemail answered. The worst thoughts went through his mind, as he rushed to his car. He thought of calling Meek and Isa, but Ethic's lessons popped into his head. Murder was something you committed alone.

"Please, please, Aria, just keep the door closed! Don't let anyone in!" Morgan shouted, as she stood with her back against the bathroom wall. Morgan was in tears and she closed her eyes as she leaned over the sink.

"Okay, okay," Aria replied, as she looked on in confusion. "Just talk to me, Morgan. What the hell is going on?"

"I just need to get out of here. I have to," she whispered. She checked her phone and the realization that it was on one percent brought tears to her eyes. "There's someone out there that I can't see. Someone who..." Morgan caught the sob in her throat.

BANG! BANG! BANG!

"Hey! Why is the door locked? Open the door. It's a line out here!"

"No!" Morgan shouted, holding up her arms to stop Aria from moving.

"I won't, Morgan," Aria whispered, sympathetically. "Who's out there that has you this afraid?"

"A guy…from my hometown. He…he…"

"He what?"

"He raped me," Morgan whispered.

Aria's eyes widened, and she reached for the door. "I will fuck that nigga up in this bitch!" she shouted.

"No, no!" Morgan protested, pulling at her arm. "Please." Morgan felt trapped and she heaved in distress.

Aria smoothed her hair and nodded. She had never seen anyone so freaked out. "Okay, we can just leave. There's a back entrance. You won't even have to pass through the front of the club. We can just walk out," Aria said.

Morgan's lip quivered, as she gripped Aria's forearms. She was holding on so tightly that her nails left dents in Aria's skin. Aria took Morgan's hand. "Just hold onto my hand and follow me. Okay?"

Morgan nodded, as Aria opened the bathroom door. Aria pushed through the tiny hallway and when Morgan saw his face she pulled Aria's arm the other way.

"Yo! Morgan!"

Morgan pushed through the crowd, practically running, as she squeezed through the small spaces people left.

She burst out of the club with Aria right behind her.

"Yo! Let me holla at you!"

She heard his voice on her heels, as she dug into her purse. *Damn it!*

Her keys were at the bottom, lost amongst makeup and bullshit and her hands were shaking so badly.

"Aye, I just want to talk to you!" The voice was closer.

"She doesn't want to fucking talk to you!" Aria said, as she turned her back to Morgan and stood between the two. They had reached the car.

The dude lifted his shirt, exposing a gun tucked in his waistline.

"What the fuck that's supposed to do? You gon' shoot me in a parking lot with cameras? I heard you like to rape women. You're disgusting. Bum-ass nigga!" Aria snapped.

Morgan pulled the keys from her purse, hands fumbling, as she hit the unlock button. She rushed inside, and Aria ran around the car, hopping into the passenger seat. The dude pressed balled fists to her window.

"I just want to talk to you! I did some fucked-up shit! I just want to apologize so you can maybe call off your people!" He screamed, as he banged on her window. Morgan put the car in reverse, but before she could pull off, Messiah's car blocked her in. She looked at him in her rearview, as he hopped out his car. He left his car door wide open as he advanced, gun drawn.

"Yo, Messiah, man..."

The man never finished his sentence. With a pistol to the center of his head, and Messiah's free hand wrapped around his throat, cutting off oxygen, the man couldn't speak.

The grim expression on Messiah's face was deadly. He knew he shouldn't pull the trigger. He was moving recklessly, but he remembered the video. Like a mental ghost, the image of her bawled up on that bathroom floor caused his rage to bubble.

Morgan climbed out of the car, timidly, terrified as she looked around. The back of the parking lot was deserted. The party was inside, but it would be letting out soon.

"Messiah, baby..." she whispered.

She would have been better off not speaking. Her saying his name, calling him baby, sounding so terrified, made him feel obligated to annihilate all her problems. Messiah's gun collided with the dude's face, flooring him.

"Messiah!" Morgan shouted. Messiah beat him again and again and again and again until Messiah was breathless. With his bare hands, Messiah beat life out of him.

"Oh my God!" Aria screamed, as she stood in the crease of the open passenger door. She had to look away because Messiah was relentless. He knew the hit that ended it all. It was like he felt his life dissipate into the air, but he kept going. He knew he would have to clean up this mess. A murder like this would put him under the jail. There was blood all over him, but as he stood over the body, Messiah felt no remorse. He looked to Morgan whose eyes were red with tears. His eyes darted to Aria. He couldn't clip her friend. He now had a witness. One he didn't know and couldn't trust. *Fuck.* He whispered in her ear.

"Go home and wait for me. Don't let your friend leave."

"Who was that? Oh my God! I was scared as shit, but that shit was so fucking sexy," Aria whispered, as she shook her head in disbelief.

"He's my…" Morgan paused because she didn't know what he was to her. "You can't say shit," Morgan stated. "Like, not a word to anybody, Aria."

"Do I look crazy to you?" Aria asked. "I didn't see shit. Don't know shit."

Morgan nodded. She checked her phone. *5:12 a.m.*

Her nerves were so bad, and she was so tired, but she wouldn't sleep. She couldn't, until she heard from him.

Another half an hour passed, and Aria fell asleep on the couch. Morgan's eyes were low when she heard the soft knock at her door. She rushed to open it. He stood in front of her, blood gone and dressed in different clothes. She fell into his arms and it felt so good. His hold, his protection, the security of being his girl. She had missed it. She trembled there, as he pulled her closer.

"I didn't know if you would come," she whispered.

"I'ma always come," he whispered.

"There were cameras," she warned.

"It's been taken care of," he assured. He nodded to Aria. "She's a problem?"

"She won't say anything," Morgan said. The gangster in him wanted to eliminate the issue before it became one, but the girl was Morgan's friend. He wouldn't unless he had to.

He took her chin between his thumb and pointer finger. She tilted her head and waited, hoping desperately that he stayed, not just tonight but forever. He took in every inch of her face because he needed a recent memory, a recent visual.

"I miss you," she gasped. "I love you so much."

His eyes fell onto her lips. Then he remembered the kiss. He was so fucking jealous. He gritted his teeth, fighting his nature, fighting his urge to take little Morgan to her bedroom to remind her that no matter the space or time, she was his. He released her chin and took a step back. He turned his back to her and took two steps before…

"Messiah…"

He turned and closed the space between them with heavy, burdened steps, pushing her so hard against the door that it banged against the wall as he shoved his tongue down her throat. Her body submitted to him, melting right there like he had put butter to a scolding skillet. He was angry with her, she could tell. His kiss was filled with it, but he would never touch her with malice. She could feel the desperation in him too and the hardness against her belly made her panties soak. She loved this boy so much. Boring or butterflies. It was a choice that every girl must make. Messiah was butterflies and Morgan didn't care about what heartbreaks lie ahead. She didn't care about the extreme lows. This high was worth it. His kisses were like sex. No dick required to make her cum. This man was a drug. He pulled away and Morgan knew nothing had changed. He was still leaving, and she was still lonely. Sure, she had friends and Bash was decent, but Messiah was life. She couldn't just let him walk away.

"This hurts. Not talking. Not being us," she whispered. "I just want us."

"Keep living, shorty. You're safe here, in the real world. It's where you belong. I'm a jealous mu'fucka, but I'm proud of you," he said. He left, and Morgan went inside her apartment to cry.

Morgan's eyes burned when she popped them open to acknowledge the buzzing of her cell phone. She was exhausted, and when she saw Bash's name, she groaned as she placed the back of her palm over her forehead. She wanted to ignore his call, but she would have to face him in class and explain herself. To avoid that awkward encounter, she answered.

"Hello?" The grogginess was all in her voice.

"That doesn't sound like the voice of someone who's trying to go on a date today. As a matter-of-fact, it sounds like a man. Your voice is deep as hell in the morning, girl," Bash joked.

Morgan laughed. He was light. Easy. Fun. He was exactly what she was supposed to be experiencing in college, but he wasn't Messiah.

"I just woke up. Actually, this phone call woke me up," she chastised. "I'm exhausted. Can we maybe take a rain check?" Morgan asked.

She had no interest in this date anymore. She had seen Messiah the night before and he had left her depleted. He had left her desperate for him and only him. Bash just wouldn't do.

"Yeah, of course," Bash stated. "Is this about the kiss? Or the guy from last night?"

He didn't beat around the bush and his questioning took Morgan off guard. *Do I even owe him an explanation?* She liked Bash and didn't want to offend him. It had been her idea to get breakfast and she was the one pulling out.

"No, it's not, Bash. I'm seriously just tired. I'll call you, okay? And when we do get together it's on me. I'll see you in class," she said. She hung up before he could respond, and then immediately dialed Messiah. When it went to voicemail, her heart ached. He had told her to live but here she was putting her life on hold, waiting for him to come back. She wondered if he was doing the same during their time apart. Morgan was too young to know that men never put their lives on pause. In love or not, they moved how they moved whenever they wanted to; and at the moment, Messiah was choosing to move away from her.

CHAPTER 10

One Month Later

The city was alive. It was Thanksgiving break, and everybody was in town for the holiday. It was the opening week of the winter festival and the five blocks that made up Downtown Flint was closed off for the festivities. It was a big deal in the city. Everybody who was anybody came out to ice skate on the outdoor rink, and those who were too cool just came to walk the streets, dressed to impress. It was like a car show, as Morgan maneuvered through the traffic. Everything from old-school, boxed Chevys to Cadillacs were fighting for parking spots. Very few people whipped foreign cars in Flint, so everyone knew who was behind her tinted windows before they even saw her face. Princess Morgan was pulling up in her baby Benz. Morgan was eager to see her people. Life at college was vastly different than her little, gritty city. Although she was grateful for the experience, she missed this…the ghetto…the everybody-knows-everybody of it all…and most of all she missed him. Things hadn't been the same since he had come to see her dance at the club. There was distance between them and Morgan hated it. He hadn't called her in a month and he never answered when she called. He would be here, she was sure of it, so this was where she would be too. She was going to get her man. He didn't even know she was back in town and Morgan was eager to pull up on him.

"So, this is where all the niggas have been hiding in Michigan?" Aria said, as she scanned the block from the passenger side of Morgan's Benz.

Morgan shook her head. "Nah, girl. These are all hood niggas with good dick and empty promises. You don't want no parts."

Aria laughed. "Dick ain't good if it don't come with a little lie on it."

Morgan hooted, as she eased into the parking lot of the corner store, parking near the driveway, and making sure to back in just in case she needed to escape quickly. You never knew how these types of nights would end. It could be carefree and filled with good times or end deadly. That was just Flint.

Morgan parked at the end of the block and stepped out the car. Red, high-waisted jeans, a red, long sleeve, turtleneck body suit, and a red, off-the-shoulder mink coat adorned her body. She had come through to murder shit. She wasn't too fancy with the footwork. A pair of all red, retro Jordan's graced her feet. She popped the trunk and grabbed her red Gucci belt bag. She wrapped it around her thin waist. Bloody fucking murder.

"You got a man. Why can't you let the rest of us shine?" Aria joked. Morgan had no insecurities about slick talk from Aria. There were no hidden innuendos in her jokes. No jealousy, because Aria had come to turn heads in her own right. She wore all black because, "Niggas think you're friendly when you colorful."

"Aye yo, red, let me talk to you for a minute!"

The catcalls began as soon as Morgan put foot to the pavement. She shook her head and rolled her eyes, as she kept moving.

They made their way to the rink and Morgan immediately located Messiah. He and his crew were the ones who drew the crowd. Morgan knew he hated the attention, but it was inevitable.

"I hope I'm not a third wheel out here," Aria said.

"His homeboys are with him," Morgan said, nodding across the street. Three, matching, snow-white BMW's sat side by side. Messiah leaned against the front of his car, his shoulder-length locs braided to the crown with the back down. Irritation teased her, as she saw the girl sitting at his side and the group of women hanging around the trio. The girl whispered something in Messiah's ear and Morgan saw red. She didn't show it, however. She stepped through the crowd.

"Aye, red, what's your name?"

"God damn. Red mean as hell. Black dress, don't break a nigga heart out here." That one was for Aria.

The thirst of the corny lines caused Ahmeek to look up first.

"Eyes up," he called out, signaling Messiah.

You better warn his ass, Morgan thought.

Messiah lifted lazy eyes to Morgan. Morgan lifted a brow, as he rubbed the sides of his mouth. He was high, she was sure. He had to be to be out here flossing with a bitch sitting next to him. She didn't do the expected. She walked right pass him, taking the stairs down to the rink.

She was forced to pause when Isa tugged on the bottom of Aria's dress. "You, I need a name from."

"What you need is some manners. This is Chanel you're pulling on," Aria said, shrugging him off. "When you get you some, then maybe I'll offer a name."

He lifted hands in surrender and smirked. "I can dig it. No disrespect," he answered, intrigue dancing in his eyes. He licked his lips, as Aria followed Morgan down the stairs.

Isa turned to Ahmeek and Messiah. "Yo...where the fuck Morgan get her from?"

Ahmeek shook his head. Messiah said nothing. He had noticed, for the sake of not being able not to notice. Aria was a beautiful girl with skin like fresh, ground coffee. It was a shade of black he had never seen before. He appreciated the aesthetic because it was undeniably pleasant, but only one girl moved him. Morgan Atkins. He tapped the girl beside him. "Time's up," he said.

"What about that thing I told you I wanted to do?" the girl said, suggestively.

"Not tonight, baby, move along to the next nigga," Messiah said, lifting from the hood of his car. Messiah had been on the verge of leaving until Morgan had shown up. Since her, scenes like this bored him. It was the same shit. A sea of groupies and dickriders.

"We still breaking out?" Isa asked.

"You know we not leaving now. This ol' drunk in love mu'fucka," Ahmeek cracked.

"You funny, nigga," Messiah stated, but offered no denial. He turned to eye the rink below. Morgan was on the ice with her friend, and like he expected, she attracted her own groupies. Men who would never put on a pair of ice skates were on the ice, stumbling all over the place, just to shoot their shot with her. She laughed, as she held her friend's hand and tried to teach her to balance on the blades. Ahmeek was right about one thing. Plans had changed. As long as Morgan was present, he had to be. He would never leave her in the city uncovered, but he wasn't trying to cramp her style either.

He descended the steps and posted up on the side of the rink. He leaned his elbows on the railing, his right and left hand flanking his side.

The outdoor rink had music playing, as the skaters struggled to do the wobble in their skates.

Isa pulled a fresh blunt from his back pocket and fired up,

passing it to Messiah. He took the weed and pinched it between his fingers, eyes locked in.

"Baby girl busting her ass all over the ice," Isa noted, grimacing as Aria hit the ground, bringing Morgan down with her. The pair laughed, and Messiah shook his head. He was amused but from the outside he appeared indifferent. Only he knew how his heart quickened at the sight of her. He was positive she knew it too, but to the naked eye, Messiah was unaffected. He hit the blunt and passed it off.

"I quit! I'm too cute to be out here looking all clumsy and goofy and shit," Aria yelled, with a laugh, as she hobbled toward the side.

The music slowed, and Morgan closed her eyes as she snapped her fingers. Messiah knew it meant the song playing was a favorite. Morgan took off on the ice.

You don't know, babe
When you hold me
And kiss me slowly
It's the sweetest thing

She was zoned in, as she glided across the ice like a pro. She did a little skip to change directions, skating backwards. She was doing all types of circles and figure eights to avoid the other people on the ice.

"Damn, she's nice with it, bro'," Ahmeek said, as he stood up straight, in surprise.

Messiah didn't speak. He just watched, as she opened her arms to him, singing the words loud, and impressively on key. She was showing out and Messiah would have otherwise been too coy to stick around. He wasn't with the public displays of affection, but it was her and she made him do things others never could. It was near negative degree temperatures outside, but Messiah warmed.

I just want to see how beautiful you are
You know that I see it
I know you're a star

He was fighting the smile he felt trying to turn him into a bitch. So, he wore a smirk instead, as one corner of his mouth turned up and he shook his head. *I'ma fuck her little-ass up,* he thought, lightheartedly. *She knows I hate this shit.* But he knew that she knew that he loved this shit. She was so unapologetic in the way that she adored him.

Where you go I'll follow
No matter how far
If life is a movie
Oh, you're the best part

Out of nowhere, the groupie from his car bumped Morgan hard. Fury streaked through him in an instant. Before Messiah could even get on the ice, Aria suddenly wasn't so novice on those skates. She was at Morgan's side in seconds.

"Bitch, I want you to pop off out here," Aria said, as she put two fingers to the groupie's forehead and pushed it. Morgan's eyes burned into the girl's eyes. A challenge.

"He has the cutest birthmark, right?" the girl smiled, devilishly.

Morgan's heart sank. The birthmark, the position of it. On his right thigh, where his dick curved to the right. Morgan scoffed, as her eyes prickled. She turned to leave the ice. She was defeated. The words were enough to knock her out in the first round.

Fuck that.

She turned and slapped fire from the girl, gripping a handful of the girl's weave as she followed through, slapping her all the way to the ground. Suddenly, two girls came off the sidelines and Aria squared up.

Bop! Bop! Aria landed two to the chin.

Morgan and Aria were at a disadvantage because they were on skates, but it was too late to think twice. They were handling their own, despite the odds. A girl came up on Morgan, but before she could deliver one blow, Messiah was on her, one hand wrapped around the girl's throat so tightly she couldn't breathe.

"Not the type of problems you want, you understand me?" he asked. The girl nodded. "Now, get the fuck on." He released her with a shove, and the groupie stumbled, barely able to keep her balance on the ice.

"Damn, Messiah, it's like that?" she asked.

"Straight like that, ho," Morgan stated.

Fire-laced eyes burned Messiah before Morgan made her way off the ice.

She and Aria sat on the bench to swap their skates for shoes. Morgan was tender on the inside, her eyes, clouding, her stomach sinking, her heart tearing. *You bet not cry out here,* she told herself. Messiah was off to the side, discussing something in hushed tones with Ahmeek and Isa.

"He's such liar," Morgan mumbled. She snatched at the laces of the skates so hard that she broke a nail.

"Mo, don't listen to her," Aria whispered. "You know how girls are."

"Nah, he fucked her," Morgan said, surely, as she slid into her sneakers. "We out."

She stood and stormed by Messiah. When he caught her elbow, Morgan eyed his hand on her skin and cocked her neck back like she was cocking a gun. Messiah knew she was about to light his ass up, but to his surprise, she laughed.

"I don't even know why I'm surprised." There was so much disappointment in her tone that it injured him.

Messiah tossed his keys to Ahmeek. "Meet me at the spot. Have one of the little niggas take my whip." He directed his attention to Isa. "You got her?"

Aria's eyes widened. "No offense, but we came together so we leaving together," Aria said, sternly.

Messiah would have lost his patience with the girl if he didn't appreciate the loyalty. She seemed solid and Messiah knew Morgan needed friends like that. "We're all going to the same spot. I just need a minute with her."

Aria looked to Morgan. Morgan nodded, and Aria followed Isa up the stairs.

Messiah knew better than to begin the conversation here. He could feel the anger radiating off her. He extended his hand, telling her to go first and she climbed the stairs. The walk to her car was awkward, silent. Their energy had been off lately, and Messiah didn't like it.

"Give me your keys," he said, as they made it to her car. "I'll drive."

She ignored him and snatched open her door. She didn't speak, as he lowered into her passenger seat.

She turned up her radio and eased out into traffic.

"Pull behind Isa," Messiah instructed. She did as she was told but turned her radio up louder.

I just want to break up all your shit
Call your mama phone let her know
That she raised a bitch
Then dial tone click

Messiah's brows lifted in impatience. He knew she expressed

her emotions through music. The lyrics flowing out of her speakers were intentional, aimed straight for him. *Fuck this shit,* he thought, as he reached for the radio and turned it off. *Fucking Cardi B.* He was insulted and amused all at the same time.

"Can we talk?" Messiah asked.

"Nope," Morgan replied, stubbornly. "What's the point in talking. You tell me it's one way when we're together and I find out it's another when you're alone. Now that I know how it's laying, I will act accordingly. No conversation needed."

Messiah pushed his seat back and sighed out his irritation. Morgan's vibes had turned from 'I love you' to 'fuck you' and he only had himself to blame. He gave her the silence she desired, in hopes that she would cool off so he could explain. Even the notion of explaining himself was foreign. It was a courtesy he never extended to anyone… until now. Messiah placed a hand on her thigh and she cringed. His stomach lurched because, until now, she had only associated his touch with pleasure.

"Don't touch me. I don't know where your hands been."

Ten minutes of silence passed until she pulled onto the curb in front of his trap house. He wished he could just take her to his home, just the two of them, but she had her homegirl with her and Messiah didn't know Aria well enough to let her know where he rested his head. She turned off the car and Messiah grabbed her keys from the cup holder. It was his way of controlling when she could leave. Before he could get out one word, she was out the door.

"You good?" Aria asked.

"Yep," Morgan said, but her short reply let everyone know she was anything but. She stalked to the backdoor, leaving footprints in the snow and on his heart…he was glad she could only see one set.

"Yo, Meek went to pick up his girl," Isa informed. "Bleu and

Iman falling through too." Messiah nodded, but he was sure it wasn't going to be that type of night. No group festivities of weed, liquor, and 'never have I ever games' that couples played and shit. He and Morgan had some things to hash out.

Messiah unlocked the door and Morgan entered first and headed straight to the living room. She took the love seat, as everyone sat down around the room.

"So, that's what you and your girl do in your spare time, Mo? Y'all laying bitches out like Ali out here?" Isa said.

"She was disrespectful," Morgan shrugged, as she flipped her hair over her shoulder. She narrowed her gaze on Messiah. "She wasn't the only one." The last part she signed.

"I thought we agreed to take a break," Messiah signed back. "The bitch is irrelevant. She don't mean shit."

He spelled out s-h-i-t with his fingers because he hadn't learned informal signs yet.

Morgan's hands were moving a mile a minute. "No, *you* instituted this break. It's bullshit. I didn't agree to this. I didn't even want it. What if I fucked somebody else during this break? Is that okay?"

Messiah's entire body stiffened, as he sniffed and flicked his nose with his thumb. Morgan knew she was dancing dangerously close to the line that flipped Messiah's rage.

Good. Cheating-ass.

"If I sucked a nigga dick? How about that? Would that be okay?" Morgan signed.

"There would be a dead n-i-g-g-a out this b-i-t-c-h," Messiah signed back. "Don't play with me, Mo."

Morgan's body ignited. She was like the proud owner of a prized Pit Bull who gloated at its aggression, it's loyalty, it's instinct to protect. Messiah was her Pit. When she yanked his chain, he barked; when she let him off his leash, he bit.

Isa and Aria sat confused, as they absorbed the awkward energy that was clearly an argument.

"Maybe we should um…I'm hungry," Aria said, as she stood. "Are you hungry? My treat. It'll give me a chance to see if there is a gentleman underneath all this finesse."

Isa stood, gripping the sides of his hat and pulling it low over his eyes. "You must think I'm one of them bum-ass college dudes you used to. I can handle the bill, Ali," he chuckled. "I don't eat no bullshit, though."

"It's late, nothing's open this late but diners and fast food spots," Aria countered.

"My boy is a chef. He'll put something together for me. We can go pick it up." Isa's thumb moved across his phone screen and then turned to Messiah. "You want me to bring you back something, bro'?"

Messiah's temples throbbed, as he gritted his teeth. He didn't even look at Morgan as he pointed to her. "Bring her back the lobster roll and fries, man, side of ranch." He went into his pocket and Morgan smacked her lips.

"I can pay for my own food," she snapped. "And I don't want that. Bring me the catfish with mac and cheese, add a small side of greens."

"I gave you the money you pulling out, so I'm still paying for it, put that shit up," Messiah said. "And you ain't even gon' eat that shit. Your bougie-ass don't even like catfish."

Isa and Aria looked at each other in stun. There was so much passion between Messiah and Morgan. Whether it was anger or love, it could be felt by everyone in the room.

"I got it, bro'," Isa said. He didn't know whose money to take so he would spend his own. He was Switzerland. He wanted no parts of picking sides in this war.

"We'll be back in about an hour."

"Aye, Is, cancel that shit with Bleu and Meek," Messiah barked. Isa nodded in understanding, before leading Aria out the house. Messiah pinched the bridge of his nose and brought his elbows to his knees as he leaned forward in his seat. Morgan had burrowed all the way under his skin and his imagination was running wild.

"Why didn't you tell me you were coming home?" he asked. This time he spoke.

"Why? Because you need a heads up? So you can pretend to be all about me when really you're out here doing you?" Morgan asked.

"Only time I'm me is when I'm with you," Messiah answered. His voice was dipped in something she couldn't identify. Deprivation, perhaps, and it lowered her defenses - slightly. "But you got your life, shorty. You got your whole life in front of you," Messiah continued, as he held out his palms like he was presenting it to her on a platter. "You got school and you got friends there, fucking college niggas all over you…"

"Is this about Bash? I don't want him," Morgan shouted.

"But you kissed him," Messiah stated.

She steeled, and guilt filled her eyes before spilling onto her cheeks. It all made sense now. Messiah's detachment. His distance. His disloyalty.

"That was a mistake, Siah," her voice was small - when she found it - and she knew she would have to put some confidence behind it to convince him otherwise. She cleared her throat and held her chin high, as she swiped a tear from her face. "I didn't initiate that kiss."

"You didn't tell me about it either," Messiah countered. He jabbed a stern finger in her direction. "The girl who calls to tell me about everything else about her day, and I mean everything, Mo…you call me to tell me how heavy your period flowing…

got me running up and down the highway to bring you stick ups and shit."

"Tampons, nigga?" Morgan corrected, in irritation.

"What the fuck ever. Got me out here caking with your spoiled-ass," Messiah spat back. "You call to tell me how the bitch at McDonald's forgot to put your Big Mac sauce on them nasty-ass burgers you be fucking with…how the little chicks at the Asian shop don't scrub the bottom of your feet hard enough and be talking in Chinese and shit about your crusty-ass toes!"

"Vietnamese, racist-ass, and my toes ain't crusty when they in your mouth!" she bantered back, pissed.

"You ringing my line to tell me the girl in your Chem class don't blend her weave with her real hair, so you be looking at tracks the whole hour…or how you have to park at the back of the lot at school because I keep you up too late and you oversleep so you miss out on all the good spots. Tell me how it is that you hit my line to tell me all these insignificant details about your day, but somehow you neglected to tell me this. I'm calling bullshit, shorty. You hid that shit from me. You lied and I ain't never peg you to be that."

"I didn't want you to overreact! It was nothing. I don't want him," Morgan argued.

"I never thought that," he answered, calming slightly because the confirmation from her mouth made it a bit better. "But you're young. You shouldn't feel guilty about kissing some corny-ass college boy. That's what you're supposed to be doing. Dating, having fun, not pledging loyalty to somebody like me. I've got years on you, Mo. I'm robbing you of the years you're supposed to be getting to know yourself. You're supposed to be about partying and bullshitting right now, not centering your world around me. After what happened at your spot that day, we need distance. Distance keeps you safe."

"I'm not interested in any of that and I don't care about being safe. I'm untouchable when I'm under you. You're all I want! This! Us!"

"It might not feel like you're missing out on something right now, but years from now, you'll resent me for it. You got the rest of your life to be tied down. You only get these next few years to be young. If it's supposed to be me and you, it'll still be there…"

Morgan scoffed. She almost laughed. She would have laughed if the notion didn't tear her in two.

"In a few years? You want me to wait *years*? You want to leave me for years?" Morgan's grief was overwhelming to Messiah's ears. "Messiah."

Fuck.

His head dropped. He knew he would be unable to keep his resolve because… well… it was his name… on her lips. It was like a spell. She was like a spell; like magic in his life that he didn't believe in but couldn't figure out the illusion she was performing right in front of his eyes. An enchantress. A damned good one at that. He had bought out every seat in her audience, just so he would be the only one to witness the mystique.

"No," Morgan whispered, denying the thought, as she shook her head. This fight wasn't supposed to go this way. It wasn't supposed to lead to this. Her bottom lip quivered. "No." That one was firmer. Determined. Forget the girl he slept with, forgo the fight, fuck her jealousy. She just wanted to fast forward, or perhaps rewind…anything that would move them by this moment…away from this conversation. "Ssiah…"

"I apologize for the shit tonight. If I had known you were coming to town I would have never put you in that position. You think I'm out here doing me, but the only time I'm free to be me is when I'm locked in that small-ass apartment with you. That's real. That's me."

"She's solid, Messiah. You don't have to worry about that. It's good, though. That they're feeling each other. It can be fun."

"Don't start getting no corny, double-dating ideas and shit," Messiah warned.

She laughed and wrapped her arms around him, as she buried her face in his chest. Nothing felt better than this, being on one accord, being together, and Morgan told herself she would do everything required to keep it this way.

CHAPTER 11

Strength was fleeting lately and no matter how hard Alani tried to crawl from the bed, her body wouldn't cooperate. Depression had a vice grip on her and it wasn't something that she could shake. It wasn't external. She could manage through her day well enough. At first sight, she looked like a pretty girl who was coping just fine...some would even call her strong and graceful for being able to retain her smile through it all. Those people weren't looking deep enough. They weren't focusing on the dullness behind her smile. It didn't meet her eyes. It was superficial and was a smoke screen that hid the internal battle she was fighting. This was hell on Earth. She barely ate because food sickened her, and sleep without pills was evasive. She couldn't close her eyes without having nightmares, so she wrote all night, penning a story so sad that her tears stained the pages of her notebook as she went along. Alani felt like she was drowning. She tried to take deep breaths to curb the sensation in her stomach. This sickness. God, when would it pass? When would it get easier? The pain was supposed to lessen with every passing day, but Alani's only intensified. Alani had quit everything. School. Work. Church. Bills were piling up in the mailbox she never checked. Bills insinuated that there was living going on inside her house. Dinner and laughter and hustle and bustle and school and work and purpose...there was none of that...no life. Just death. She lived in a cubicle of hurt; and although she knew that living in that space was destructive, she couldn't step out of it. She couldn't see through what she was feeling. She hadn't even been to visit Nannie. The hospital had called her daily about the decision of Nannie's medical care, but Alani just couldn't. She couldn't be responsible for pulling the plug. She knew that once she pulled that plug, her life would end too. It would be too much loss to sustain. She would give up. A wave of nausea swept over her and she felt her entire face prickle. She rushed to the bathroom and lifted the toilet seat as she heaved up clear fluids. There was nothing to throw up. Alani hadn't nourished herself properly in over a month. She was surviving on just enough to keep her alive because she questioned if she wanted to stay that way…alive…breathing…without her daughter.

Alani kneeled in front of the toilet, gripping the seat with her head lowered.

"Mmmm," she groaned. She sucked in air through her nose. *God, please. God, please, just make it stop,* she prayed.

"Arghh!" She threw up, again. Apparently, God wasn't answering calls at the moment. She reached for the handle and flushed the toilet before struggling to her feet. She grabbed a water bottle and opened the medicine cabinet for toothpaste. Her eyes fell on a lone tampon that sat on the shelf. Her eyes widened, as she staggered backward. She sat on the edge of the bathtub and covered her mouth.

When was my last period?

Alani rushed to her room and snatched her phone from the charger. She frantically unlocked it and opened the calendar.

No, no, no, no, no.

Her menstrual was late. She hadn't felt like herself lately, but she was grieving. She wasn't supposed to feel like herself. She would never feel like herself again.

But the nausea, and the lightheadedness, and the exhaustion.
I can't be pregnant by him.

It felt like the room was spinning and she had to reach out for her headboard to keep from falling. She rushed into the bathroom and brushed her teeth. She threw on leggings and a hoodie, before snatching up her keys.

Alani's leg bounced nervously, as she drove to the local pharmacy. She grabbed a test off the shelves and didn't even bother paying for it before heading to the bathroom. No way would she survive the drive home without knowing. She couldn't pee on the stick fast enough.

God, please. God, please.

She wanted no mistakes, so she purchased the one that gave written results. It was the longest two minutes of her life. Her stomach tightened in angst as she squared off at one end of the stall while the pregnancy stick sat on the back of the toilet at the other end. She had palms to both walls, bracing herself for impact.

Pregnant.

Alani crumpled to the floor, right there in the dirty stall.

She kicked the aluminum wall, as torment ate through every fiber in her body. "Aghhh!" she screamed.

How had she let this happen? How hadn't she thought it might occur? Of course, she was pregnant. He had helped himself to her body so many times that night she had lost count. She remembered being depleted when they were done. Like her body wouldn't be able to produce another orgasm for months because he had used them all up. He hadn't used protection. She hadn't even felt compelled to ask him to because she trusted him. Alani couldn't bear the thought of having him inside her. He was growing there, and it felt disgusting. She wanted to dig him out herself.

What have I done?

It took everything for Alani to peel herself off that bathroom floor.

Just make it to the car.

She couldn't hear anything around her. Her racing heart drowned out all sound and her tears blurred her vision.

Before she had been oblivious to what her symptoms added up to, but now that she knew, the feelings inside her were intensified. It was unbearable.

"Hey, Miss. You have to pay!"

The man in the red vest came from behind the counter and gripped Alani's elbow to stop her from exiting the store. She blinked eyes of confusion up to him.

How could I let this happen?

She felt responsible. She had let him in, and when she had discovered the horrible truth, she had done nothing to prevent this. She could have taken the Plan B pill the very next day. *It should have been the first thing I thought of. How could I not think? I didn't think.*

A sob escaped her, as she reached into her purse and pulled out a twenty-dollar bill. She handed it off to the man without speaking, then retreated to her car. So many possibilities sprouted in her mind, as the revelation of a new baby hit her. *Their* child. *His* baby. A phantom pain bolted through her frame and she tensed. She could never raise a baby with him. It wasn't a solution to their problems. There was no answer to the things that had broken them apart. It was something you just had to let be. But it was a baby and babies were gifts. Alani shook her head. This one was a curse. A brief notion of raising this baby alone crossed her mind but images of Kenzie in her mind erased that idea almost as quickly as it had formed.

I can't.

She picked up her phone and opened her browser.

She typed in the words. *Planned Parenthood.*

She wasn't even this type of woman. She didn't even believe in what she was about to do, but she had to. There was no other option and she needed it done as quickly as possible. It couldn't wait. Waiting would only extend her torture. She wanted to be done with every part of Ezra Okafor, even if she had to commit the greatest sin to accomplish that.

"God, please, I just don't understand why this is happening to me," Alani whispered. "I know what I'm about to do is wrong, but I can't keep this baby. I just can't. Why would you even give it to me? Please…please…" Alani's pleas were filled with desperation and confusion, as she threw her burdens on the altar of the church. This pregnancy had brought her to her knees. "Why would you even trust me with another one of your angels? I didn't protect the first one. I failed her," she sobbed. She had failed at many things before. It was a part of life; but being an inadequate mother was not only embarrassing, but shattering. She couldn't shake this fog of misery. She was lost and there was no compass to help her navigate out of these troubled waters. No man to lean on, no mother to wipe her tears. Just loneliness. "Please, just give me clarity, Lord, give me strength because I'm breaking. In your name I pray. Amen." Alani used the back of her hand to wipe the wetness from her face, as she composed herself. She stood to her feet. Even that took so much effort. She was struggling with the decision to get rid of this baby. She didn't want to share a child with Ethic, but Alani was a woman who didn't impregnate easily. It had taken years for her to conceive her daughter. There had been so much time spent wondering why everyone around her seemed to sneeze and get pregnant while she had been barren for years. She had felt like less of a woman and Cream had called her such. He had beaten her down so badly during those times, crushing her self-esteem, calling her worthless. She had believed him, because what was a woman for if not to give a man a child? She had prayed so hard for a baby and then came Kenzie. *How did I mess up something I prayed so hard for? I should have loved her better...taken better care of her.* During her pregnancy the mystery was solved. Alani was diagnosed with endometriosis. She had to have a perfect pregnancy to even deliver a healthy baby and she had been willing. She had eaten right, she had stayed off her feet, and taken her vitamins. She had done it, and then she had neglected that rare gift.

Now, without even trying, without ever thinking it was possible for lightning to strike the same spot twice, she was somehow pregnant.

Her appointment for the abortion was tomorrow, but it felt sinister to destroy something she knew was unnatural for her body to even produce...life...rare life...and she was just going to snuff it out. It was like God had handed her a second gift and she was too ungrateful to accept it. *I can't raise his child. He took my baby. I can't trust him with a piece of me.*

She turned and walked up the long aisle of the church. Passing the recreation room, she noticed the girls from the pageant and her feet stopped. She peeked through the glass window to see Bella sitting in a chair alone. Every other girl in the room was with their mother but Bella. Alani frowned.

"God, please bring someone to her life that can fill that hole," she whispered. As if Bella could hear her, she looked out the window. Her entire face lit up when she noticed Alani. Bella waved, and Alani felt like she was put on the spot. She wanted to hurry out the door, but her feet were glued to the floor. Bella looked so much like her father that Alani shivered. She gave a polite, flat-lipped smile and waved back before tearing her feet from the floor and rushing down the hallway. She grabbed her jacket from the coat rack and slid her arms inside. The voices filtering from the office caused her to linger.

"I don't think she'll be able to participate, Pastor. She doesn't have anyone reliable to take part in the ceremony. We really should enforce the application process for next year to avoid girls with circumstances like hers. She's being raised by a single father and her mother is deceased. They aren't even members of the church. The prep for the debutante is six months long. Every time she has to sit through a practice or an event without a mother, it will make the other participants uncomfortable. This program may not be for her."

Alani's chest tightened, as she made her presence known.

"Alicia, if you're discussing Bella Okafor's involvement in the pageant, there really isn't much to discuss, right, Saints?" Alani asked, with a challenging smile. "This is a community church with a community outreach program. The fact that Bella doesn't have a mom should be even more reason why she gets to participate. I mean, we're all Christians in here, right? That's the *Christian* thing to do. I would hate for us to punish a young girl, and for what? Having a dead mother? In that case, maybe I should be punished too for having a dead child?"

I wish your ass would kick Bella out this pageant.

Alicia White was the church hypocrite, clapping, singing, and praising her way through Sunday mornings, but sleeping with a married man Monday through Saturday. She was phony, and Alani would put all her shit on blast if Alicia tried her. Truth be told, she was no example to any young girl. Her homewrecking-ass didn't need to teach Bella or any other girl anything for that matter.

Challenge burned in Alani, as she cocked a brow.

"Of course I'm not suggesting that we kick her out. We will just have to accommodate her, I guess," Alicia conceded.

"That would be in your best interest," Alani stated, with a fake smile. She nodded to the pastor and then turned on her heels.

"Bourgeoise-ass bitch," Alani mumbled, on her way out the door, feeling ashamed that she was acting up in the Lord's house, but praying God didn't count it against her.

Ethic stepped inside the hospital room and was shocked at how grim it felt. The energy in the room was low. The blinds were drawn shut, the lights were off. It felt like a broom closet where someone stored miscellaneous things, instead of a room where one hoped healing would take place. Ethic smelled chemicals, and oddly, the scent of "hospital". He didn't know what it was, but ever since he was a child the inside of hospitals had a very particular scent. Like death lingered just around the corner like trash waiting to be taken out on trash day. Much to his dismay, the woman in the bed seemed to just be rotting there. Neglected. He walked over to the window and let in the light. A nurse walked into the room and startled when she saw him.

"Oh! I'm sorry! I didn't realize Ms. Hill had a visitor. She doesn't get very many," she said.

He frowned in concern. "No one's been here?"

The woman gave a sympathetic smile and shook her head.

That concerned Ethic. Where was Alani? If she wasn't even visiting her aunt, he could only imagine what she was going through.

"How is she?" Ethic asked.

"She's just ticking. No progress in health, no decline in health," the nurse answered.

She went to take Nannie's vitals and Ethic crossed his arms, observing. When she began to peel back the covers to change the bed pan, Ethic turned around and stared out the window.

"During the day, the blinds should be open. The windows too. Let in the air," Ethic said.

"She doesn't know the difference," the nurse responded.

He turned to the nurse, a stern look covering his face. "That wasn't a suggestion," he said. The nurse was rolling the covers back over Nannie's body when she paused to take in his serious glower. She nodded.

Ethic nodded to the bed pan. It was filled, almost overfilled with waste.

"She should never be that soiled. Just because no one's visiting doesn't mean no one's watching," Ethic said, as he pulled out a neatly folded band of hundred-dollar bills. He stepped hard-bottomed Ferragamo shoes across the tiled floor and peeled off 15 one-hundred-dollar bills. He handed it to the nurse. "I want her treated better. Monitored closer. Her body massaged for blood circulation. Her hair combed and her body bathed daily. No skipping. I'll drop this off to you once a week to see to these things personally," he instructed. "Treat her like a person."

The nurse took the money and nodded. "I could get fired if..."

"Between us," Ethic stated.

She nodded and breathed out a sigh of relief.

Ethic peeled off 200 more dollars. "And get some flowers in here," he instructed.

"Yes, sir," the nurse said.

He sat down next to the bed. "And let her doctor know I'd like to speak with him, please," he instructed.

The nurse left the room and Ethic peered into the face of the old woman that Alani loved so much.

"I believe there is a billing issue as well," the nurse prodded. "Perhaps, you should stop at the nurse's station before you leave."

Ethic scoffed. Billing. Money. They were keeping her under their care without actually adding the care part to the medical treatment all for the sake of a dollar. He pulled out his wallet and pulled out a platinum card. "Run it up for all I care. Just make sure she's taken care of. The best possible."

The nurse nodded and then left the room. Concern was at the forefront of Ethic's mind. This desolate, abandoned room didn't make sense, unless there was something wrong. He had fought against every notion he knew to give her space, but if she wasn't here, where was she? Cream entered his mind and he wondered if she was safe. He couldn't continue to stay away and second-guess that. It was time to see about her.

Alani had to grip the top of the clipboard to stop her hands from shaking. She sat in the clinic, fighting the worst bout of nausea yet. She didn't remember it being this bad with her daughter. It was crippling, and she just wanted it to end. Her leg bounced, nervously, as she looked around discreetly at the other women in the room. Some were pregnant, some were there for the same reason as her…to end pregnancy, others had children with them. Alani tried not to look at the babies in the room. They seemed to stare at her lately, like they could sense her conflict about the child she was carrying. It was like every baby she saw in that room was beseeching her not to murder one of their own. With their lovely baby scent and those adorable, but somehow delving gapes, they were pulling at her conscious. She felt haunted and knew that she was about to add another ghost to her life. She just couldn't keep this child. This baby would make her love a man she shouldn't love. Severing the connection and ripping the roots he had planted in her was the only way for her to stop loving him because, somehow, she still did. She was guilt-ridden over that, over loving him... God, loving him so much even while hating him.

"Alani Hill."

Alani looked up at the black woman in scrubs. They were pink with little ducks on them and Alani's eyes teared. Those scrubs seemed so childlike, so cute, like they would be interesting to little eyes. She was hormonal and emotional, and she was certain she was depressed, and it all broiled on high inside her, making her angry at the woman for wearing those damn scrubs. *This is an abortion clinic. She should be wearing black. It's a fucking graveyard in here.* Her bottom lip felt heavy and Alani bit it to inflict a little pain to give her something to focus on besides the dread inside her. She stood and followed Ms. Duck Scrubs to the back.

Alani walked into the small room and sat on the bed.

"I'm going to get some vitals and draw some blood first; then, conduct an ultrasound. That okay?" she asked.

None of this is okay.

The word "yes," slipped from her mouth. It was like a blur. She felt tightness around her arm, felt the puncture of a needle, then something cold against her chest, then her inner wrist. It was all so routine.

"I'm going to step out for a quick moment, so you can get undressed. You can put the gown on and peek your head out when you're ready for me to come in."

Alani nodded.

Why do I have to do this?

There was a scratching on the door to her soul, like the stray cat that sometimes came to her home, begging, scratching against her screen because Alani had made the mistake of setting out milk one time. Her baby was scratching, pleading, begging her to choose differently. Her body was on autopilot, as she removed her clothes, taking the time or stalling for time and folding them neatly on the chair beside the bed. Suddenly, she wished she had called him. Ethic would have been there, next to her, holding her hand, coaching her through this. Somebody had to hold her hand through this. *Why is it just me?* A sob escaped but she chased it down, swallowed it back inside and bit that lip, bit it so hard that she tasted blood. *You're all you got. It's only you now. Having this baby is wrong. Get it over with.*

She slipped into the gown and peeked her head out the door. The nurse walked back in and Alani climbed onto the bed.

"We're going to do the ultrasound now. See how far along you are so the doctor can determine the best way to proceed."

Alani felt the cold air kiss her skin, as her gown was lifted, and a large piece of paper was used to cover her private area.

"I'm applying a cold gel."

Alani tensed and turned her head away from the monitor. Tears leaked out the side of her eyes and onto her left shoulder. A steady hum filled the room and Alani broke. She knew what it was. She could feel it. That rhythm, the drum, a pulse. It was her baby's heartbeat. Proof that Ethic had made magic of her body and gotten her pregnant when a second pregnancy should have been near impossible for her. Ethic versus endometriosis. Of course, Ethic had won. Before she had found out he was the devil, she had deemed him godly.

"You're six weeks along," Ms. Duck Scrubs said.

It's been six weeks since I've seen him. Six whole weeks since he snatched my heart out of my body and left me with this.

"It should be an easy evacuation. You're not that far along. You can do a medication abortion. It's two pills. One now, in office, and another one in 24 hours that will empty your uterus. It'll feel like a heavy period."

"No. I need to walk out of here empty. I need it done now. Right now. If I leave here and it's up to me, I won't take the second pill," she protested, slightly panicked.

"Okay, if that's what you prefer," the nurse said. "The doctor will be in shortly."

Alani heard the door open then close and she was grateful because the cry she was trying to tame was too strong to keep inside. Her breasts bounced up and down, her stomach twisted, and she wept. She wept like she never had before. It was cut short when the door re-opened and a white woman wearing a white coat walked inside.

"Ms. Hill, my name is Dr. Simmons. I'll be performing the procedure today," the woman said.

Procedure? This is murder. This is cold-blooded, pre-calculated murder.

Alani nodded, as she sniffed away her emotion.

The doctor sat on a rolling stool and frowned in concern. "Have you explored all your options? You're still very early on in this pregnancy. You have some time to decide."

"There's no time. It has to be done now," Alani whispered.

The doctor nodded and pulled out two stirrups from the bed.

"Okay," she said. "If you'll put your legs up and scoot your bottom toward me, I can examine your cervix. My nurse is going to give you a sedative. You won't be completely asleep and there will be some pain, but it will be minimal."

The nurse handed her a cup of water and three pills. Alani

swallowed them down in a rush.

Alani bit her lip harder, as she laid down. As soon as she felt the speculum enter her, the tears returned. Instant anger hit her. *Why is he not here? He did this! Why does he get to sit the hard part out!?* Even though she hadn't told him, she hated him for putting her in this position in the first place; for doing something so sinister it forced her to live without him. He was to blame, and it was a bitter truth that was too tart to live on the human tongue. *I wish he never told me. Why couldn't he just let us be happy?*

She was so distraught her legs shook.

"Ms. Hill. I can't perform this procedure in good faith if you're this emotional. I think waiting would be..."

"Just get it out of me!" Alani screamed, as she hyperventilated. Her chest heaved up and down, as panic seized her. Her legs were spread open and they trembled as the cold stirrups kept them propped up. Her womanhood was exposed, and vulnerability sickened her already weak stomach. "Just get him out!" She placed her hands over her face, as tears rolled down her cheeks, filling her ears. She wasn't even thinking of the life she grew inside of her. She was thinking of Ethic. He had spread through her like a disease, infecting every inch of her soul. She could feel him with each beat of her aching heart and it was killing her. The connection that had once breathed life into her was now slowly draining her. Having his DNA inside her, evolving, growing, it only multiplied what she felt. Every time her hormones doubled, so did her emotions. Nature was performing miracles inside her body and Alani hated it. His seed buried inside her womb was a cruel joke. The idea of what they had shared producing a tangible, living, breathing example of their bond was changing her, convincing her that somehow, someway, just maybe she could forgive him. Alani could never. Would never. "God, please just bleed me dry of him. Get him out. I can't take this. I just need him out my system," she whispered.

"Ms. Hill," her doctor said, soothingly, as she gave a look of concern.

Alani knew she had to get it together. She had to force herself to mask the insanity she felt because no way would any doctor do the procedure in her current state of mind.

"I think you need to take a few days to really consider this."

Alani heard the dreaded words and she shook her head, as sobs rushed from her mouth before she could stop them.

"I'll give you a few moments to get dressed," the doctor said.

Alani sucked in a deep breath and looked at the ceiling. She cleared her throat.

"Please. I'm fine. I'll sign whatever you have," she said, her voice eerily settled. "Just do it today."

The doctor opened her legs and Alani held her breath so that she wouldn't cry.

Alani felt like she was crazy. The rage and resentment that coursed through her made her chest physically burn. Hours passed before they would allow her to leave.

"You're very emotional. We would like for you to speak with one of our counselors before you check out," the doctor had said. Alani had just gone through the motions, answering the questions she knew they would want her to. Whatever made her look sane. Whatever sounded right. Then, she had rested, sleeping as she let the sedation wear off. She stood and dressed slowly. Her hands shook. Her emotions were so potent that she couldn't control them. She balled her hands into fists and placed them on the exam table before leaning against it, hanging her head in angst. My God, how could one man cripple her so? Flashes of their one night played in her mind and she popped her eyes open to avoid the memory. It was the reason she couldn't sleep. He lived in her dreams. His new home was behind the lids of her eyes. She could still feel the way his manhood had parted her lips and imprinted a path from her womb straight to her heart, as he made love to her from behind. He had only entered her once, but somehow, she had memorized the rhythm of his stroke, as if he had been her lover for years. It felt like she was mourning the end of a marriage - not some fling. Ethic had planted not only a seed that she was growing, but roots that were too stubborn to be pulled. Her heart felt like someone had taken razor blades to it and she could feel it bleeding inside her chest. She was standing there, fully functioning, lungs taking in air, but she was suffocating. She dressed and stormed out of the office. She didn't even know how she made it home, but when she pulled up and saw that Tesla sitting in front of her house, pure dread seized her. *It took you six weeks. Six fucking weeks to come check on me.*

Alani's thoughts were all over the place. How could she be mad at that? She had convinced herself that she hadn't wanted to see him ever again, but had she only told herself that because he wasn't showing up anyway? She was confused. Irrational. Enraged. She was going crazy. He was driving her crazy. Thoughts of the baby was pressing on guilt and resentment inside her. Why did he have to show up today? Of all days? Why now?

Fate.

Ethic climbed from his car and Alani froze. It was like when she saw a spider and clammed up, thinking it would somehow jump on her, or attack her before she could find the bleach, or the broom, or air freshener, or whatever other random thing she would try to use to kill it because her ass never had bug spray. She needed repellant for Ethic. Something to kill him and exterminate him from her life. She waited for him to say something, to do something.

"Lenika…"

His tone was broken, like setting eyes on her was excruciating. She didn't know if it was the fact that it was obvious that she had been crying, or that she had lost a massive amount of weight, or if she just looked pathetic, but he was visibly wounded at first sight. When he started for her, Alani started for her door, rushing, scrambling with house keys, to try to beat him so that she could close the door and lock him out.

"Go away!" she shouted, as she stormed into her house. His strong palm against the wood prevented her from closing it in his face. She gripped her keys in one hand and ran her other hand through her short hair in exasperation, as she spun in a circle. "My God! Why are you here?" she screamed. "I can't do this today. I can't. I can't! I just can't!"

Ethic was on top of her, holding her face in both hands, staring down at her so intently. His wet eyes bore into hers.

"I just want to breathe you in for a minute, baby," he whispered. So tortured, so pained. He placed his forehead to hers and drew in a deep breath. It reminded her of the Little Mermaid, like he was sucking her soul from her body, taking her voice, robbing her of her choice. He was touching her. He loved her. She felt the potency through the heat of the palms of his hands, as she withered in his hold. He couldn't touch her like this because she would never get rid of his black ass.

"What do you want from me?" she yelled, her wet face contorted in suffering.

"You," Ethic said it as if it was just that simple. "I've opened my eyes every morning since you walked out my life and I know I'm alive. I see my kids, I feel my pulse. The world around me is moving forward, but I'm stuck. I'm making it through each day, but I'm not breathing, Lenika. I can't fucking breathe without you." He held her face so tightly it almost hurt. His hold was filled with need, as he loomed over her, his head bowed slightly into the side of her face in shame... in pain. It made her feel a bit of satisfaction that he had been suffering too. He hadn't just gone about his life like nothing had happened. He felt it too. She wanted to run from the room, but the sincerity of his words had glued the soles of her feet to the floor. Was he hurting? Were his insides twisted, his head clouded, and his heart split open the way hers was? She believed he was. She hoped he was.

"Then die," she said.

Ethic pulled a gun from his waistline and Alani's eyes widened as instinct caused her to tense. Of course, he kept a piece on him. He was a killer disguising himself as a good man. It was a part of his deception. Alani felt foolish all over again. Just the sight of the gun in his hand, inside her house, caused a rage to bubble inside her, outweighing the notion of fear. Was it the same gun he used to...*God, is it?* The trepidation that flashed in her eyes made Ethic's stomach hollow. "You're afraid of me." He knew it. He had known it ever since he visited her the day after admitting the truth, but each time he saw her react to his presence it injured him all over again.

Her lip quivered, violently, as she tried her hardest to pull it together. She was a weakened woman. It was something she had never been before losing her child, but that type of loss changes a person. She didn't know if she would ever find her strength again.

"What did I do to you?" He asked. He held the gun out for her. The feeling of his rough hand as it briefly connected against her butter-soft skin caused her to suck in a baited breath. He felt it too. The connection. The spark. Like flint against stone, they just reacted to one another. "I took life from you. I owe you life. I'll give you mine, if that's what it takes to let you know how sorry I am. Take it." Alani wrapped her hand around the gun, feeling the weight of it in her small palm. Ethic placed his hands around hers and forced her to press the gun into his chest. "Pull the trigger, Lenika. You want revenge, I understand. It's yours. I'll give that to you. I'll give anything to you, do anything for you. My heart you already own. If it's my head on a silver platter, you can have that too. If I got to put my life in your hands, then so be it. Just love me. Just before you pull that trigger… just love me. I can't function out here. I'm at war with your baby's father and I can't do what I need to do. He shooting up my businesses and putting my kids in harm's way, but I can't react because I don't want to bring *you* more pain. I don't want to bring any more death to your life. I don't want you to bury anyone else, so I'm not doing what I should do. I'm not moving how I know to move. I'm at a disadvantage because you make me weak. Cream wants revenge. He wants war and I'm going to lose, because I can't take anything else from you. So, I'm right here, Alani, surrendering, losing the war to you because that nigga can't kill me. I would never let him. It's fucking amateur hour with him. I'll tag his fucking toes, but that will hurt you and that's the last thing I want to do. So, you end it. You pull the trigger, but just love me first. Just let yourself love me before you take my life."

Alani's eyes flooded, as she gripped the gun in both hands. He pressed against the barrel, his stare on her, her stare on him. He was fearless, as Alani's finger rested on the trigger. If she chose to pull it, he would deserve every bullet. The intensity that filled the room felt like water filling her lungs.

"Just do it. I'm dead out here without you anyway," Ethic said. "I'm tired of losing." He wasn't talking about war now. He was talking about love. Ethic was tired of losing love.

Ethic had never, would never, put his life in anyone else's

hands. He knew he would be leaving his children behind, but this was the only way to rectify his wrongs. Cream would stop his quest for revenge and Alani would get her peace. He knew Mo would take care of Bella and Eazy.

She'll make sure they are okay.

He had taught her how to pick up the pieces after death. She knew the routine well from losing her own father so young.

"You have kids," she whispered, as her face melted in pain. Her brow wrinkled, torment caused the vein in the center of her forehead to strain. "Why did you do this to us? How could *you* do this?" she sobbed, jabbing the gun into his chest. Alani was split in half, hatred filling her on one side and stubborn love that refused to dissipate consuming the other. "Could you love me? If I murdered your child?" she asked. "Would you forgive me? Would you still want me? If I took one of them away from you?"

Even the thought of it seared him on the inside. He couldn't stop the display of emotions that took over his face. His eyes darkened against his will and his forehead creased in distress. It was an involuntary reaction to the notion of her bringing harm to his children. It was a natural, parental, instinct to protect that which you brought into the world. She recognized it, instantly.

"You couldn't, could you?" she scoffed. "But you expect me to. I know that you're sorry. I can feel it. I lay in bed at night and I can feel you tossing and turning all the way across town. That's the type of hold you have on me and it's choking me. It's killing me, Ethic!" She couldn't steady her breathing, as the words spilled from her distraught lips. "I know what time you close your eyes every night. At 3:10, every fucking night, because it's when the agony let's up, just a little bit. It's when I'm able to hate you the most because whatever love you keep awake, alive, is weaker when you finally fall asleep."

Ethic's red eyes revealed shock, as she spoke the truth.

"I felt you on the inside of me, Ethic. One of your children in my womb," she said, as she gripped the front of her t-shirt passionately. "Two heart beats inside my body. One from me, one from you. God, I thought about calling you a million times. I thought about what sharing a baby with you would mean, what it would look like? What it would feel like?"

Ethic couldn't keep his hands to himself, as she lowered the gun. He cupped her crying face, pressing his forehead to hers. She was so weak, broken, like glass and her sharp pieces were cutting him. Her affliction was unbearable, and he felt it. He was plagued with guilt.

"My baby?" he whispered. She nodded, as he wiped the snot from her nose with one swipe of his thumb. Nothing about Alani repulsed him. She was him. She didn't know it, but from the moment she let him between her legs, Ethic had infiltrated her. She carried him with her, souls tied.

"Your baby," she confirmed. "Maybe a beautiful little girl like Bella or a busy little boy like Eazy. *Our* baby. Can you believe that?" she asked, with a scoff, as a hint of a smile appeared on her lips and her eyes drifted to a place that wasn't the present, a place where she could still love him, and a place where he had never killed her child. A fake place that didn't exist. She was off in her head and Ethic noticed how zoned out she was. He frowned. In a flash, she came back to the reality where only suffering existed. "All this energy, the love that we felt that night, the passion I've felt ever since the first time I saw you, all wrapped up in a beautiful baby. I see it when I sleep. Could you even imagine?" she asked. Her lips were so close to his that they touched when she spoke. He was breathing her in, desperately absorbing her essence.

"I can imagine," he whispered, as he closed his eyes, a single tear falling down his cheek. "I want that. Don't take that from me. Have my baby. I swear to God, I'll take care of you. I'll love every single fiber of that pain away. I'm begging you, Lenika, and I don't beg, but I'm fucking begging you. I need you. I can see it so vividly in my mind."

"And that's the only place it will ever live," she said, her voice suddenly turning cold. He opened his eyes and pulled back from her. The disdain in her stare shattered him. "I could never let a piece of you grow inside me. I went to the doctor and got rid of it. I sucked the life right out of me. I could never betray my daughter and raise a child with you. You killed my baby, so I killed yours. Now, I'm a murderer, just like you. So, hate me for it, hate me the way that I hate you," she cried. He would have never guessed Alani was capable of such malice. She had built up the fantasy in his head just to tear it down. A scorned woman had a special way of hurting a man, of hitting him low, of digging her nails deeply into a wound.

Her words were worse than bullets. He stumbled backward, as he folded his lips and swiped his hand over his mouth to stop himself from speaking his emotions. Alani saw the change in his eyes. She recognized the shift in his disposition. She had shown him the devil inside her, the worst possible version of herself, the woman that could be spiteful, the one that operated out of hate. The bitch that lived inside any woman if you crossed them badly enough. Alani had a lot of bitch inside of her, these days. She could be the worst kind when she wanted to. Ethic had never given her a reason to bite him, until now, and he had discovered that her bite was nasty.

"You see that feeling? That pit?" she asked, as she used the gun to point to her belly. "That disgust that you're looking at me with? Now, imagine if I had birthed that baby and spent years allowing you to love it, to nurture it, to protect it and then I erased it like it never existed. Imagine I snatched that shit right out of your life, leaving you with only memories. That hate you feel right now would be worse. It would be unforgivable. What you did is un-for-give-able. Fuck our baby and fuck you."

Alani raised the gun.

"Pull the fucking trigger. PULL IT!" Ethic surprised himself, as he shouted. He advanced on her, gripping her chin as he pressed her into the wall. It was like his actions weren't even his own. They didn't belong to him because as he was making the moves, he was regretting them all in an instant, but he couldn't stop himself. He had never handled a woman so roughly. He was powered by fatherhood, powered by an instinct to protect. So many frustrations had built inside him over the past six weeks. He knew he had no right to be angry with her. The logical part of him understood why she had aborted his child, but the part of him that had waited to love her his entire life was enraged. He disregarded the feeling of steel against his abdomen, as one of his hands wrapped around her neck and the other tightened around her chin. No woman had ever pushed him to his limit in this way. He knew it was no excuse because he was a man and his actions were his and his alone, but Alani was a different breed. There wasn't a naïve bone in her body. She was tough, and he was her adversary. Alani didn't fight fair with her enemies and Ethic had to tell himself to calm down. Nobody had ever disrespected him so blatantly, but she wasn't just anyone, she was his future and he had squandered it. He loosened his grip, but kept her hemmed against the wall, his eyes burning into hers. It was at that moment that Alani understood. *This* was the man who had killed her family. This man, with his flared nostrils, eyes like the darkest hour of night, and undeniable rage was the one responsible for her turmoil. She hadn't been able to reconcile how the caring man she had fallen for had done the unspeakable acts, but she had awakened the blackest parts of him with the admission of an abortion. Now, she recognized the gangster he hid so well. Alani was a mess. She wanted to keep up the callous visage but seeing him so affected by the loss of the baby they shared hurt. It was pain on top of pain, wrong on top of wrong, and the tears clouding his vision caused hers to multiply. She abhorred this. This fucking unbreakable, disastrous, toxic bond they had created.

"I will never fuck with you! I never fucked with you to begin with. You're pathetic! You were spending so I was taking. Fuck you!" she roared. Alani spewed every lie she could think of that would damage him. It hurt her to even say them, but she just wanted him to hurt. She just wanted to spread some of the pain around a little because she had extra to spare.

"It's funny how quickly I can flip that switch. Love to hate," he said, in an eerie calm and with a snap of his fingers. He was seething. The thought of her killing his seed went deeper than just losing a child. She was severing their connection, erasing the brief moment in time that they had been allowed to co-exist. Her revelation caused him to love and lose a baby all in one moment. It was a baby he would have cherished, a baby that he knew was the one thing that could possibly keep him from losing her. It was a miracle and she had squandered it.

BOOM!

Alani heard the blast but didn't even remember pulling the trigger. She knew she had done it, however, when Ethic released her. He stumbled backward, shock taking over his face, as he looked down at the growing blood stain on his white, V-neck t-shirt. He looked back up at her and horror seized his entire body when he saw her lift the gun underneath her chin.

Fuck all this shit.

"No!" he shouted. He watched her white-painted nail curl on the trigger and his heart stopped.

CLICK!

Ethic lunged for her, fighting against the burn in his stomach as he tried to get control of the gun. She twisted and turned, as he wrestled her to the ground, fighting the pain that traveled through his entire body. The bullet seemed to be playing pinball inside him, as he felt the burn spread from his stomach to his chest. He struggled to pry the gun from her hands but Alani kept pulling the trigger, persistent about flirting with suicide. She kept it aimed snugly under her chin. CLICK! CLICK! He knew it had to be God that had caused the gun to jam repeatedly because it was a fully-loaded, semi-automatic pistol. It was designed to spray effortlessly. Alani's brains were supposed to be splattered over the floor.

"Let it go," he grunted, as he struggled to breathe while gripping her wrists tightly.

She sobbed, as he pried the weapon from her hands and his blood continued spilling out of him. He wrapped his arms around Alani, her back to his chest, as he leaned against the wall. Ethic could barely catch a breath, his blood poured from him.

He gritted his teeth, using all his strength to keep her held against his body, but he was fading. He was losing a lot of blood. It covered him, it soaked her, but he still refused to let her go. His mind spun, wildly. *I did this to her.* He had pushed her to the point of no return. Her hyperventilated cries filled his ears.

"Shh," he whispered, kissing the top of her head as her grief caused her to roll onto her side. He hoisted her into his lap, rocking her as he held her. "Why would you do that? Hmm? Why would you do that?" he cried. The shock from being shot had worn off and he was close to blacking out, but he gritted his teeth in determination, afraid to let her go. He could die right there on the floor of her small foyer and accept that as fate, but to see her try to take her own life was a punishment greater than death. He wasn't sure if she would try to finish the job, so he bit into his jaw, forcing himself to stay alert.

He gripped her with one hand and reached for his pocket with the other.

It's in the fucking car, he thought, in despair.

He was grateful when he heard the knock at the door. Someone had heard the gunshot.

"Daddy? Alani?"

What the fuck is she doing here?

"Bella, baby, don't come in!" he barked. "You have your phone?"

"Yeah, Daddy, what's going on?" she called through the door.

He hated for her to walk into this scene, but he needed her. He panted, as he began to cough up blood. He was struggling to stay alert. Alani just laid in his arms. He wondered if she was hurt. The way that she had stopped fighting, he wasn't sure.

"Daddy?" Bella called, unsurely.

"Call 911, baby girl," Ethic struggled. "Tell them you need an ambulance. Give them the address and wait outside for them to arrive, okay?"

"Daddy, are you okay?" Ethic could hear the worry in her voice. "Where's Alani?"

"Call them now, Bella!" It was all he could manage before his vision blurred and everything faded to black.

CHAPTER 12

What part of the body is this?" Messiah asked, as he lifted Morgan's foot, placing his tongue between her toes. Morgan smiled. She had been doing a lot of that lately. Messiah was back in her bed and nothing had ever felt so right.

"Phalanges," she moaned, lifting her eyes from her biology textbook and smiling down at Messiah. He took his time giving attention to each one as he sat shirtless at the end of the bed. His tattooed body was a distraction. Her eyes took him in, appreciating each ripple of his muscular build. The way his Nike sweat pants hung low on his hips, exposing those deep, V-cuts and the beginnings of his pubic hair made Morgan pull her lip between her teeth. He was a distraction, a sexy, tempting distraction.

"What about this part?" he asked, as he snaked his tongue up her leg.

"The tibia," she whispered. "Siah, I'm supposed to be studying." Her protests were in vain because he kissed further up her leg.

"We studying, shorty. Stay focused," he chastised. She smiled...a million-watt leer that tightened his chest. He shook his head in disbelief. He wasn't even sure how she did what she did to him. All he knew was he felt like he was worth something in her presence...like, if he took a bullet in these streets, finally somebody would mourn his loss.

"What?" she asked, wondering what was going through his mind.

He kissed another part of her body. "Nothing, shorty," he answered. "What's this part?"

"The patella," she whispered. "Seriously, I have a test."

"And I'm going to make sure you ace that mu'fucka," he assured. "This?" he quizzed, planting a soft kiss on her thigh.

"Femur," she said. He came up between her legs, parting them as he moved her panties to the side.

"What's this?" he asked. Messiah opened her lips and flattened his tongue. He licked her like he was trying to stop ice cream from melting down a cone and she quivered.

"Hmm," she moaned.

He smirked. "That ain't an answer, shorty."

"I don't know. I might need you to do that one again," she teased.

Messiah lowered his head and gently pulled the hood back from her pearl. Wrapping his mouth around it, he gave it a wet kiss, before sucking it gently.

Morgan's entire body bucked, as he spread her thighs wider and his head moved in circles. Morgan felt her body crushing her study guide and destroying the papers beneath her, but she could care less. Messiah was giving her a crash course and she was determined to pass. "The clitoris."

"Nah, wrong answer," he said, as he put his face back in her treasure. He kissed her swollen lips, and then flicked his tongue on her clit. It was quick, like he was popping her for being a bad girl by giving him the wrong answer.

"Hmmmm," he groaned. Morgan was a weakness. She made the center of his chest so tender that he was almost afraid to indulge in her. If he ever had to go without her again, he knew withdrawal would cripple him. He placed his hands under her and her ass filled up his palms as he pulled her into his face. She had picked up a few pounds. She called them the freshman 15. Messiah called them the *Messiah 15* because he was fucking and feeding the shit out of Morgan's spoiled-ass. He appreciated that she was gaining in the places he loved the most. The dancing kept the additional weight toned and the feel of her thickness made Messiah's dick brick in anticipation.

"Siah, wait…ooh, baby, shit. You're distracting meee," she whined, closing her eyes. Messiah smirked because her protests were accompanied with hip winds as she pushed herself into his face, adding pressure the way he knew she liked it.

"This the most important question. I got to make sure you get it right. What is this?" he mumbled, as he continued to deliver French kisses to her middle.

"I said, clitoris!" she shouted, in pleasure, arching her back. Messiah always ate her pussy like he was starving. Like she was Saturday morning pancakes coated with thick Alaga syrup that he was trying to clean off his plate.

"Wrong," he moaned. "Fuck, shorty, you sweet than a mu'fucka." He pulled her clit between his lips and moved them side to side like he was spreading ChapStick evenly. Morgan went wild. Her toes curled, as her head fell back. "Now focus, smart girl." She loved when he talked to her while he was between her legs, kissing her inner thighs between each word. Messiah made Morgan feel like she was enough, and after feeling inadequate for most of her life, she loved him more than anyone for seeing past her flaws. "What's this? You better get it right this time or I'm gon' fuck you up."

Morgan wanted to play dumb, she wanted to answer incorrectly on purpose. She knew it would provoke the beast out of him, but the way her orgasm was building, she couldn't hold out any longer. "It's Messiah's pussy. It's yours, baby. It's yours," she cried out, her entire body was held hostage in euphoria. She exploded.

Messiah's rare smile was reserved for only her and she reached down, grabbing his locs, pulling him up. He hovered over her body, propping up on his elbows to make sure he wasn't too heavy as he stared into her face. He took in all her features, admiring her. Morgan was exquisite. She was like art and Messiah got lost in trying to figure out her mystique. "Yo' mama must have been a fine mu'fucka to make something like you," he said.

She smiled. "My mama was the shit. She was so beautiful. Her and my sister were just effortlessly pretty. I remember I used to just watch them all day. Both of them would walk into a room and immediately everyone's eyes would shift to them."

"Shit must be hereditary then, shorty, because you're describing yourself right now," Messiah said. "I used to have to tear my eyes off you when Ethic was around."

Morgan laughed at that. "My mama would have loved you. Raven too. Even though she would have acted like she didn't because that's just how she was. She was bourgeois as fuck." Morgan's eyes lit up when she spoke about her family. "My daddy would have hated you, though."

"If I had a daughter and she brought me home, I would hate my ass too," Messiah admitted.

"It wouldn't have mattered. I want what I want and that's you," Morgan replied. He didn't even know how this girl had captured his heart. Women his age had tried to tame him to no avail, yet somehow, 18-year-old Morgan had burrowed her way to his core, imprinting herself into his life. He couldn't remember how he had ever survived a day without seeing her. She was a requirement for his sanity. She was good for him. She provided a purpose to life besides chasing money and power. "I love you," she said. Her eyes sparkled whenever she told him. He still wasn't completely comfortable hearing the sentiment. He had never been blessed enough to receive it before, and she saw him blush in unease. If his skin wasn't dipped in deep melanin, he would have turned red. "You are worth loving, Messiah, and it's a blessing to be loved by you. Am I loved by you?"

"You know you are," he answered, as he burrowed his head into the side of her neck, resting there, as he put half his weight on the bed, the other half on her. She rubbed his back, gently.

"You never say it," she whispered, listening to his breathing go heavy. He was all man. After he ate, he slept, especially when his meal was Morgan. She nourished his soul, balancing all his bad with a bit of her good. He lifted his head and craned his neck back so that he could look into her eyes. There was insecurity in her. He could see it and he hated it. Life had been hard for Morgan for many years. He just wanted to make her happy. He wanted the time they spent together to feel easy. Messiah would go to any length to erase the pain of her past.

"I might not say it all the time or even every time, but you will never see a day where I don't love you, Mo. Even after my last breath is gone, that is the one thing that will never change. Ain't a thing promised in this world, except that. No matter what. You hear me?"

She nodded. It was so easy for him to comfort her heart; and although she was young, Morgan hoped his words were true. She never wanted to be without him. Her phone rang, and he gave her a quick peck on the lips before lifting from the bed. He grabbed her cell from the night stand. "It's Bella," he said, as he tossed it to her.

She caught it, and just before she answered it, he turned and said, "Oh yeah, by the way. A plus, shorty." He shot her a wink and she blushed, feeling her face go red as she answered the phone.

"Hey, B, what's up?" Morgan answered.

"Mo, it's daddyyyy!" Bella's hysterical voice filled Morgan's ear and she sat straight up in the bed.

"What? What happened? Where are you? Where is he?" Morgan asked.

Bella was hysterical. There was so much noise in the background, so many voices.

Is that a siren?

"B!" Morgan yelled.

"He's bleeding, Mo. He's been shot!"

"Oh my God," Morgan hopped from the bed. "Is he okay? Bella, is he awake?" Morgan's eyes misted.

"I'm getting into the ambulance. I'm at Alani's."

"Alani's!" Morgan shouted. "Why are you there?"

"I just wanted to talk to her about the pageant," Bella cried. "When I got here, I found them. Mo, please come home! There's blood everywhere! I don't know what to do. I don't know what to do," Bella cried.

"Go to the hospital in the ambulance. I'll get Eazy from school. I'm on my way," Morgan shouted, as she jumped up. Messiah emerged from the bathroom, hearing her panic.

"What's wrong?" he asked.

"Ethic's been shot," she stammered. Her eyes burned with tears. "Bella's headed to the hospital!" Morgan's face furrowed in anguish, immediately imagining the worst.

"Come on, I'll drive you," Messiah said.

Morgan showered and dressed in haste. Within 10 minutes, they were racing down the highway toward Flint.

Messiah picked up his phone and dialed Isa's number. "Bro' what's the word?" Isa answered, coolly.

"You tell me, G," Messiah asked, his tone low and impatient. "Big homie got touched today."

"I don't know nothing about that, bro'. On God, nothing's

moving this way. Streets been silent the way we like 'em. We just racking up the count on this paper. You think ol' girl baby daddy wet that nigga?" Isa asked.

"I don't know, but I'ma find out," Messiah answered. "Shut the shop down and be ready to lay anybody moving out the ordinary down."

Messiah hung up the phone and reached across the car for Morgan's hand. She held onto him tightly but remained silent, as haunting thoughts filled her mind.

Morgan raced into the emergency room with Messiah in tow with Eazy on his back. "Bella!" she shouted, as she rushed toward the waiting room. When she saw Bella she ran to her, wrapping her up in a hug so tight that Bella could hardly breathe. Bella broke down in Morgan's arms.

"What happened?" Morgan asked, pulling back and placing her hands on Bella's shoulders while looking her in the eyes.

"I don't know. I just wanted to talk to her. I just went over there to ask her about the pageant, and when I got there, I heard yelling inside. Then, there was a gunshot. Then, I recognized Daddy's voice. He told me to call 911 and to stay outside, but I went in, Mo. I went in and there was all this blood and he was holding Alani on the floor in a pool of blood," Bella said.

Messiah had been on the phone, ordering his team to lock down the entrances and exits of the hospital, but when he heard Alani's name his head turned in recognition.

"Nobody came out? After you heard the gunshot? It was just Ethic and Alani?" Morgan asked.

"Nobody came out," Bella said, her lip quivering.

Messiah pulled a wad of money from his pocket and handed Bella a twenty-dollar bill. "Why don't you take Eazy to the vending machines and get some junk. We might be here for a while. Your pops is going to be fine. He's strong. That's my word, okay?" he said. Bella nodded and then took Eazy's hand and walked down the hall.

Morgan looked up at Messiah.

"Did she do this?" Morgan asked, as she gripped Messiah's forearm. "Messiah, is this my fault? She shot him!"

Messiah sighed. A lot had happened since Morgan's rape. A lot had transpired from that one event; and although it wasn't her fault, she was the root of it all. "It ain't your fault, Mo. There's a lot between him and her. A lot that Ethic has kept to himself," he said, in a low tone, as he pulled her close and whispered the words in her ear. "This ain't on you, shorty." He kissed her cheek. "It might have started with you, but Ethic and Alani have taken it way beyond you. The nigga raped you. It was a price to pay for that, but unfortunately a little girl got caught up. There's a price to pay for that too. Ethic's been tiptoeing around that nigga, Cream, because of her, but I'ma handle it. I'ma fix it. I promise you."

Morgan nodded, a chill ran down her spine at the memory of her rape. She never talked about it and the mere mention of it brought tears to her eyes.

Morgan was breathless, as she tried to process the information. Her rape had sent their lives spiraling out of control. Messiah put a reassuring hand under her chin, lifting her eyes to his. "You're safe, you hear me?" he asked.

Morgan was trembling, and Messiah added, "You don't got to ever fear a nigga another day of your life, Mo. I'm not Ethic. I don't have an off switch. I shoot first, so a nigga better think twice before he even look at you the wrong way. You're always safe with me." He kissed her lips, not caring that they were in public. Morgan was his to protect, his to love, and he wanted her to know it, and he suddenly had an overwhelming need for Ethic to know it too. Bella and Eazy walked back into the waiting room. Morgan took a step back, putting an appropriate space between her and Messiah.

"B, are you sure you didn't see anyone else there?" Messiah asked.

"No, it was just Daddy and Alani. Daddy was holding her in his arms when the paramedics got there. He wasn't breathing, and she was just sitting there, leaning against him. Her eyes were real low. An ambulance took her too," Bella said.

"I knew she was bad for him," Morgan whispered, as she took a seat, pulling Eazy onto her lap. They waited for hours, anxiety filling them, as Morgan tried to remain strong. She was the oldest. If she fell apart so would they, so she hid her worries, despite the growing dread in her stomach. Morgan had already lost one father. She didn't want to lose Ethic too.

"Maybe you should call Lily to come get the kids," Messiah whispered in her ear. "It's getting late." Eazy was dead weight in Morgan's arms so she knew he had fallen asleep, and Bella was leaning on her shoulder, snoring lightly.

"Nobody's leaving. He wouldn't leave us here alone," Morgan said, through teary lenses. "It's important that we are all here together. He'll want to see their faces when he wakes up. God, please let him wake up."

"He will," Messiah said, leaning down to kiss the top of Morgan's head. Messiah was desperate to hit the streets to find out where the immediate threat lied. His temper was boiling, and Messiah had been keeping it contained since walking into the hospital. He needed to run the streets. He needed to murder, terrorize, reign but he was trying something new with Morgan, putting her needs before his own. She needed him at her side, so he stayed, despite his trigger finger itching.

"Are you the family of Ezra Okafor?"

Morgan looked up and she tapped Bella's leg to wake her. She stood with Eazy still sleeping in her arms. "I'm his oldest daughter. Is he okay? Can we see him?"

"You can, but I want to prepare you for what you are about to see. The bullet ricocheted throughout his torso. He has three fractured ribs. A quarter of an inch to the right and that bullet would have hit his heart. We've removed it. He's in the ICU, but he isn't awake. We have him on a ventilator to allow him some time to heal from the injuries sustained. They are critical. When we think he's strong enough, we will try to pull him off to see if he can breathe on his own. You will want to think about next steps, just in case it comes to that," the doctor informed.

Morgan had to reach out for Messiah's forearm to stop her legs from giving out. Ethic, the man who protected everyone around him for so long, had been touched. "Next steps?" Morgan's throat constricted, as her heart split in half. One half was with Messiah, in love and happy. The other was dying with Ethic. Bella fell into her already full arms and they held each other.

"I'll take you to see him now. Family only," the doctor said.

Messiah took Eazy from Morgan's arms, without ever waking the young boy. Messiah rested Eazy's head on his shoulder. "You and Bella go," Messiah said. "I'll be right here when you get out."

Morgan nodded. She and Morgan followed the doctor down the hall.

Nothing could have prepared Morgan for what she saw when she walked into Ethic's hospital room.

"Daddy?" Bella's voice was almost inaudible. Morgan gripped her hand, as they inched toward the bed.

"No!" Morgan whispered. "What did she do to you?" Her lip quivered, as Bella buried herself into Morgan's embrace. Morgan was unsteady on her feet and the room spun a little. *Please, don't die.* A sickness invaded her stomach and she had to grip the edge of Ethic's bed to stop from falling. His skin was greasy and

ASHLEY ANTOINETTE

stretched from the thick tube they had lodged in his throat. His parted lips were swollen, and dried blood rested in the corners of his mouth. There was so much blood that his bandages had already stained and were beginning to bleed through the hospital gown too. Morgan turned to Bella, facing her fully, as they cried together. Bella faced the door, because if anyone was forced to face Ethic, Morgan knew it should be her. *This is all my fault.* The way his chest moved up and down, as the machine pushed air into his lungs, looked unnatural. Ethic was dying before her eyes. The man who had rescued her time and time again was helpless in front of her and there was nothing she could do.

"Mo?"

Morgan didn't want to pull back from their embrace because she couldn't gain control over her emotions.

"Ma'am. We just have a couple questions." Those foreign voices forced her to release Bella. She sucked in air, turning toward the door as the sight of the two, plain-clothed detectives forced her to pull it together.

"My name is Detective Adams, and this is my partner…"

"What do you want?" Morgan interrupted. She took in the black man standing in front of her. She observed it all, his close-cut haircut, his scrutinizing eyes, his ashy knuckles that extended a card. She didn't take the card. She left it lingering in mid-air.

"We need to get a statement from Bella Okafor," the detective stated, as he retracted his hand, tucking the card in his breast pocket.

"She doesn't have anything to say to you," Morgan stated. "And it's a little insensitive for you to come in here right now." Morgan was defensive, as she placed one hand across Bella's chest as if she could shield her from these officers of the law. "A parent has to be present during the questioning of a minor and the only parent she has is lying in here fighting for his life."

"Ma'am, we're just trying to do our jobs and find out who is responsible for this. We're here to help."

Morgan didn't trust cops. She remembered when her father had gotten shot all those years ago. She and her sister had run from the authorities, sneaking out of the hospital because CPS had wanted to separate them. Morgan wasn't letting anyone take Bella and Eazy away. The less information she gave them, the better. *They'll have to do their jobs, for once.*

"It's okay, Mo. I'll answer their questions," Bella said, softly. Morgan looked at her in uncertainty. She wasn't sure if Bella knew what to say or not to say. There was a code to follow when dealing with the police and Bella was young. If she said the wrong thing, it could put their entire family at risk.

"What were you doing at Alani Hill's house?" the detective asked.

"She's my mentor in the debutante pageant at my church," Bella said.

"What was your father doing there?" the officer countered.

"She's his girlfriend," Bella said.

Morgan's neck snapped in Bella's direction.

"When you arrived, who was present?" The officer was digging, trying to piece together the puzzle of events that had left Ethic near dead and a woman mentally inept. Alani hadn't uttered a word since arriving at the hospital, and her visit to the abortion clinic was unknown, so the police were suspicious of drug usage. She was lackadaisical and zoned out from everything around her.

"Alani, my dad, and a man. I think his name was Cam, or something with a C," Bella stated. Morgan's stomach filled with butterflies, recognizing Bella's lies. *What is she doing?*

"Cream?" The officer inquired, looking at his partner before putting intimidating eyes on Bella.

"Yeah, I think I heard her screaming that name. Cream, no, she said." Bella's eyes filled with tears. "Then, I heard the gunshot. I ran up the walkway and knocked on the door. I heard her crying and my daddy yelled to tell me to call the police." The story was drastically different from the one she had given to Messiah.

"The backdoor was open when we arrived. The shooter probably ran out the back. It would explain why she didn't see him. Have the backdoor dusted for prints," the detective mumbled to his partner.

The officers finished taking Bella's statement, making notes in a pad. He scratched his temple and said, "If we hear something, we'll be in touch. We may need to speak with her again. Maybe come down to the station to make an ID if we get a lead. Do you think you will be able to recognize his voice again if you heard it?"

Bella shrugged. "I don't know. I was so scared."

"I think that's enough," Morgan interrupted. "We just need some privacy with our father."

Morgan nodded, and when the officers left the room she closed the door. She turned to Bella.

"What the hell was that?" Morgan asked.

"Alani shot him for what he did to her daughter," Bella whispered, with tears in her eyes. "She doesn't deserve to go to jail."

"How do you know about that?" Morgan asked. "There's more to that story, Bella. Ethic is a good man. It was an accident."

"I know, but he hurt her bad, Mo. You didn't hear her, when he told her what he did," Bella paused, as a tear fell down her cheek. "The way she cried. The way he cried with her. Daddy loves her, Mo, and I know that she shot him, but he wouldn't want her in jail. He would want to keep her safe. Even after she shot him, he sat on the floor, holding her while she just cried. They love each other!"

"Fuck her!" Morgan shouted. "What about him? Bella! You don't shoot someone you love! Do you know who her baby daddy is? She could have been setting Ethic up the entire time! When did he even start seeing her? Why would he trust her? You can't lie for her!"

"Around the same time you started seeing Messiah," Bella stated. Bella's tone was so matter-of-fact that Morgan knew there was no point in denying it. Morgan was taken aback, as the rest of her protests jammed in her throat. "I'm not a baby anymore, Mo. I have eyes. Alani looks at Daddy the same way you look at Messiah. I don't know what happened today, but she's family. I need her, Morgan. She hugs me, and it feels like I have a mother, like she could be my mother."

"She's not though, B," Morgan whispered, sadly, as tears came to her eyes. She could see the void in Bella. There was a hole inside Bella that she was desperate to fill. Morgan understood it. She lived with the same hole; only she had two of them because her father was dead too. "She's not your mother. The police probably have her finger prints on the gun already, Bella. There's probably gun powder on her hands."

"No, they don't because I hid it!" Bella shouted.

"You did what?" Morgan asked, in disbelief. "She's the enemy! She's not family. She's one of them!" Morgan argued, losing her cool at the thought of Lucas' hands on her body flashing through her mind. She snapped her eyes closed and drew in a sharp breath.

"But she doesn't have to be! She needs a daughter and I need a mother! Her baby daddy is a bad guy. He hit her! He hurt Nish! So what if I lied on him? If they think he's responsible, he'll go back to jail and everybody will be safe. Then, they can be together. She loves my daddy! They just need time to make things right! She needs time to forgive him," Bella cried. She stormed out of the room and Morgan didn't chase her. Life had taken them down this disastrous path and it had all started with her. She sat next to Ethic's bedside and looked down at his serene face. She leaned over the bed and kissed his cheek, and then climbed onto the small space beside him. Her tears raced out of her, as soon as she placed her head on his shoulder.

"Please, wake up," she whispered. She sniffed loudly and then swiped away a tear, only for another one to replace it. "You've got to wake up," Morgan whispered. "We can't lose you."

CHAPTER 13

Alani sat staring blankly at her red-stained hands. "Ma'am. We'd like to clean you up. Get you out of the bloody clothes and wash you off," a nurse said, using a calming tone. Alani shook her head but didn't respond. She didn't want his blood off her hands. She wanted to see it, to feel it. It was proof that she had done something to get retribution for her daughter's death. It made her feel less guilty for the love sickness that she suffered from. She had shot him. Ethic, the man that had made her whole. The love of her life.

No, my daughter was the love of my life. I shot her killer. I did the right thing.

Alani was losing her mind. The vindication she felt was weighed down with concern. How she could want him to suffer and survive at the same time was beyond her. This entire situation was out of the scope of her understanding. It was said that everything happens for a reason, but she couldn't fathom why this had occurred. God couldn't have designed her path to include worshipping her child's murderer. Was he dead? Had she killed him? Did she even want to kill him? She had just reacted. Hearing him say he hated her had caused her to snap. Who the fuck was *he* to hate *her*? When all she had ever done was love him. From the very first time he had wrapped his arms around her, Alani had coveted him so dearly that it felt like she had discovered an unchartered emotion, something beyond love. Worship, perhaps.

What she felt for Ethic was scary. It was so deep that it was outside the realm where human emotion registered in the brain. It was in parts of the psyche that scientists had yet to figure out; like the undiscovered depths of the ocean, or stars too distant to be seen with the naked eye. Her feelings for this man were all-consuming; and for Alani to open to him, after guarding herself for so long, was a miracle. She had trusted for the first time in years, only to be deceived. He had told the ultimate lie, inflicted an unhealable hurt. That's why she had shot him. That's why she had pulled the trigger. Still, she wondered.

My God, did I kill him?

She doubled over, sobbing, as she hid her eyes with her Ethic-covered hands. The nurse looked to her in sympathy.

"I'm going to give you a minute. I'll be back to check on you soon. The doctor should be in shortly," the woman said. Alani couldn't even lift her head to acknowledge the woman. She just continued to weep.

A knock at the door came minutes later, but Alani just couldn't function. It was this bottomless pit that had caused her to turn the gun on herself. It was the greatest hurt she had ever felt. It was greater than the day she buried her daughter because it was laced in guilt, then dipped in longing for something she could never have. She couldn't speak because no one could possibly understand her burden. She was going crazy. That much she was sure of. The moment she felt the gun under her chin, she knew that all reason had abandoned her.

"Alani?"

Alani lifted her head to see Bella, sticking her head through the cracked door. Bella slid inside and closed the door, opting to stay close to it as she looked at Alani. Alani's chest jerked, as she fought herself, trying to gather herself in front of Bella but she was choking on grief. It just kept spilling out of her. She could feel Bella's fear from across the room. Bella's eyes were wide and brimming with anguish. Alani squeezed her eyes closed and shook her head from side to side. *What about her? I shot him without even thinking about his children,* she thought. Her chest hit her thighs, as she leaned over, unable to hold herself up as she sat on the exam table. She was wrecked, overwhelmed, and understanding of the type of remorse that Ethic had. She wasn't a bad person. She had made an emotional decision, a bad one, despite how justified it felt at the moment. She felt Bella's hand on her back and she looked up in shock. The sadness in Bella's eyes tore through Alani like a storm and she leaned her head into Bella's palm as Bella touched her face.

Alani gripped Bella's hand. It wasn't nearly as small as her Kenzie's had been, but still had the softness that only the skin of a child could possess. Alani's shoulders hung with sorrow, her heart aching as Bella squeezed her hand. It was a gesture of dependency, something her daughter used to do when she was urging Alani to fulfill some need, some basic motherly duty that only Alani could provide. Alani's heavy lids closed and kissed the inside of Bella's wrist, causing Bella's chest to quake. Emotions that Bella had held inside for years were threatening to erupt. Things that Bella couldn't say aloud, insecurities that she had never shared, feelings of bitterness that she had never wanted to admit she had all bubbled inside her chest. They all came blubbering out of her as she lunged into Alani's arms. Alani clung to Bella, rocking her back and forth. "I'm so sorry," she whispered, as she caressed the back of Bella's hair.

"It's okay, Alani. Everybody needs a little forgiveness sometimes," Bella said.

Alani pulled back in stun. How had this little girl become so wise? Bella had just made the hardest notion sound so simple.

Adults had a way of muddling things up, of overly complicating things. Children saw the world for what it was - black and white. For Bella to see Alani for more than the sum of her sins and to see value warmed Alani. It cracked right through her depressed soul. Alani was grateful for little Bella in that moment.

"Where is he?" Alani's voice came out broken. "Is he dead?"

Bella shook her head.

"Can you take me to him?" Alani asked. Alani walked through the hospital, holding Bella's hand. She looked like something from a scary movie, blood-covered, and in shock as she took slow steps to Ethic's room.

"I did this," she whispered, covering her mouth with four fingers, stopping in the doorway.

She crossed the tiled floor slowly until she was standing right in front of him. She had to look away to stop from throwing herself right over him in mourning.

"What have I done?" she whispered. She now knew why God claimed vengeance as His own. It didn't serve a purpose amongst mortals. It didn't relieve any pain, it only added more to the equation. Alani had made a stupid decision when she had pulled that trigger, and now she was burdened with remorse. If he died, she would leave his children fatherless. His life for Kenzie's didn't make her feel better. It wasn't right at all. Nothing could make up for her daughter's death, she had been stupid to think this would be the answer. Killing Ethic was like killing herself.

God, please fix this…fix me.

"Get away from him!"

Morgan came storming into the room with Messiah.

"Mo! I told her she could!" Bella shouted.

"Bella, you're a little girl, you don't give permission to anyone to do anything, especially not her. Stay out of it!" Morgan demanded.

She set fire-laced eyes on Alani. "Get the fuck out of our father's room before I send you to meet your daughter and brother, bitch."

Messiah shot shocked eyes to Morgan. Those weren't her words. That wasn't her at all. That was him, taking over her body, and speaking threats that she couldn't deliver, but ones that he could at her command.

"Shorty," Messiah corralled. "It's been a long day for everybody. Why don't we let everybody breathe for a minute?" He pulled her arm and turned her to him. Morgan buried herself in his shoulder.

He pierced Alani and felt a bit of sympathy for her. She stood there, trembling, visibly affected by Morgan's words and the consequences of the actions she had taken that day. The daughter comment was a cheap shot, which is why Messiah had refereed.

Alani looked to Bella.

"You don't have to go," Bella defended, voice small, eyes hopeful.

Alani nodded. "I do, Bella. I don't belong here. I hope your father will be okay," she whispered, before fleeing the room.

"You load the clip first. There's 16 in a clip," Messiah said, as he placed the gold, metal bullets inside a thin, rectangular-shaped clip. Morgan mimicked his movements with the gun she daintily handled. "That's a nine-millimeter. It should feel good to you. There's kickback, but not too much for a girl."

"Messiah, is this necessary?" she asked, placing the gun down.

Messiah popped his clip into his pistol and racked it back before placing it on the table next to Morgan's. He looked her in the eyes.

"If you want to love a man like me, it's required, Mo; and

if you gon' be throwing around boss talk like you did in that hospital room, it's very necessary. You're commuting to school now so that you can be here for the kids while Ethic is laid up. I'm not comfortable with my girl being accessible like that. I have enemies, Mo, and not just Cream. Bella's story has the police on him, so he's probably lying low, but he's still out there somewhere and until I find him, we have to be careful. I've done a lifetime worth of shit for niggas to look at you and see a target. Your last name makes you a target. You know how many niggas around this city your daddy ghosted coming up? He was a fucking king around here. He left wives without husbands. Children without fathers. He took people brothers away. All these old beefs, vendettas against you for so many reasons, and you don't even know it. A nigga who don't mean you no good could be staring you right in your face and you wouldn't know it until it's too late. I will always rock a nigga to sleep behind you, but what if somebody catch you on the rare chance that I'm not there to protect you? I want you to be capable of protecting yourself. I never understood why Ethic kept you so sheltered or why your sister was so sheltered. Naïveté will get you killed. I'm not letting that happen to you. I need you to know how to wet some shit up without thinking twice, if you ever need to. You hear me?" Messiah pinched her chin, as he spoke, and then kissed her lips. Beauty and her beast.

Morgan submitted into him, to him, for him, every time. He was her king.

"I swear I get so high on you," she whispered, tracing the print of his dick with her fingertip. He was always semi-hard for her, never soft, because she simply made his blood pump by her presence alone. She could feel him reacting to her touch.

"Later for that, shorty," Messiah said, as he tapped the tip of her nose with his finger. "Stay focused, this is important."

She groaned and threw her head back, pulling a chuckle from Messiah. He was turning her into a freak. She wanted it more than him, these days.

"Now, you got your clip loaded?" he asked.

She picked up her gun. "Yeah."

"Good, now insert it into the bottom," he instructed.

She did.

"Now, pull it back to put a bullet in the head. Finger on the outside of the trigger," Messiah said.

"Like this?" Morgan asked, as she followed his directions to a T.

"Perfect," he approved. "Never put your finger on the trigger until you're ready to shoot. You see this button on the side? That's the safety. You flip it and you see red. It's ready to go. If you don't see red and you pull the trigger, nothing's going to happen."

"How am I supposed to remember that?" Morgan asked.

"It'll become second nature to you. I'ma teach you something my brother taught me a long time ago to help me remember. All you got to do is say red means dead," Messiah coached.

Morgan lowered the gun and smiled. "Your brother? You have a brother? You never mentioned your family before. I feel special. You're opening up to me," Morgan beamed, and Messiah shook his head. He hadn't even meant to let that much slip.

"Stay focused," Messiah said. "Say it, Mo. Red means dead."

"Red means dead," she repeated. "If I see red, the safety is off, and the gun is ready to shoot. Got it."

Messiah got behind her and kicked open her legs. "You need balance to hit something."

Morgan turned her gun sideways and poked out her lips. Messiah gave away a leer.

"You been watching too much *Menace II Society*," he said. He reached around her with both arms and straightened her grip. "One hand on the handle, gripping it, the other underneath that hand, supporting it." Messiah was standing too close to Morgan. She felt his manhood pushing into her behind and tremors went up her spine.

"Yo, you so unfocused, shorty, it's crazy. I'm questioning how you ace all those tests you be taking," he chuckled. "I tell you what. Every time you hit the target inside the lines, I'll kiss that pussy real good for you," his voice lowered in lust. He kissed her neck, right behind her ear and her head fell to the side, giving him access. If she missed every single shot, he was still putting his mouth all over her. It was already in his mind now, but she didn't know that. They were gluttons for one another and one another alone. Young and passionate, obsessed and blinded. Neither cared to do this thing of theirs any other way.

"Ssss…" She sucked in air between clenched teeth. "Let me focus."

"A'ight, Shorty Doo-Wop, let's see you bust something," he said, as he lifted defensive hands and took a step back.

"Show me first," she said.

Messiah picked up his pistol from the table. Safety off…aim… BANG.

He ripped a hole through the center of the paper man's forehead.

"Such a show-off," she smirked.

She repeated the steps and her heart pounded.

"Aren't I supposed to wear the headphone thingies to block out the sound? Ethic always wears those when he comes out here," Morgan said.

"Ethic's a gangster. He ain't gone freeze when he hear a gunshot. He can afford to protect his ears. You need to hear the shot. You need to get used to hearing the blast. You should be so comfortable you can fire without flinching. Now, quit stalling," Messiah said.

Morgan steadied her aim. Flicked off the safety. *Red means dead.*

BANG.

Morgan didn't even hit the target. She relaxed her arms, taking the tension out of her shoulders and pulled the trigger again.

BANG
.

"Keep bussin'. You got 14 left," Messiah yelled, over the blast.

BANG. The third shot hit the paper but not within the lines.

Morgan paused and readjusted her aim and then let all remaining 11 bullets fly.

"Safety on, pop the clip out, check the head," Messiah said, as he relieved her of the gun. He hit the button to bring the target toward them. She was decent. She needed work, but for her first time, he could see potential. "We out here every day for a few rounds," he said. He put the guns back onto Ethic's artillery wall. Ethic's property was so massive that it was nothing to build a gun range in the backyard on some of his land. It would come in handy to show Morgan the ropes. Messiah turned and headed for the door.

"Homeboy, where you think you going?" Morgan's voice halted him.

He turned to her and she held up her target like it was a report card. "I see five shots inside the lines, playa."

Messiah smirked and licked his lips. She had put in work, now it was time for him to do the same, only Messiah was going for overtime.

CHAPTER 14

I can give you $39,000," the car dealer said, as he sat across the desk from Alani.

"It's a 2019 with only 700 miles. It's practically brand new," Alani replied. "They're 60-k new and it's loaded."

"That's what I can do," the man said, with a shrug.

Alani stood and shook her head, knowing that the salesman was cutting her a raw deal. She headed for the door. She had decided to sell her car. Even though she needed the money, it was a visual reminder of Ethic. It had always felt like an inappropriate gift, even before she had found out what he'd done. It just wasn't her. She was a simple woman and didn't need that type of luxury. She didn't even feel right behind the wheel. It garnered too much attention and Alani detested being in the spotlight. She had bills overdue and nothing to her name. She needed this money, but she wasn't going to give away her car for less than it's worth just because she was desperate.

"Forty-five," the dealer said, as she placed her hand on the door to the exit.

"Fifty," she countered.

He nodded, and she felt relief flood her. She was rid of it and the money would go to good use. She saw a Prius sitting on the used side of the lot. "How much is that car?"

"The Prius?" he asked.

She nodded.

"Fifteen," he answered.

"I'll take that and a check for the rest," she decided.

When she drove off the lot, she felt like a new woman. She felt more like herself than she had in a long time. She didn't realize that she had felt pressure being with Ethic. They hadn't even established a real relationship and somehow it felt like she had to glamorize herself; like, she was in a constant chase to prove that she could upgrade. Her house, her life, her clothes, all seemed beneath him. Now, she was a regular girl, driving a regular car and it felt familiar. It felt nice. Alani had lost herself and she was in the process of trying to get reacquainted with who she used to be. Shooting Ethic had been a turning point for her. She was out of control. Her depression had gone too far, and she just wanted to get a handle on her life. After stopping at the bank, she headed to the hospital. She was so unsure about so many things in her life, but one thing was certain, she had to find some type of peace. After what she had done, she was lucky to be walking around free. She had gone to the other side of crazy and it wasn't a place she wanted to remain. She was in pain, every single minute that her eyes were open, but she was trying and that was better than it was before. She walked into the doctor's office on the first floor and signed in at the front desk.

"Is this your first visit?" the receptionist asked.

"Yes," Alani said, blowing out a breath to fight the tension rising in her. She was so anxious, so troubled, but she just kept breathing, in and out. It felt like she would pass out. She didn't know why she was so nervous, but after what she had almost done, she just wanted to make sure everything was okay. "I filled everything out online. My appointment is at one o'clock," Alani informed.

"I see all your information here. Have a seat and we'll call you back shortly."

Alani sat, wringing her fingers while her leg bounced up and down.

"Alani Hill?"

Alani stood and followed the nurse back. She noticed her pink scrubs. It was appropriate. An obstetrics office was a happy place, a pink and blue, boy-or-girl type of place. She couldn't believe she was sitting in it. Alani felt nervous butterflies in her stomach. She was still pregnant, by Ethic Okafor, the man who murdered her baby. She didn't know how she would handle it. She wasn't even sure she would keep this baby after it was born. It didn't seem right, but killing it also felt extremely wrong. There was no right, no wrong, there was just confusion, but Alani had experienced enough loss. She didn't want to lose this too. With the type of love she and Ethic had shared, she wouldn't be surprised if she was carrying an angel that would change the world. The best parts of Ethic were beautiful. The most delicate and amazing qualities in a man she had ever seen. The worst in him was also the most terrifying she had ever known. This baby would take all his good and all her good. It would bring love back to the world, even if she wasn't the one that reared it. She was grateful that the doctor had refused to perform the abortion, even after Alani had ordered her to. She had forced her to sleep off the sedative and think about it before making such an irreversible decision. Guilt burned through her for carrying a child by Ethic, but this baby wasn't to blame for all that had gone wrong between them. A baby was a blessing, especially where an injured womb was concerned. She wasn't supposed to give birth to one child, so two felt extraordinary. Still, her daughter weighed on her so much that Alani felt like crawling in her bed and dying. She had forced herself to stop that part. The rotting. The wallowing. She had to put one foot in front of the other, no matter how hard it was. She wondered how things might have been if Ethic had never told her. Would he be there with her? At her first appointment? Would he want this baby? He was the most loving father she had ever seen, so she assumed he would be present.

It could have been such a beautiful thing.

Alani was escorted to an ultrasound room where she undressed and laid down on the bed. It was the same routine but a different experience, and when she heard the steady, strong beat of her child's heartbeat, she laughed out in joy. She had stressed enough to induce a miscarriage, and she hadn't been sure how the sedatives from the abortion clinic would affect the growth of this child. She was grateful that all was progressing normally. She had spoken so much negativity, hate, and regret over this pregnancy. Even still, she was struggling to bury her natural reactions of regret and hate. Her initial reaction had been devastation and she was relieved to know that the curses she had spoken over this baby hadn't destroyed it.

The appointment went by flawlessly. She was eight weeks along and in the throes of the worst parts of pregnancy. Morning sickness plagued her every day and her breasts were so tender that even the fabric of her bras hurt them. It seemed that she was also battling sinus infections from the extra blood the baby produced in her system. Alani was having a hard time and she had no help. There was no one around to make sure she ate, no one rubbing her feet at night, or holding her hair while she threw up. She had no family to provide this child. It was another reason why she didn't think she was suitable to raise it. She had no support and she was in a bad place in her life. Every aspect had hit a low point and she didn't want this child to struggle. Financially, spiritually, mentally, emotionally...Alani was at war with herself. A baby didn't fit into the picture. She walked to the fifth floor where Nannie was. She was ashamed at how much time she had let pass without coming to see her or even checking in with a doctor. Alani was in denial that she was getting ready to lose her. Amid this storm, she just couldn't bring herself to deal with such a life and death decision. She was so out of sorts and emotional these days she didn't trust herself to make the right one. She walked into the room and stopped in surprise as she saw the dozens of floral arrangements that filled the room.

Who sent all these?

The room was so bright, and the scent of fresh lavender and sage filled the air. A natural oil humidifier blew mist into the room. Alani went to the bed and sat on the edge. She grabbed her great aunt's wrinkled hand. It was soft, freshly moisturized, and her nails were painted.

"I'm here, Nannie," she whispered. "I'm sorry I've been gone for a while. I've been having a rough time. I need you, old lady. Please, wake up."

"Oh! Another visitor!"

Alani turned to the voice and watched a nurse walk into the room.

"Another?" Alani asked. "I'm her caretaker. Who else has been here?"

"I think the gentleman is her son. He first came a few weeks ago, strolling in here in a suit and ordering everyone around. He sends her fresh flowers every few days and has hired a manicurist to come to paint her nails and toes every week. A massage therapist comes to rub her down. It's so very sweet. He's a patient here now and he has his nurse bring him here every day. He sits here and talks to her. I think he thinks she can hear him. Sometimes, he reads," the nurse said.

Alani's eyes produced so much emotion. *He's awake*, Alani thought. She had called to check his condition almost every day since shooting him two weeks ago, but she wasn't family, so no one would give her information. She had tried to visit but

Morgan had put Ethic under a security protocol that only allowed certain people to visit. Morgan had specifically prohibited Alani from being able to, but since she was already in the hospital as a visitor to her aunt, she wondered if she could sneak past security. Suddenly, she had an overwhelming desire to see him.

"Whatever he's doing, it seems to be helping. Her doctor has seen increased brain activity on her scans since he's begun visiting."

"She's going to wake up?" Alani asked, voice full of hope.

"We don't know, but she's doing better than before," the nurse said.

"I think there are some things I need to handle. I've been sick and couldn't return calls, but I was called about insurance bills..."

"No, her son has taken care of those. Her care is being covered by him," the nurse informed.

Alani scoffed in wonder.

"Do you know what room he's in?" Alani asked.

"Eighth floor, room 14," the nurse responded.

She turned to Nannie and leaned down to whisper in her ear. "I'll be back, Nannie. I promise." She kissed her cool cheek and then pulled the blanket up to warm her lovely aunt before walking out. Alani had an overwhelming urge to tell Ethic about their baby. She was pregnant, and it was his. He deserved to know. Hurried steps carried her through the halls of the hospital and butterflies filled her stomach. She just wanted proof that he was okay. She just wanted to lay eyes on him to ease her soul a bit. She wasn't strong enough to do what she had done and not have remorse. She had been unstable when she had pulled that trigger. She was still battling something, but it wasn't who she was, it wasn't the type of retribution she wanted. She knew that there was nothing that could ever make up for her child's murder, not even revenge.

Her eyes followed the numbers outside the rooms on the eighth floor.

Room 800. 802. 804.

The closer she got the more nervous she became. She was sick to her stomach and this time it wasn't because of the baby. It was the baby's daddy. Her breaths were so shallow that Alani felt lightheaded. She saw room 814, ahead. The door was closed, and no one stood outside the door. It was the middle of the day, so she assumed his children were in school. If she wanted to see him, now would be the only time to do so.

Fighting guilt and nerves and angst and shame and so many other things, she approached the door. She reached for the knob but the visual through the small, glass window on the door caused her to release it as if it were burning hot. Ethic wasn't alone. He wasn't even awake, but Dolce sat at his bedside, doting over Ethic, stroking his face and kissing his lips, as if she had loved him her entire life.

That's the girl he was with that night at the diner.

Jealousy seared her now even worse than it had then because now she felt entitled. Sure, she had shot his ass, but he had deserved it, but he was still hers, more hers than this bitch's who was all over him.

What are you doing? He killed your baby? This isn't what you want, she told herself.

It was in that exact moment that Alani decided fate for them both. They wouldn't know one another. They couldn't. She would have this baby and give it to two parents that deserved it because she and Ethic could never co-exist.

She backpedaled from the room. She didn't know that her heart could break any further but there was something about seeing Ethic loved on by someone else that annihilated her.

I just need air.

She couldn't get out of the hospital fast enough. The beginnings of winter welcomed her, and she gulped in the icy air. Her phone rang, and she fumbled to open her purse to retrieve it.

"Hello?" She was so emotional that her voice cracked.

"Alani?" The voice was full of angst. She could hear the tears through the phone.

"Bella?" Alani asked.

"Can you come to my school? I need your help," Bella cried. "I started my period and I'm bleeding through my clothes. I called Mo and she didn't answer. I know I'm not supposed to be talking to you, but I don't have anyone else to call."

Alani's heart couldn't take much more. These Okafors bounced her around like a yoyo. Ethic with his shattering and Bella with her innocence that acted like glue trying to piece together what her father had broken.

"What school, baby?" Alani sighed. "Can you drop me your location?"

Alani's phone dinged.

"I'm on my way," she answered.

The entire way, Alani wondered if she was crossing a line. She had connected with Bella and couldn't just break the promise she had made her. They were friends and she had a feeling that it wasn't just Bella who would benefit from their bond. She walked into the school and into the office where Bella was waiting. Her face was full of embarrassment, but Alani recognized relief when their eyes met. Bella was happy to see her, and the way Alani's chest eased, she knew she felt the same.

"Everybody saw," Bella whispered.

"Oh, baby girl," Alani cooed, as Bella hugged her. Alani removed her jacket and tied it around Bella's waist. "Let's get you out of here, okay?"

Bella nodded, as Alani signed her out. She was surprised that the staff gave her no trouble about leaving with Bella, but there was no resistance. They climbed into the car and Alani pulled away.

"Is this your first period?" Alani asked.

Bella nodded, her chin to her chest. Alani reached over and grabbed her hand.

"Hey…"

Bella lifted reluctant, shame-filled eyes.

"It's okay. It's your body doing exactly what it's supposed to do. You're becoming a young lady, Bella. That blood is just blood. No different than a nose bleed. There's nothing to be embarrassed about, sweetheart. Do you know why your body bleeds once a month? Has anyone ever talked to you about it?" Alani asked.

Bella shook her head.

"Okay, well, let's get you home and I'll explain to you what's happening with your body and you can ask me anything you want. Is that cool?" Alani asked.

"Yeah, that's cool," Bella whispered, as a small smile broke through the sadness on her face. Alani smiled too and released Bella's hand, putting her eyes back on the road. Suddenly, her heart didn't hurt as much because she wasn't totally alone. Glue. Little Bella was definitely glue.

"What you doing here, ma?" Ethic asked, as he brought hazy eyes to Dolce. He groaned, as he used balled fists to lift himself slightly and reposition himself in the stiff hospital bed. Hers was not the face he had envisioned when he felt the soft lips on his face as he slept. In his dreams, it had been

Alani. The reality that met him when he opened his eyes was a disappointment.

"I heard about your shooting. It was all over the news. They've arrested someone," Dolce said. "I know we've been through a lot. I know we haven't spoken, but Ethic...we have history. I couldn't *not* come. I called Mo and she put me on the visitor's list."

"Get out, Dolce," Ethic whispered. Ethic's frustration over not seeing *her* face...of not knowing where *she* was or how she was doing had him in a foul state of mind. He had no patience for pretenses and politeness. Dolce wasn't who he wanted. She would never be what he wanted. Alani had put a bullet in him and she had been the first thought to enter his mind when he had found his way back to consciousness, after four days of flirting with death. Fuck nice. He didn't want Dolce in his space. In that chair. That chair, near his bedside where wives sat when their husbands were ailed, belonged to one woman. *With her crazy-ass,* Ethic thought.

"Ethic..."

"It just ain't you, Dolce. Women who try to force that, who weasel their way into that spot, those are the ones who end up disappointed...bitter. When a man cheat. When a man lies," Ethic struggled the words out because his pain was high and talking was a struggle, but he needed her to hear him loud and clear. "Most men would take you, would sleep with you because you're beautiful, would wife you knowing they ain't really in it all the way, then they would cheat on you, they would dog you and keep you right at home in pocket because they know you ain't going nowhere. I'm not trying to do that. You're just not her." He hadn't meant to say it, but he was so deprived of Alani that she infiltrated his thoughts at the wrong time. Her name fell off his lips mid-sentence at times, when he was thinking of something completely unrelated. She had him stapled up, ass out in hospital gowns, not even eating solid foods, and not an ounce of love had been erased for her. It was either love or insanity... perhaps a little of both. Anybody else would be in the dirt for what she had done; instead, she was in his soul, taking up residence.

"Her?" Dolce asked, wounded by his words. "This is about that bitch from the diner, isn't it? That broke, busted, basic, bum-ass..."

Ethic was unamused, as Dolce went on her tangent. Women were always comparing, always judging based on superficial things. None of which mattered. A man wanted who he wanted. If she was at a low place when he met her, he would uplift her. It just took the right woman to make a man want to put in the effort.

Ethic blew out a tired breath. "This is about you and it's about me, telling you that whatever we had... or didn't have. Whatever it was, it's over. You should move on."

"I gave up everything for you," Dolce asked. "I moved to this shitty town for you."

"I didn't ask you to do that," Ethic stated.

Dolce scoffed and stood. Her stilettos, ones he had bought her, clicked across the floor, as she opened the door. "Your karma will be a bitch, Ethic," she whispered, before slipping out.

"She fucking shot me," he whispered, in disbelief, with a chuckle that made his entire chest rock in pain. He found no comedy in his circumstance but the disbelief behind her moxie floored him. He couldn't hate her if he wanted to. He couldn't even say he blamed her. Life wasn't black and white. No person was only good or bad; they were only human, and humans had a little of both inside. Her good parts were phenomenal and made him feel like he was worth something. He just needed to talk to her...to find her. He was desperate to lay eyes on her, but first he had to regain his strength. He had a lot of healing to do and he suspected she did as well.

Morgan came storming into is hospital room.

"Bella is with her," Morgan said, urgency and disdain in her tone.

Ethic grimaced, reaching for the remote that controlled the bed. He lifted the top so that he was sitting up. "Who, Mo? Who has my daughter?" Something seized him. The possibility of Bella being in danger had him ready to lift out of this bed and go find her.

"Alani!" Morgan shouted.

Ethic's worry eased, as he focused on the pain inside him. It was so overwhelming it took his breath away. "I need the doc, Mo. The pain is...just go get the doctor."

Morgan stood in disbelief. Her face scrunched in worry and fear. "Ethic, that woman has Bella. She called me and told me she started her period at school. I was in class, so I couldn't answer, but she left a message. I left as soon as I heard it and I get to her school and I see that Alani signed her out. How are you not worried about that? She shot you!"

"I deserved it," Ethic stated, simply. "Now, Mo, the doctor."

"So, I'm just supposed to not do anything?" Mo asked.

"She's fine. Alani won't hurt Bella," Ethic whispered. "I need you to allow whatever it is they have be. Just let them be, Mo."

"How can you trust her after what she did?" Mo was livid. "After what her brother did?"

Ethic saw that Morgan was fighting something. There were issues lingering from her rape that she hadn't addressed. He motioned for her to come to his bedside and Morgan took stubborn, anger-filled steps toward him. She had always been his most difficult child, but he loved her with his entire being. He groaned, as blinding agony shot through him as he moved over to make space for her. She climbed into the bed next to him and rested her head on his shoulder. He felt her tears as they landed on his skin. She wrapped her arm around his elbow.

"Alani is nothing like her brother, Mo, and I can trust her because your sister taught me that people can change after making a mistake," Ethic said.

"Raven would have never hurt someone she loved. She would have never hurt you," Morgan defended.

Ethic loved the way Morgan loved and remembered Raven, but she was ill-informed. Raven's connection to Mizan is what ruined her entire family. It was what got her father killed. Ethic wouldn't tarnish her image. He wanted Mo to keep Raven on that pedestal, but Ethic knew that he had fallen in love with Raven despite those things.

"She made a lot of mistakes, Mo. Mistakes that hurt a lot of people, but I still trusted her enough to love her. I trusted her enough to bring you both into my life. I love this woman, Mo, and I know that's hard for you, but I'm going to do everything I can to love her correctly…everything I can to repair what I've broken…if she'll allow me to. Now, I see something in you that's broken too, something new since the rape."

Morgan's breath caught in her chest, as she tripped over it, her chest quaking as Ethic peeled back her layers.

"Talk to me, Mo. How can I fix that?" Ethic whispered, turning his head and kissing the top of hers.

"They just took something," she cried. She couldn't explain to him that even now when she had sex, willingly, when Messiah was inside her, she had to work around the terror of being touched before she could get to the pleasure. It was like her body was owned by men and not hers to control. It was like her 'no' didn't matter, and even though with Messiah it was always consensual, it still felt a little bit unsafe, like if she said no, he could still take it. He wouldn't but he could if he wanted to.

"Men have the power to take pieces of me. That night, with two different men, they took two pieces. There are holes where those pieces used to be. I don't know how to fill them. It feels like I'll always have to say yes to a man, because what's the point of saying no? They'll just do what they want anyway …like that night."

"Mo, your voice matters, kid," Ethic whispered. "It matters. Your no is strong, and you can't be afraid to use it. Don't give your power away. Women are the most powerful creatures on Earth. Yes, men are stronger, but women are sharper. Women are thinkers. Those holes will never be filled if you don't talk about how you feel. Turn that pain to power, baby girl, and if a nigga ever misstep…"

"I know," she interrupted, before he could finish.

Ethic called the nurse and they replenished his pain medication and Morgan stayed right there, tucked underneath him, until he fell asleep. This conversation, this relationship with the only father figure in her life, was refilling her, replenishing, rebuilding those pieces Lucas had taken. She was terrified for him to repair things with Alani. Ethic had never really brought a woman into their lives, over the years. Dolce didn't count. Morgan had always known his interest in her wouldn't lead to anything serious. Alani felt life-changing and she hoped his new connection to Alani wouldn't interfere with the way he viewed her. Bella and Eazy were his blood-born kids, she was just the orphan he had taken in. *I'm grown now. He'll move on with his life with Alani and I'll lose my entire family.* It was her greatest fear. It was the real reason why she had banned Alani from visiting. As she rose from the bed, she released a heavy sigh. *God, please let him always look at me as a daughter. Please, don't let this woman come into our lives and destroy everything. Keep her where she is. We were fine without her.*

Morgan knew that wasn't quite true. She, Bella, and Eazy were fine without Alani, but Ethic...poor Ethic, was always last, always lonely, and he needed someone. Morgan just didn't want it to be her.

CHAPTER 15

Alani entered the church and sucked in a deep breath. It was one of the hard days. It was raining, and she was sulking. She needed prayer. She needed strength and she always felt that when she was under this roof. She hadn't realized how much she relied on her faith until after Kenzie died, but God was like a crutch to her. When she was having trouble walking, she leaned on Him. She heard laughter coming from the banquet hall and she made her way in that direction. When she stepped inside, she saw the group of young girls sitting in a circle on the floor with their mothers at their sides.

"If I could give advice to my 12-year-old self, it would be to always trust my instincts," one woman said, as she looked into her daughter's eyes. Sadness took over her, when her eyes found Bella, sitting alone in the circle with no one by her side. Alani crossed the floor.

"So sorry I'm late," she interrupted. She rushed over to Bella.

Alicia White, the church ho, looked up at Alani in surprise.

Alani squeezed into the space next to Bella.

"I didn't know we were waiting for you," Alicia said, in confusion.

"I'm Bella's mentor," Alani said. Bella turned to her with glossy eyes and smiled so big that Alani felt like fireworks were erupting inside her. She didn't know how she was going to hide her pregnancy from Ethic if she was in Bella's life twice a week, but she couldn't just abandon Bella. Her time with Bella the other day, after picking her up from school, had been the happiest Alani had been in a long time. Something inside her truly cared for Ethic's daughter. She couldn't see this motherless void and not fill it. She just couldn't.

"Okay, what are we doing? Giving advice to the babies?" Alani asked. "I'll go next." She turned toward Bella and held out her hands to her. Bella grabbed on tightly. "Okay, let's see. If I could give my 12-year-old self advice, it would be to always love yourself. Love everything about yourself, even the things that you think are no good because they are extraordinary. There is only one you and God made you perfectly in His image. Love that image every time you look in the mirror because you are beautiful, and you are valuable. Never let anyone treat you like you are cheap." She didn't mean to get emotional, but sitting there looking at Bella, beautiful Bella, with her kind eyes and her identical face to her father's, Alani saw family. Alani wanted this little girl to be hers. She had to remind herself that she wasn't and that there was a good reason for that. A murderous reason. Her father was a murderer. Alani and Bella made it through practice. When it was time to go, Bella asked. "Can I come with you? For a little while?"

"Oh, umm, I don't know, Bella. Your dad probably wouldn't want that…"

"Can I call him?" Bella pushed.

Before Alani could answer, Bella was dialing the number; and just as Alani feared, she put her father on speakerphone.

"B, baby girl, Daddy misses you. I need some of that sunshine in here with me."

Alani's entire body reacted to the sound of his voice, and flutters filled her womb.

She had to lean against the wall to stop from falling.

"I'm coming later. I promise. I just finished debutante practice, and guess who came?" she asked.

"Who's that?" Ethic answered. His tone was distracted, as if he was doing other things and Alani pictured the woman from the diner doting over him. She seemed like the type of woman to hog his attention. Her stomach soured, instantly.

Alani felt like she would hyperventilate. She turned her face from Bella and closed her eyes. Wetness sealed her lids and she sucked in air, and then blew it out slowly. His voice. His baritone. It was doing something to her.

"Alani. She's going to mentor me for the pageant."

A pause. A long one and Alani held her breath. She had a feeling he was holding his too. She heard him clear his throat.

"You must be special for her to extend her time like that, B. Make sure you thank her, okay?" Ethic answered. There was something in his tone. Something heavy.

Does he not want me to? Bitch, of course he doesn't want you around his daughter. You shot him!

"Can I go with her for a little while? Practice just ended, and I just want to spend some time with her."

"Did *she* ask *you*, Bella? You can't put her in an awkward position, baby girl. Alani has a lot going on. You can't force yourself..."

"I asked her, Daddy, but she said yes. She would have just said no if she didn't want to," Bella answered, her words rushing out like they did when she was upset.

"Is she with you?" Ethic asked.

"She's right here. You're on speaker," Bella revealed. Alani's eyes widened.

Please, don't ask to speak to me. Please...please.

"Can I speak to her? Take me off speakerphone, B, and give her the phone."

Alani wanted to run. She faced Bella as the 12-year-old brought expectant eyes up to match her stare. Alani reached for the phone and it felt like it weighed a million pounds in her hand. She brought it to her ear, but she couldn't speak. All she could do was breathe. She knew he was listening because she was listening to him too. His breathing was like her favorite song. He was still breathing, and it brought her to tears because if he had died, she would have never forgiven herself. Turmoil lived in her. The part of her that he still possessed, the piece of her that had loved him once, loved him still. It was a mustard seed of love, but it was powerful enough to combat all the hate she harbored. She tried to decipher that breathing like it was Morse code. Was he angry? Had he meant it when he said he hated her? Bella wrinkled a confused brow, as she looked on, wondering why no one was speaking. Love appeared complicated to a young girl. What she saw from two, silent adults was an unspoken conversation that said so much.

Alani cleared her throat and said, "It's fine, she's always welcomed, if you're comfortable with that."

Another pause. He was thinking. She knew him enough to know that he was searching for what to say first. There was so much that needed to be addressed, who would know where to start?

"She's a lucky girl," Ethic said.

Alani returned Bella's phone and Bella put it back on speaker.

"So, can I go?" she asked.

"Yeah, B, you can go. Take care of my girl," Ethic said.

"Of course," Alani answered, weakly.

"I was talking to Bella," Ethic shot back and then he was gone.

That one sentence told her he held no resentments. How could he hold none? How could he not hate her?

I could have killed him.

Ethic's love knew no limits and Alani was floored. She led Bella out of the church and to her car, in complete disbelief of how Ethic could be so dreadful but so incredible all at the same time. She wished she could love like that, without boundaries, but boundaries were necessary. Boundaries kept guns out of her hands and kept her out of the woes of depression. Boundaries kept them separated; and as long as they were separate, they were safe.

"Come on. I'll take you somewhere fun," Alani said.

Alani made the quick trip across town, and when she pulled up to the bookstore, Bella looked out her window and frowned.

"*This* is where you go to have fun?"

Alani laughed aloud at Bella's blank expression. "Come on, I'll show you how I get down," she replied, as she got out. Bella hustled across the parking lot behind Alani and they entered.

"Do you smell that?" Alani asked, as she took a deep breath.

"Umm... smell what?" Bella asked, skeptically.

"Books. Thousands and thousands of pages of books," Alani said. "It's my favorite thing about the bookstore. It's the reason why I won't get one of those iPad things you have. Nothing can replace the feel of a good book in your hand, and a good book..." Alani sighed. "My God, a book can make you feel like you are miles and miles away."

Bella frowned. "You're talking about the book like it's a boy you like?" Bella smiled, and her chest lifted in amusement.

"Oh, baby girl, I have 10 boys I like. My book boyfriends put your daddy to shame," Alani said. She said it so effortlessly, as if Ethic had truly been considered that - her boyfriend. Alani counted them down on her fingers. "Let's see. There's Carter from The Cartel, there's A'shai from a book called Murderville, There's Basil's fine self from The Streets Have No King. You'll see. I'm going to put you up on game, little girl."

Bella followed Alani down the aisle, as she browsed the shelves. "The Cartel, huh?" Bella said, in intrigue.

"No, ma'am. The Cartel is for grown folks. I'm going to start you off small."

"I mean, I like to read but I wouldn't call it fun," Bella shrugged, as she trailed behind Alani.

"That means you're reading the wrong things," Alani said.

"Try these," Alani suggested. She perused the shelves, scanning the spines of the books, like a librarian, until she found what she was looking for. She picked out a book.

"Lord of the Flies," Bella read, taking the book from Alani's hand. Alani held up a finger, as she moved to the next shelf. She located another one. "The Coldest Winter Ever," Bella whispered, taking the book before following Alani to one more aisle. "I Know Why the Caged Bird Sings?"

Alani started her off with an assortment of genres - all classics. You could never go wrong with the classics.

"Now that we have the books, we need snacks because you can't sit in a bookstore all day and not eat when it gets intense inside those pages," Alani said. She sat her bag down on a table and Bella placed the books down beside it. Grabbing her wallet, Alani hurried over to the counter.

"I'll take iced, black tea with stevia, a squeeze of honey, and heavy ice, a red velvet cupcake, pistachios, and a banana," Alani ordered. She knew it had to be pregnancy cravings because she hated bananas, but she had an overwhelming urge to eat one. "What about you, Bella?"

Bella stuck her hands in her back pocket. "I'll take... umm. Chips and a pop..."

"No pop; it's horrible for you," Alani said, reciting something she used to tell her daughter.

"Tea then. The same as hers," Bella said, complying without

protest. "And a flatbread pizza, I guess."

Alani paid for the food and they took their snacks back to the table. Alani scooped up the books and her bag.

"I thought we were sitting here?" Bella asked.

"Nope," Alani said. "Follow me."

They entered the children's section and Alani paused. It was where she used to bring her daughter every Saturday. She went all the way to the back where there were dozens of bean bags in a corner.

"Best seat in the house," Alani smiled. She sat with her snacks and Bella immediately reached for the purple book with the red lips. Alani had predicted that, so she took it. "Nope. You earn this one. Start with The Lord of the Flies, then a little Maya Angelou, then I introduce you to Winter Santiago," Alani said. She held up the book as bait and Bella grabbed her first challenge. The pair laid out on the bean bags and it took no time for them to get lost within the pages.

Alani heard all types of gasps and sound effects coming from Bella, as she read about the group of young boys turned savages. Alani chuckled but only kept reading her own book. This felt so familiar that Alani forgot that Bella was attached to Ethic. It felt natural, as if they had come to this same bookstore and bonded over book boyfriends for years.

"Jack is my book boyfriend," Bella said.

"Jack!" Alani protested. "He was the bad guy!"

"Sometimes, the bad guys protect you better," Bella shrugged, but Alani took pause. Bella had a way of saying things that penetrated Alani, without even knowing it.

"Maybe, Bella," Alani whispered. "I'm going to the restroom. I'll be right back."

Alani stood, and the entire room felt like it was tilted. Her equilibrium brought her crashing to her knees.

"Alani!" Bella screamed, as she scrambled to her side.

"Ma'am, are you okay?" a store worker asked, as she too came to Alani's aide.

Alani's mouth was cotton dry and it was hot. "I just need some water," she whispered, closing her eyes.

Alani?" Bella was worried. Alani could hear it. The last thing she needed was Bella telling Ethic about this.

"I'm fine, baby girl," Alani assured. She planted a cautious foot onto the ground and then held onto the worker, as she stood straight up. Everything in her stomach came up. She reached for the trash bin and hugged it to her chest, as she threw up.

"Ma'am, we can call security or an ambulance if you need help," the worker asked, empathetically.

"No," Alani said, shaking her head. "It's not serious. I'm fine. I'm pregnant."

Bella's eyes widened, and Alani could see Bella putting the truth together in her head.

"By my daddy?" Bella asked.

"Bella…" Alani whispered.

Bella smiled. "It's by my daddy, isn't it?" Bella's excitement couldn't be masked. "You're having my daddy's baby?"

"Bella, listen to me," Alani placed the trash down and chose her words carefully. "Ethic can't know about this. Please, don't say anything." She knew she was wrong for asking Bella to lie for her, but Ethic's awareness would just complicate things. If he knew there would be no keeping him away.

"But why? He would be so happy," Bella asked, confused.

Alani felt her body betraying her and she rushed to the restroom. She barely made it, kicking in a stall door and heaving in the first toilet she came to.

Bella came in moments later with Vernors pop and crackers. Alani reached for it, in desperation, and gargled with the first sip, before spitting it into the sink. Vernors was her childhood remedy for everything. Nannie had given her the bubbly soda every time she complained of a cold or a stomach ache and like magic it worked. This time was no different.

"Your father can't know, Bella," Alani pleaded. She knew getting close to Bella was too much. Bella was a direct link to Ethic and Alani wanted no parts of him. She snatched paper towel from the dispenser and wiped her mouth. Bella nodded.

"Okay, I promise. I won't say anything." Alani had a feeling it would be the first time Bella lied to her father. Alani felt like scum.

"Can I see?" Bella asked.

Alani lifted her shirt to reveal the tiniest bump. It was still so early along but because it was her second child she was showing slightly. With clothes, there was no noticeable difference, but Bella's hand located the small change, instantly.

"Wow, you're so small," Bella said.

"I've got a long way to go," Alani whispered.

Bella bent down. "Hey, you in there. This is your big sister out here." Bella smiled and stood, before throwing her arms around Alani's neck.

"He's been waiting so long for you," Bella whispered. "I won't tell him, but hurry and stop being mad at him because he needs you, okay?"

Alani was speechless. She couldn't respond to that with words. She simply nodded and led Bella out the restroom. It was time to take her home.

CHAPTER 16

L aughter filled the hospital room, as Ethic sat around with the three most valuable possessions he owned - his children.

He was tired of being trapped in this room; tired of calling it home. He was ready to be discharged so he could spend Christmas with his family. He was in pain, but it was manageable, and his wounds were healing. The fractured ribs were the worst part and that would take months to heal. He couldn't spend that time in the hospital. It was time to get back to living, time to get back to her. Alani saw his daughter almost daily and he had yet to get a glimpse of her. She picked Bella up from school and dropped her off at the hospital after their time was done. It had gone from once a week to almost every day and he had noticed a drastic change in Bella. The things she conversed about were maturing, her views of the world were expanding, even the subject matter she was reading about had evolved.

We gon' have a talk about the book with the red lips, though. Got my baby running around here talking about book boyfriends.

Overall, he could see the effects of the debutante pageant helping her. The time Alani was committing to Bella gave him hope that one day she would forgive him. Last he had heard, Cream had been arrested. The brilliant lie Bella had told was the perfect trap to remove the threat he posed. He hated that his baby girl had to be involved at all, but her wit had surprised him. He knew she had done it to protect Alani. He could see her getting more attached to her by the day, and he understood, because Alani was infectious. She was every bit of the woman he thought she was. A woman who took no shit. She loved hard and hated harder. She was real, and he couldn't fault her for the things he had done to harden her. The fact that she was still soft, still loving for his baby girl, meant the world. His only fear was if Alani pulled away. He knew Bella was sensitive and it would devastate her, so Ethic would have to play things carefully to ensure that Alani didn't run off.

"Daddy, Christmas Eve is in two days, will you be home by then?"

"You know I wouldn't miss it, big man," he said.

Ethic was more than ready to be home. He could relinquish Morgan of the responsibility she had taken on, give Lily some much-needed time off and a bonus, then focus on healing his body. The doctors had poked, prodded, burned, cut, stapled, and sewn him like he was a science experiment. He needed some holistic healing, some mental, and spiritual cleansing because so much negative was breeding inside him.

"I know you're eager to get back to school, Mo," Ethic said. "After Christmas, you can head back to your place. I know you miss your freedom. I appreciate you holding me down, baby girl. I'm real proud of the way you've been handling things," Ethic complimented. "You heard from Messiah?"

The question caught her off guard. "Um, yeah, he comes around to check on us sometimes, make sure we don't need anything," she lied. Truth was, after the kids went to sleep, Messiah pulled up on her every night. She wished she could just be transparent about Messiah with Ethic, but she knew him, he would never approve as long as Messiah was in the streets. If there was anything Messiah loved more than Morgan, it was the streets. They had raised him. She knew if he had to choose, she would lose, so they were reduced to sneaking around, hiding their affections for one another from everyone except a select few.

Ethic examined her from head to toe, studying Morgan.

"You know you never have to lie to me, right?" he asked.

Morgan felt a gnawing at her gut. The truth would cause conflict. She never wanted to be in a position to choose between the love for her family and the love for her man. She simply nodded, "I know." She stood, ready to run from the hot seat Ethic was trying to place her in. "We should get going. We'll be back in the morning for your discharge."

Ethic nodded, as he pulled himself to his feet. Alani had done what no man before her had ever been able to, lay Ethic down, and he was having trouble getting his body to work the way it used to. That bullet had aged him. He felt like he would break every time he moved. His body hurt everywhere.

"You don't have to get up, Ethic," Morgan said.

"I do, Mo. I really do," he groaned. "I've been in this bed for too long. I'll walk you guys to the elevator. I can manage that." He grabbed the rolling walking pole where his IV hung and took slow steps behind his kids.

"Daddy, I want the PS4 for Christmas. I hope I get it. Man, I hope I get that!" Eazy said.

"You put it on your list, big man?" Ethic asked. "Santa might bring it."

"Daddy, Santa isn't real. I'm not a baby. You don't have to fake," Eazy said.

Ethic stalled.

"Yo, what you talking about Santa ain't real, man? I know homie personally. I'll dial him up right now."

"My friend said Santa was his mom. He said she put the gifts under his tree every year."

"Your friend is probably a little bad mu'fucka who didn't deserve any gifts from Santa, so his mama had to put gifts under there instead," Ethic said, slightly perturbed. *Bad-ass little nigga ruining my big man's childhood. He not even seven yet.*

Ethic wanted to retain Eazy's childhood as long as he could. All his children were growing up and it saddened him. They gave him purpose, and when they were all gone, moving on with their lives, he knew he would be lost.

"Can I go to Alani's on Christmas Eve?" Bella asked.

"Why are you constantly with her? Your pageant is months away. Is it necessary for you to be there every day?"

"Is it necessary for you to be a bi..."

"Yo!" Ethic stopped Bella, looking at her in disbelief. He had definitely been away from home for too long. His baby girl had lost her mind. "Be a lady, B."

"Sorry, Daddy," Bella whispered. "Can I go? If I don't go, she's going to be alone on Christmas. How is that fair?" Ethic thought of Alani spending her first Christmas without her daughter and Nannie. He could spare Bella. His daughter seemed to want to spend her holiday there anyway. He wouldn't deprive her. Even though Alani refused to be a part of his life, it felt like they were sharing custody of a child. Like they were too bitter for words and only did what was best for Bella, only Bella wasn't Alani's to be obligated to.

"You'll spend a few hours at home and then I'll drop you off," Ethic said.

"What about me?" Eazy said. "I want to go to Ms. Alani's. Why does she get to go all the time?"

Shit, Ethic felt that. He wanted to go too. "It's a girl thing, big man. Besides, if you leave Daddy too, what am I going to do? Me and Mo will get lonely," Ethic said. He would let Bella have her time with Alani, but he wasn't too keen on Bella staying nights in Alani's home. The neighborhood wasn't the safest and he had done too much dirt there to ever truly feel comfortable with his child resting there; but it was Christmas, and it was what she wanted, so he obliged. He'd have to put shooters on holiday pay in order to rest well while Bella was there.

Bella smiled and hugged him, a little too hard, but Ethic took it all in before they piled into the elevator. Tomorrow couldn't come soon enough. He would be going home to them.

He pulled his cell phone from the pocket of his sweat pants. He had some dreams to make come true and only two days to do it.

He sent out numerous text messages, as he made his way down to Nannie's room. Everything had to be perfect this Christmas. It had been a rough year, he felt obligated to spread around a little happiness. He couldn't leave without telling the old woman goodbye. He was an everyday fixture in her room and he talked to her, using her as therapy to get the ghosts of his past out his head. He had lived with them for a long time. Having a sounding board had done him well. It took him 45 minutes to make the trip to her floor. He refused help. He wouldn't have it at home, so he needed to get used to maneuvering through the pain. By the time he sat down in the chair next to her bed, he was exhausted.

"Hey, beautiful," he said. "They're cutting me loose tomorrow. I want to go to her. It's like the snap back of a rubber band for me. No matter how hard she pulls away, I just want to get right back. How do I get back to her, huh? I just love her," Ethic said, as he rubbed one hand over a closed fist. "More than anything." He stood and placed a hand over one of hers. He squeezed it, before taking steps toward the door.

"Hmm."

Ethic thought his mind was playing tricks on him, until he heard it again.

"Hmm."

He turned toward the bed.

"I need some help in here!" he shouted. "She's moving! She's trying to talk!"

Nannie's eyes fluttered in confusion, as she tried to speak. The tube down her throat prevented it, but she was coming out of her coma. She was moving, and Ethic felt like he was witnessing a miracle.

He was happy for what this would mean for Alani. Happy like the old lady had been the one to raise him his entire life. It gave him comfort that she would have comfort now, and he eased back to his room because he didn't want to ruin the moment when Alani arrived.

The scent of Pine-Sol wafted in the air, as Alani stood in the middle of her kitchen, a head scarf tied around her short hair, long, tube socks on her feet, a pair of tights and hole-filled t-shirt covering her baby bump. It was Christmas Eve and she had expected misery, but God had given her a gift. Nannie wasn't home yet. She probably wouldn't be for another week, but she was awake, and she was going to live. Alani's heart had a brief respite from all that it had endured. Christmas wouldn't be dismal like she had anticipated. There would be some bitter because it would be her first Christmas without Kenzie, but there would be a little sweet too. She heard a horn honking and she peered outside. A blanket of snow covered her walkway. Even her foot prints from the night before had filled in and were non-existent. When she saw Ethic's Range Rover pull in front of her house, she froze.

"No, please, no. Don't get out the car," she whispered. "What is he doing here?"

He exited and walked around to the passenger side to open the door. Bella emerged. She carried a huge gift bag filled with presents. Ethic held his daughter's wrist and walked her through the deep snow, stopping at the bottom step to the porch.

Alani jumped back from the blinds, when he looked up at her window and she closed her eyes, anticipating the knock at the door.

She couldn't not answer. Her car was there. They knew she was home. She looked down at her belly. It was noticeable. She grabbed her waffle weaved robe and slid into it, tightening it to conceal her stomach before going to answer. When all she saw was Bella, she sighed in relief.

"Merry Christmas!" Bella shouted.

Alani looked behind Bella. The Range Rover was empty, but he wasn't behind her.

"He's not coming in," Bella whispered. Alani sighed in relief and then hustled Bella in out of the cold.

"What is all this? Why aren't you at home with your family?" Bella asked.

"You are family," Bella said. "I have gifts. Good stuff. Not the cheap gifts most kids get at the school Christmas shop. Daddy lets us go into our bank accounts and spend $2,000 on gifts for each other every year. Eazy and I got you stuff this year."

"Eazy too?" Alani asked.

Bella nodded. "But it's tradition that we can't open them until midnight."

"Midnight it is, I guess," Alani said. She was in shock that anyone had even thought of her today. She hadn't expected any of this, but she was flattered, honored even. She heard an odd

231

sound outside and she rushed over to the window. Ethic's truck was still there.

CRUNCH
CRUNCH
CRUNCH

What the hell is that sound?

She walked around to the kitchen window and peered out to find Ethic in her driveway. He had located the shovel she had meant to use a day ago and was clearing her driveway and walkways of snow. She saw the painful grimace on his face and knew he shouldn't even be out in this weather. He wasn't nearly close to being healed and he was outside doing what good men did on a snowy day...what husbands did on a snowy day. She scoffed, in disbelief. He never missed a detail. He was the man you didn't have to ask for anything, he just provided. He was the type to fill your gas tank on Sunday night, so you would be covered during the week. He was the man that had a hot bath waiting for you when you walked through the door and kept up with your oil changes every three months. He never had to be reminded, never fussed at. He didn't leave room for error. She watched him through the slits of her blinds, unable to not take peeks for the entire 30 minutes it took him to finish. She expected him to come to her door afterward, but he kept his word and drove off without interruption.

Bella had made herself comfortable in the La-Z-Boy.

"Umm... little girl. Come in this kitchen. You spend Christmas with me, we have to follow some of my traditions."

Bella beamed, as she arose from the chair and followed Alani into the kitchen.

"You know how to cook, B?" Alani asked.

"Lily taught me a few recipes," Bella said. "I always make the crispy brussels and green bean casserole when she needs help in the kitchen."

Alani snapped her head over to Bella, frowning.

Ethic know he should be ashamed of himself.

"I'm going to teach you to make cornbread dressing," Alani said. "Wash your hands and then grab eggs, corn meal, onion, bell pepper, smoked turkey legs, chicken stock and butter from the refrigerator. The dry stuff will be in the pantry."

Alani and Bella spent hours in the kitchen. After preparing the dish, Alani had to round out the meal. A full spread sat on the counter by the time she was done, and she had a red velvet cake in the oven.

"That was slave labor!" Bella cried. "My feet hurt!"

Alani complained. "If your feet don't hurt, your food ain't good. One day you'll have a family of your own and you'll remember today. You'll cook that meal with love the same way I just cooked it with you. Soul food is about pouring your heart into your food. It's about doing it with the people you care about, about making memories," Alani said.

"Now, we have a memory," Bella added.

Alani smiled. "Yeah, I guess we do, baby girl." She ushered Bella out of the kitchen. "Can't hang out in here. The cake might fall." She hated when Nannie used to say that to her as a young girl and it tickled her that she was now repeating the words to Bella.

"I'm not even hungry anymore," Bella said, with laughter.

"The chef usually hates to eat after all that work," Alani schooled. "You can take most of it home. I won't eat much of it."

"So, can we break tradition a little bit? I have something I want to give you," Alani said.

Bella looked at the clock. It was 11:30 p.m. She shook her head. "Okafors have strict Christmas rules. No gifts until Midnight."

Alani lifted her hands in defense. "Okay, okay."

"Have you been sick lately?" Bella asked, her eye brows dipping in concern.

"It's getting better, Bella. Every day," she said.

Alani tried not to talk about her pregnancy, especially with Bella. She didn't want her getting attached. Alani didn't even want to be attached. Once this baby was born, she could move on with her life. She was writing her emotions, filling up chapters in a book that she hoped to publish. She would use all her loss to gain something, to help others gain something. That was the plan. She had even met a woman named Noni at the doctor's office who was having trouble conceiving. She was at the stage of considering adoption and the two had exchanged numbers. Alani hadn't called yet, but she was considering it.

"I can't wait to meet him or her. Do you know yet?" Bella asked.

Alani shook her head. "Not yet," she answered. She didn't want to tell Bella there would be no introduction, no celebrating, no merging of families. Alani knew she couldn't witness Bella holding her child and keep her resolve to give it up. No, she would deliver the baby alone and sign away the rights immediately. It would hurt but it was better than the alternative...the abortion.

"Why don't we change into pajamas and put on A Christmas Story?" Alani suggested, changing the subject.

"A Christmas Story?" Bella asked.

Alani rolled her eyes. "Oh my God! How is Ethic raising y'all over there?" she asked. Bella laughed. "Go change and I'll meet you down here in 10."

Alani took her cake out the oven and put it on the stove to cool before heading upstairs. When she saw her daughter's room light on, she froze. Her feet seemed to be tied to blocks they were so heavy. She staggered down the hall and looked inside from the hallway. Bella stood in front of Kenzie's desk, holding a picture in her hands.

Alani was stuck. If anyone else had trespassed into Kenzie's room, Alani would have spazzed, but with Bella she swallowed down everything that felt intrusive. She took a deep breath.

"She was very pretty," Bella whispered.

"The prettiest," Alani whispered back.

"Alani, I'm sorry that she's not here," Bella said.

Alani shook her head and pushed down her grief. It was Christmas. She didn't want to feel grief. She just wanted one day to unwrap presents and enjoy a meal with this lovely-spirited girl who had come into her life. She just wanted to be 'merry,' damn it.

"Me too," she croaked. "I'll be downstairs when you're ready."

She knew Bella was curious, so she let her stay in Kenzie's room. It took her 10 minutes to join Alani in the living room.

"I know it's your first Christmas without your daughter, but it's my first Christmas to know what it feels like to have a mom," Bella said. Alani was staggered by her words. She didn't want that pressure of trying to fill motherly shoes for Bella because she knew she would disappoint. Being Bella's mother meant being connected to her father and Alani just couldn't. Not knowing what to say, she reached for Bella's hand and gave it a gentle squeeze.

"Christmas Story?" she asked.

"Christmas Story," Bella answered.

They woke up the next morning on Alani's couch. Alani's feet were tucked underneath her, and she leaned her head on the arm of the sofa, while Bella's head rested on Alani's hip. The movie had stopped playing hours ago. It was still dark outside, which told Alani it was early morning hours. She lifted Bella's head gently, replacing her hip with a pillow and then draping her with a throw.

Alani went to her the kitchen to wrap up the food. She would send it with Bella. She wondered if she was just doing the logical thing or if she felt like feeding Ethic and his family somehow placed her in his thoughts on Christmas Day. Like, if she nourished the man he wouldn't forget her. She sat at the kitchen table and unlocked her phone, scrolling to his name. Just allowing herself to look at his contact information was progress. There were days before where just the sight of those five letters together, E-T-H-I-C, had felt like a knife being twisted in her belly. She typed the words *I'm pregnant.*

I'm Pregnan-
I'm Pregn
I'm P

She second-guessed each letter until nothing, but a blank screen remained. She couldn't tell him. He would want this baby. He would want her, and it was something that she could never allow. Even if she had this child and placed it in Ethic's custody to raise, she would want to be a part of the dynamic. Creating a new family erased her old one. It diluted her hurt a bit; and although she didn't want to feel it, she didn't want to forget Kenzie. The pain was all she had left. Her hormones had her thinking of the possibility of repair with Ethic. It was the exact reason why she hadn't wanted this baby to begin with. She brewed herself a cup of tea and then sat silently, watching Bella sleep soundly, as if she was right where she belonged.

Later that morning, Bella awoke with so much excitement. Bella's level of maturity fluctuated daily. Sometimes, she felt like she was a teenager, other times she felt like she related to Eazy. She was in a peculiar place in her life where people accepted both childish antics and maturity. Alani saw the kid in her this morning and it made her smile. Bella came into the kitchen, carrying the huge bag.

"Is all that for me?" Alani asked.

"Daddy let me bring one of my gifts from under the tree, so I would have something to open Christmas morning, but the rest are yours," Bella informed.

Alani reached into the bag and pulled out a huge and exquisitely-wrapped box.

"That one is from me," she said, giddily. Christmas had a way of enchanting folks and Alani felt a bit of glee, as she watched Bella's eyes twinkle in anticipation. Alani removed the wrapping paper to find a mustard-colored box. The words *LOUIS VUITTON* were pressed into it. At discovery, she knew it was too much.

"Bella, I can't…"

"Daddy said you would say that, keep going," Bella said.

She pulled at the ribbon and pulled off the lid to find a huge, checkered-print, brown, tote bag.

"I wanted to get you a diaper bag, but since you don't want Ethic to know, I figured this could kind of serve as the same thing. It's a Monogram print, GM, Neverfull."

Alani laughed at Bella's description. What 12-year-old went around talking about *Louis Vuitton* with so much knowledge? Ethic's 12-year-old, that's who. She was flattered.

"You bought this with your own money?" she asked.

Bella nodded.

"Thank you, Bella," Alani said, genuinely. "I don't know what to say."

She reached under the table and pulled out her own gift bag. "Maybe except, Merry Christmas," Alani returned, sliding it over the table for Bella.

Bella wasted no time tearing into the wrapping paper. She pulled out the book first. "Letter to My Daughter," Bella read.

Alani teared up, as Bella opened the first page.

"It's signed?" Bella whispered, in disbelief. "After I read her first book, I Googled her. She's dead. How is this signed?"

Alani cleared her throat. "Well, that book was intended for my little girl. I bought it for her the day she was born, and when I went to see Ms. Angelou speak years ago, I got it signed. I never got the chance to give it to Kenzie. She wasn't old enough. She wouldn't understand, but I would like you to have it. For days when you feel alone, and you need a little motherly advice."

"I don't feel alone anymore," Bella whispered.

Alani knew those lonely days would return. Bella simply wasn't hers to nurture forever, so the book would come in handy. Bella was too young to truly know it's worth, but the tears sparkling in the young girl's eyes told Alani that Bella was assigning her own value to it. "Thank you, Alani. I promise to take really good care of it," she whispered. Alani reached across the table and feathered Bella's tears, wiping them away.

"You're welcome."

Bella let out a smile and a laugh that was laced in a sob. It was happiness breaking through years of grief.

"There's more," Bella motioned. Alani nodded to Bella's small bag.

"For you too," Alani said. "And there's something for Eazy in there too."

Alani reached inside the bag and pulled out a necklace. It was silver.

Or is this platinum? Is this a real diamond?

"Did your dad buy this?" Alani asked. If he had, Alani was prepared to send it back.

"No, Eazy picked it out," Bella said.

I guess rich kids have good taste.

The necklace had a small angel, diamond pendant on the end and it shined effortlessly under her dim, yellow lights.

"Wow, thank you…I mean, thank you both, Bella. Please, hug him for me," she whispered. It made the Pandora charm bracelet she had gotten Bella look like it had come from a bubble gum machine. If Bella was used to opulence like this, she would hate it. Alani cringed, as Bella opened it.

"A Pandora bracelet! Agh! All my friends have them at school! Thank you!" That one earned Alani a huge hug.

Alani motioned for her wrist. "I have the same charm," she said, pulling at the tiny cross bead that hung from her own.

"You have one more thing," Bella said.

Alani reached in and pulled out a large, flat, square box. It looked like it held a certificate or something. Alani released the document to find documents with her name on them.

"What is this?" she asked, as she glanced up at Alani. Bella shrugged. "I don't know. That's Daddy's gift. I told him it was lame but…"

Alani pulled out title deeds to every house on her block.

"If you do it with this house you can do it with the one next door and the one next to that. Before you know it, you're a black woman with a whole block…with assets."

She remembered his words from their first date and she looked up at Bella in disbelief. A Christmas card lay inside, and Alani pulled it out. Her fingers shook so badly, she could barely open it.

Assets. Merry Christmas.
--E

She kept flipping through the paperwork to find signed contracts between Ethic and contractors. Workers who were set to start demolishing and rebuilding things at the top of the year. Pre-paid labor and her name was the contact person on everything. Her name covered all the deeds and the tax receipts, which had been paid up for the next five years. Ethic had bought the block for her and her mind was blown.

Her neighbors lived in these houses, some lots were abandoned all together, but land held value. For years to come, they would be hers. She was speechless.

"It's a dumb gift, right?" Bella interrupted.

Alani blinked disbelieving eyes up to Bella. She opened her mouth to speak but could only offer the shake of her head. A man that loved a woman put her in position to elevate.

The sound of a car horn made Bella rise to her feet.

"That's my dad. Merry Christmas, Alani," Bella said.

"Wait," Alani whispered, as she handed Bella the box of packaged food. "You cooked it. It's only right you share it with your family." Alani kissed Bella's cheek and opened the door for her, making sure to shield her body behind it as Bella walked out. Ethic stood against his car, waiting to open Bella's door. Alani knew she should thank him, but the part of her that would never heal simply avoided his gaze and closed the door; because no matter what, he was still her child's killer. Nothing could erase that.

Messiah sat in his house. He had spent many holidays alone, but this one felt especially forlorn. This year there was someone he would rather be spending the snowy day with, but she was across town, locked away in a castle because she was playing princess instead of being his queen. He was in a mood and he didn't feel much like being bothered, so when Morgan sent him a Merry Christmas text he had ignored it. He wanted her all the time. He had grown accustomed to being with her everyday while

Ethic was in the hospital. It had been two days since Ethic had been released and Messiah hadn't seen her face. It had him in a zone. The knock at the door pulled him from his seat. He walked over to the door and pulled it open.

"Messiah!"

The little boy ran into his arms.

"What up, li'l G? Merry Christmas," Messiah greeted, as he gave a signature handshake to the little, brown-skinned boy. "Them locs getting long, boy."

"Shorty Doo-Wop," Messiah said, as he stood and embraced the kid's mother.

"Don't Shorty Doo-Wop me. You not answering the phone, now?"

"Yo, Bleu, for real. Not now," Messiah said.

Bleu Montclair was one of the very few friends Messiah cared for in the world. Isa, Ahmeek, Bleu. That about rounded out his circle. He had seen her at her worst, so she never judged him at his.

Bleu waltzed into his house. "Well, Saviour wanted to come tell you Merry Christmas, since you didn't show up to dinner." She held up Tupperware. "I brought you food."

"Thanks, Bleu," Messiah said, as he sat on his couch. He motioned for the Christmas tree. "Saviour, man, why don't you hop up under that tree and dig out you and your mama gifts."

"You put up a tree this year?" Bleu asked, in astonishment. Messiah felt a streak of embarrassment warm him, as he waved her off. Morgan had him on some corny shit and she didn't even show up.

Bleu took him in, eyes sparkling in shock, as she shook her head. "This girl is changing you, Messiah. You're different with her."

"Mom! He got me a Nintendo Switch!" her son shouted, in excitement. "Thanks, Uncle Messiah!"

Messiah smirked. At least somebody was happy on Christmas. "You're welcome, man," Messiah said.

Bleu looked on with sympathy-filled eyes. "Messiah, just tell her. If you love her, you have to tell her. If she finds out from anyone but you, she'll never forgive you," Bleu advised.

"She'll never forgive me anyway, so I just got to run up the clock with her while I can," Messiah said, voice low and pained. "I'm going to lose her and I ain't talking about breakup to make up shit, sis. I'm talking about lose the one good thing I ever knew. I'm selfish with her, trying to squeeze all the time in I can get before it's over. It's gon' fuck me up. I can feel it."

Bleu's eyes were dreary clouds of emotion.

"Mom, this one is for you," Saviour interrupted, handing her a small box.

Bleu took it and reached into her bag to retrieve Messiah's. She handed it to him.

She opened her box, pulling out a platinum, heart-shaped locket. She opened it, already knowing what picture would be inside. She smiled. "Thank you," she whispered.

The doorbell rang and Messiah stood.

"You didn't open your gift," Bleu said.

"I'll get around to it. Whatever it is it isn't necessary, B. You staying clean and taking care of your business the way you do, that's gift enough for me," he said. "Noah would be proud."

The bell rang again.

"That's our cue," Bleu said. "Come on, baby."

Saviour followed Bleu to the door with Messiah trailing them. She opened the door and there she stood - Morgan.

"Oh," Morgan faltered, as she took a step back at Bleu's presence. Her mind went to a million places, as confusion spread through her. She saw Messiah walk up behind Bleu, shirtless and barefoot, looking like a whole ho. He was comfortable around this girl and the basketball shorts he wore pronounced his print through the fabric. Her eyes took in Saviour.

"Hi, I'm Bleu. It's really nice to meet you."

Morgan's chest eased some. She had heard him say the name before, the night they had fought at his trap house.

Messiah stepped up. "Mo, this is my friend, Bleu, and her son, Saviour."

Morgan was uncertain on what she was witnessing, but the girl's vibe was kind, almost sympathetic, like she knew something Mo didn't yet.

"Nice to meet you," Morgan said, in a polite but not overly friendly tone.

"She's pretty, Uncle Messiah?" Saviour asked.

"Aye, stop trying to steal my girl, li'l homie. I'ma give you one of these," Messiah said, holding up a balled fist.

Saviour laughed and Morgan relaxed. She had been acknowledged as his girl. The kid had called him Uncle. Bleu was indeed just a friend. She sighed in relief.

"See you later, Messiah, and open that gift!" Bleu yelled, as she stepped off the porch.

"Yup," Messiah called back.

"I thought I was gon' have to fuck you up," Morgan said, with a smirk.

"I thought I was gon' have to fuck *you* up," Messiah shot back, as he pulled her by the wrist into his body.

"I'm sorry. I couldn't get away," Morgan whispered, as she wrapped her arms around his neck and buried her face in the center of his chest, kissing his skin. "Merry Christmas, babe."

She was plain today in tearaway track pants that hung low like a boy and a midriff camisole and a baggy jean jacket over it. A bigger Moncler puffer kept her warm. He pulled the coat off and kissed her forehead. Messiah was a king amongst peasants, but when Morgan was around, he was the peasant around the queen.

"I want to give you something," Messiah said. She followed him to the living room and he reached under a couch cushion and pulled out two things. He held a velvet box in one hand and a set of stapled papers in the other. His face was serious, conflicted, pained even. It unsettled Morgan's soul.

"Messiah, what is it?" she asked.

"It's a ring," he said. "It's a ring that a man gives a woman he wants to spend his life with. Not a man like me, a square-ass nigga, one of them college boys," Messiah whispered. "I'll never be that, Mo. I'll probably never be able to be that, but I want you to have the ring, a ring from me, to know that I loved you as much as any man can love a woman. When this is over, and you've learned what not to accept in a nigga because of my fuck ups, you'll find somebody else. That man will be smart enough to not mess it up, but I want you to always have something to remind you that if I was able to, I would have made an honest woman out of you, Mo."

"Messiah, why are you talking like this?" Morgan whispered. "Are you leaving me?"

"No," Messiah answered. "No, Mo, but one day you're going to leave me, and when that day comes, I want you to have that ring."

Morgan opened the box and her breath caught in her throat. It was beautiful. Three, simple, flawless karats from Tiffany's wrapped in platinum. It wasn't gaudy. It was classic and timeless. Morgan loved it.

"I don't want anyone but you. I'll wear this ring, Messiah, but I can tell you that nobody will ever change my last name if it's not you," she said. Messiah shook his head. "Look at me," she said. Their eyes met. "I promise." She took the papers from his hands. "What are these?" Her eyes scanned the documents and then went wet. "Life Insurance? Messiah, who's dying? Why are you doing this? A million dollars?" she asked.

"I'm living wrong, and if a nigga ever catch me slipping, I want to make sure you're straight. No matter if you're with me or not," he said.

"This doesn't feel like a gift, Messiah." She cried. "This is our first Christmas and you're making it feel horrible. I don't want any of this. Why are you planning for stuff like this?" she whispered.

Messiah sat down and pulled her into his lap. He planted soft lips to her clavicle, as he placed his hand inside the band of her pants. He feather-stroked her clit through her panties. "That feel better?" he asked.

Morgan sighed, as she felt a silky wetness penetrate the fabric. He went inside her panties to access it without boundaries, working her clit with his thumb while sliding two fingers in her depths. She sucked in air. "How about that, baby, that feel better?" Her face twisted in pleasure, as she nodded.

She felt him rising beneath her, hardening, pushing against her. She stood and looked back at him because she knew where his fingers were going next. He sucked her off his fingers. He was nasty when it came to her and he made no apologies for it. She unsnapped the buttons down the sides of her legs, turning the pants into a skirt. He lifted it as she worked her way down onto him.

"Dance on it, shorty," Messiah grunted.

"There's no music," she gasped.

"Make some for me," he whispered, as he gripped her waist.

Morgan closed her eyes and rolled her hips.

"One. Your smile don't have to say no more," she sang softly, almost in a whisper, as she rode him.

"Two. Your guidance and all the things you show me." His finger tips dug into her sides. She danced, slow, and sensual, as she rode that reverse cowgirl.

"Three. The way you look at me, when you say I love you-oo--oo." Her voice floated like the sounds of birds singing on a sunny day.

"Four. Your headstrong personality. Five. Your take charge capability."

She bit her lip, as she went down low, touching the base of him, and then bounced there.

"Six. I love the way you cook for me. Beef roast, white rice, and gravyyy."

Messiah groaned under her, as he admired the visual.

"Damn, shorty. Keep going."

"I'll give you 25 reasons why I'm really in love with you," she sang softly, damn near whining because he was fucking her back now, meeting her with upward strokes, as she rolled her wetness with intensity.

"I can give you 25 reasons why I'm neverrr leaving you..."

Messiah had to bite into his bottom lip to add pain to all the pleasure she was bringing him.

"Mo, shit, shorty. You got to slow down," he whispered. The combination of things she was pulling out of him had him ready to explode. Her voice, the sight, and the peculiar rhythm that only she could find was too much to take.

"I can give you 25 reasons why I'm really in love with you..."

"Shit, ohhh, shit," Messiah's head fell back against the back of the couch and he didn't even give a damn that he wasn't worth shit tonight. It had been two days of no pussy, after having her every day for weeks straight. He couldn't hold out.

"Let it go, Ssiah," she moaned. With her blessing he let his orgasm go. Morgan didn't care that she hadn't cum. This wasn't about her. It was for him....to show him...that he wasn't going anywhere. She stood and turned to straddle him. She brought her face close to his, massaging the nape of his neck as their noses touched. She whispered. "I can give you 25 reasons why I'm never leaving you."

Christmas night was for lovers. Ethic always believed that man and wife could find no greater joy than watching the seeds they had sown open gifts and share in laughter all day. After the kids were put to bed, husband and wife, woman and man, would indulge in one another. It was how he always thought it should be. Fire burning in the fire place, music playing in a darkened room, his body, on top of her body, fighting pleasure to ensure that his children didn't stir. Instead, he sat on the floor of his home, the remnants of wrapping paper strewn about, as he sat with a plate of love in his hands. It was the only piece of her he could taste, her cooking, the bomb-ass homemade dinner that she had sent home with Bella. Snowflakes fell outside his window. It was a cold night. Shit, it was a cold life. The meal only half filled him. He was famished and in need of something else, someone else. Alani skipped in his mind like a scratched record of a love song. He missed her so much that it hurt. It hurt worse than the fucking bullet she had plugged him with.

I would have shot me too.

Oddly, it only made her more desirable. Her ability to defend that which she loved. A mother's strength was unmatched when it came to her offspring and Ethic found it admirable. It was the code he lived by. It was a love he wished his children knew. A motherly love was foreign to them, but it was second nature for Alani. She was strong and true. When she said something, she meant it, no bending. When she had told him to stay away from her, she wasn't like other women who said it only to get a man to plead to come back. Alani meant every word. He had violated her request and she had taken action to reinforce it. She was more gangster than half the soldiers he knew working corners. He knew plenty niggas who barked big but never came off the porch to bite. Alani had proven that she didn't speak just to speak. It was the reason he hadn't pushed harder to see her after being released from the hospital. Bella had come home smelling like Alani, and Ethic had held her so tightly just to get a piece of that beautiful woman. He picked up his phone, and before he could think twice about dialing her number, he tapped her name. It rang until it went to voicemail and he ended the call, in disappointment. His stomach turned. Destroying his chance with this woman had made him question if he had ever loved a woman before her. Losing the others hadn't felt like this. Even Raven hadn't devastated him so. This felt life-altering, like he was a different man after her. She made him question if he was as honorable as he deemed. The buzz of his phone and her name on his screen surprised him. He slid the bar to the right, in angst. There was no delay. There was no ego or want to play it cool. He answered that mu'fucka like he had been sitting by the phone waiting all day.

"Lenika," he said.

She didn't answer but she was there. He could feel her. He held the phone so tightly that he thought he would break it. She didn't want to talk, so he wouldn't talk, but she had called him and that was enough. He knew she needed his energy.

She's having a rough day.

The remedy to her hard days, to her impossible moments, was his touch and, apparently, this silent connection. So, he obliged her. His stomach tightened, as his throat dried and he felt the burn of emotion stir in him. He was broken. She was broken.

They were pieces of the picture they had tried to draw together. Remnants of something that used to be beautiful. He rubbed his free hand over his head.

Fuck this.

He stood and snatched up his keys, kicking his feet into construction Timberland boots, headed out into the cold, not even caring to put on a coat. She was still there. Still breathing, still listening and he heard the hint of a cry she was stifling. Ethic raced across town, fighting snow and ice, until he was sitting in front of her house. He hopped out of the Range and rushed to her door. "Open the door, baby," he said. He knocked at the door. He heard her gasp, and when she was on the other side of the door, he felt her. She was like a magnet pulling him and he rested his head against the wood, still holding the phone to his ear. Her head rested in angst on the other side.

Ethic's lip trembled, not from the cold of outside, but the chill of her heart. She wasn't going to open the door. He felt it. She wanted too, but Alani wouldn't be Alani if she allowed that door to swing open. "Open the door for me, Lenika. Please, baby," he whispered. There was a full-blown cry on the other end of the line now and he had to squeeze the bridge of his nose to stop his own from running free.

"I can't," she whispered. The call disconnected, and the lights went out inside, as Ethic staggered backward. Frustration mounted in him and he hit the door with flat palms. He leaned into that door, as he felt her on the other side walking away, pulling her energy away, further and further with every step. He nodded, lip trembling, jaw locked, teeth clenched. He retreated to his truck and pulled off into the night, with the heavily realization that what they had couldn't be revived.

CHAPTER 17

Five Months Later

Alani had forgotten how taxing pregnancy could be on a woman's body. She was seven months and there was no longer any hiding behind clothes. Her belly was round and a beautiful brown. Tan stretch marks ran over her skin like interstate lines on an old-school map. A slightly darker line had appeared almost overnight, straight down the center. Whatever she had eaten had her baby boy going crazy inside her. She was so over this pregnancy. It had been rough, and it had been lonely because once she began showing, she had been too afraid to leave the house. She didn't want Ethic finding out under any circumstance, so she was confined to her house. When she was brave, she ventured to the neighboring houses to oversee the work that the contractors had begun over the past few months. Church for pageant practice, the doctor's office, and home. That had been her only outings. She even had her groceries delivered. Nannie was home but not quite back to herself. She had months of therapy ahead of her to try to repair the damage that had been done. Nannie wasn't speaking. The part of her brain that controlled speech had been affected by the stroke, but Alani had faith that God would heal her. If Alani had listened to the doctors, she would have unplugged her great aunt months ago. It was a miracle that Nannie had even opened her eyes again. Alani believed God had a few more tricks left up his sleeve. Nannie was bedridden most of the day and Alani didn't mind caring for her but her days were still lonely. Bella made things easier when she visited. She was Alani's confidante. She came over to read with Alani and watch old, sappy movies that only made Alani cry. Alani had felt a fairytale love like the ones in those movies. It had been more than a script, more than a fantasy, but it had transformed into a horror, like the director of her life had gotten the genre wrong.

She felt a sharp kick to her abdomen and she lifted her shirt to see the metamorphosis of her skin, as a distinct nudge poked through her skin. She placed a hand over it.

She closed her eyes and took a deep breath. "Calm down in there. You're killing me, love," she whispered.

Ethic had respected her space. They were both busy healing from one another, along with the physical things that ailed them. She was grateful for his absence. Even when he dropped Bella off, he never came in. It was like he had given up after that night on her porch. After that, he never intruded on her space again. Every time she saw the tail lights to his car pull away, energy left her. It was like he had hooked a tow up to her heart and hauled it out of her chest, every time he departed. The hurt was still very real, too real to deal with sometimes, and on those days, she wished she had never met him. There were still days that she wished the baby in her stomach didn't exist. She was human, and human beings were fickle creatures. They ran around in rat races and mazes, trying to figure life out. Alani only knew one thing for certain, she was broken-hearted and no amount of time could mend it. She would carry a scar around with her from Ethic for all her days. Noah could build an ark of massive proportions and the tears she cried would still drown it. It just wasn't something she could ever get over.

Not ever. Not now. Not in five years. Not in ten. A lifetime's worth of sorrow was a part of her. Like blood. Like bone. Like muscle. Like organs. If you cut Alani open, sorrow would be as present as any of the others. Christmas night had broken her. She had sobbed into her pillow well into the morning. She had cried so much that she made herself sick. She had gone to the hospital for dehydration. Since then, it had been a roller coaster of ups and downs, all the while the baby boy in her stomach flourished.

Alani went to Nannie's room and peeked in to find her sleeping. The ringing of her phone pulled her back down the hallway to her bedroom. She sat on the bed, Indian-style, as she grabbed her phone off the charger. It was a FaceTime from Bella.

"Hey, baby girl, what's up?" Alani answered. She immediately gagged at her swollen features. Her face was so fat, and her nose was spread so wide. She felt anything but attractive, but Bella insisted on FaceTiming instead of calling when they spoke.

"So, I was thinking, I have a new book boyfriend and his name is Midnight."

Alani hollered. "No, baby girl, Midnight is taken. I'm sorry. Maybe you can have Bullet or something," Alani joked.

"Bullet!" Bella shouted. "We might have to fight over this one."

Alani laughed hard, her belly quaking, as she rubbed it with one hand. "How was school?" Alani asked. She moved her hand to her hair, feathering it. Her hormones had her hair growing back nicely, but Alani had grown fond of the cut. It felt like dead weight had been cut off.

I'll need to call Margo and see if she can squeeze me in.

It was the pregnancy brain that had her thoughts jumping from subject to subject, but she was listening. She was always an open ear for Bella.

"It was fine," Bella answered.

Alani squinted her eyes as she took in Bella's appearance. "I feel like you're wearing makeup. Mascara and eyeliner. Who's the boy?"

"What boy?" Bella asked, turning red.

"The boy that has you wearing makeup," Alani said. "Apparently, you've graduated from book boyfriends."

"His name is Dionte," Bella whispered. "He doesn't even know I exist."

Alani shook her head. "And soooo you're wearing makeup to get him to notice you?"

Bella shrugged. "All the other girls wear it. They dress different too, but my daddy is so strict. I can't really wear what they wear. He pays attention to them. I don't know. I just thought it would make me look older."

Alani felt something sear her. Protectiveness. That's what it was. Pure, old, maternal instinct. Bella was kicking up dirt inside her heart, uncovering the part of her that she thought had gone into the ground with her daughter. "Older? How old is this boy?"

"Fourteen," Bella answered.

Alani raised a brow. In the hood, kids were fucking by 14. *Who the hell is this little boy?*

"Well, Bella, the last thing you want to do is get his attention for the wrong reasons. Those girls with the makeup and the stank clothes..."

She elicited a grin from Bella with that comment.

"They have to put all that stuff on because they aren't full on the inside, B. They want to all look the same and all dress the same, talk the same, flirt the same, attract the same boy. When you don't feel beautiful in here..." Alani pointed to her own chest. "You have to dress the outside up with extra stuff to fool other people. I know who you are on the inside. I know you've been taught to love yourself, because I had a small taste of that same medicine from the person who gave it to you."

"My dad?" Bella asked.

Alani nodded. "Nobody makes a girl feel as beautiful as your daddy," Alani whispered. A beat of silence took over her, but she pushed it aside because this wasn't about her. This was about Bella. "Subtlety and being unique is pretty; overdoing it and being more of the same makes no sense. How is he supposed to notice you if you're doing the same thing as everybody else? Nobody looks like the prize. He just thinks he has options because there are so many of the same thing that he doesn't have to treat any of you special. Be special, B. You're beautiful and your spirit, your friendship..." Alani paused to take a breath, as she placed a hand over her heart. "He would be lucky for you to choose him, not the other way around. Fall back, wipe off the extra stuff and be you. He'll notice. Trust me."

Bella nodded.

The sound of glass breaking caused Alani's neck to snap to the side as she peered into the darkened hallway.

"What was that?" Bella asked.

Alani stood, the phone still facing her but worried lines wrinkling her forehead.

"I don't know," Alani said in a low tone. She walked to the window. There was a car in front of her home. A Cadillac XTS sat in front of her house and Alani frowned.

"Alani?" Bella said. "I can't see you."

Alani reached for the switch in the hallway, but nothing happened. "The lights are out, Bella. Hold on, baby."

Alani was half way down the hall, near the overlook and she looked down to her first floor. She took another step and glass sliced into her bare feet. "Shit!" she shouted. She looked up. The light bulb had been busted out and then he stepped from the shadows.

"Bitch, you tried to send me to jail for that nigga?"

Alani's bladder failed her, and she felt panic, as urine ran down her leg.

"Alani? Who is that? Alani!" Bella called.

Cream slapped the phone from her hand, sending it skidding down the hallway floor. He wrapped callous hands around her neck so swiftly that Alani couldn't even think about running.

"I didn't," she whispered. "Cream, please. I didn't," Alani gasped, as she clawed at his hand. Technically, it wasn't a lie. She hadn't said a word. Bella's story was enough. The police had tried to speak with her before speaking to Bella, but she was mentally inept…too traumatized to speak to anyone. The psychologists had called it a mental lapse, a breakdown from all the tragedy she had experienced in a short period of time. She hadn't uttered a single word until Bella had come to her room that night. When she had found out about Cream's arrest, she did nothing to reverse it either, however, so perhaps she was guilty. Perhaps, her time had come to pay. *If he kills me, it all ends. It all just goes away. This baby, this hole inside me. It just all fades to black.* "You're pregnant, La?" She heard the heartbreak in his voice and she couldn't help but wonder when he had started loving her so much. When had he ever shown her that he cared enough for this to hit him to this magnitude? Or maybe it was because he knew whom she was pregnant by. That was the sting. This was an ego thing, a disrespect thing, it had nothing to do with love. Once a man felt disrespected, it became a dangerous thing. Cream's need to prove that he was the man, that he was more gangster, more capable, more malicious than Ethic would be taken out on Alani. She could see it in his eyes. "You having that nigga baby? You just replacing my daughter? Like she didn't exist?"

She felt that. She felt it in her bones because she battled with those exact sentiments, daily.

"I'm not, Cream. I didn't know who he was. I haven't touched him since then. I swear," she cried. "You know me!" she was screaming, pleading, and his grip was loosening. "She was my everything, Cream. When you were cheating and lying, she was my happiness. I loved her with every bit of me."

Cream released her and rested his back against the wall. His face was different. There were scars from the beating he had taken months ago, and his eyes were dark, deadly, troubled. They both were so haunted.

"The nigga killed my baby," Cream whispered.

Alani's eyes were pools of remorse, as she stepped bloody feet toward him. She reached up to hug him and he placed his hands on her belly.

"I'm sorry, La," he said. She pulled back, brows dipped in confusion. *Sorry for the beating? Sorry for the glass? For the blame?* He didn't leave her guessing long. "I got to kill his."

He shoved her so hard that she went flying over the ledge of her second floor. The thud that she made when she hit the floor echoed through the house. Pain exploded in her like a bomb had been detonated, but she couldn't move. She couldn't even scream. The shock of the impact stunned her. All she could do was pray that Ethic would feel her because she still felt him...every day and every night she felt his energy. Hers was leaving her and she needed him. She finally needed him. *God, please let him come.*

"Daddy, I have to tell you something," Bella said, as she stood at the bottom of the basement steps. His eyes were closed, and his torso was turned to the right, praying hands rested against his chest, as his legs lunged deeply. He didn't answer. She knew he was zoned out, in mid-session of an intense yoga routine. He had been doing that a lot lately, escaping the real world and retreating into his mind. He had spent more time in the basement than he ever had before.

"Daddy!" Bella's voice was forceful, urgent, and Ethic's eyes opened. He had never heard her sound like that before. He saw trepidation, felt it even, radiating off his little girl. His instinct to fuck shit up over her reared its ugly head. "We need to go to Alani's."

"Not now, baby girl," Ethic said.

He was trying to flush Alani from his system. This yoga session was directly related to the thought of her invading his brain, now here was Bella bringing her up.

"Daddy, it's important," she said. She was twiddling her fingers and sort of bouncing in angst. She resembled Eazy. It was the little dance he did when he had done something and was afraid to tell the truth about it.

Ethic released a sigh to curve his impatience and stood to his feet. He grabbed his towel from the floor and wiped the sweat from his body. Something was up. He let his silence pull whatever Bella was hiding right out of her. She was his daughter. He knew when something was wrong, and he knew just how much pressure to apply to get her to spit it out.

"I have to tell you something and you're going to be mad," Bella whispered. Her eyes couldn't contain the tears, if she wanted to.

"What did I tell you?" Ethic asked, calmly.

"If I tell you the truth you'll never be upset with me, but that's the thing," she paused. "I've been lying. I've been lying for a long time."

Ethic's brows lifted. Bella wasn't naturally dishonest. His body tensed, as he thought of what could be so bad that she had told an ongoing lie. Something where Alani was involved.

"I just really need to get to Alani's. She might need help and I just want to make sure she's okay," Bella rambled. She had backpedaled away from the truth and Ethic knew it had to be bad.

"Why wouldn't she be okay, Bella?" Ethic asked, as he slipped a shirt over his head.

Bella's bottom lip was heavy and quivering.

"I think that man is there with her. The one from before. Her daughter's father," Bella whispered. "We were on FaceTime and something happened. Someone was in her house and then she dropped the phone. I think he hit her."

Ethic's feet moved before his mind could process the information. Cream was supposed to be locked up. Had he gotten out? How had he missed that? Ethic was taking the stairs, two at a time, and Bella was on his heels. He was trying to be a different man, a less violent man, one Alani could see fit to forgive, but...

If that nigga lay a hand...

He couldn't even think the thought. He grabbed a jacket and stepped into shoes as he picked up his phone, dialing her number. It rang in his ear and he was halfway out the door when Bella finally released her secret.

"Daddy, she's pregnant!"

CHAPTER 18

Ma'am, can you tell me your name?"

Alani laid on the stretcher, her neck stabilized, as she was being rushed through the halls of the hospital. Four people surrounded her and they all spoke at once, urgency lacing their tones.

"Umm..." She took a deep breath. She was dazed and disoriented. The throb in her head was so loud.

"Alani. Alani Hill," she stammered.

"Alani, can you tell me what hurts?" the doctor asked.

Alani was still in shock. "Nothing. I mean, my baby. How is he? I can't feel anything. I can't feel him anymore," she rushed out, panic seizing her.

Her head was ringing and her back ached, but she didn't care about herself. She just wanted to know that her baby was okay.

"My doctor works here. Dr. McEwen," Alani said.

"Let's get Dr. McEwen here, now!" the woman in the white coat, standing over her said. "Alani, we're going to get an MRI of your brain and make sure there's no internal bleeding, while we wait for your OB. Is that, okay? Is there any pain anywhere?"

"My head. It's pounding, and my back," she whispered. She blinked away tears. She was terrified. Everyone around her was moving so fast and their expressions were so grim. They lifted her. "My aunt. She lives with me. She had a stroke. She can't be there alone."

"Your aunt is the one who called the police, Ms. Hill. She's just fine," the woman said. "Let's just focus on you, okay?"

They transferred her from the stretcher and laid her on a sliding platform before she was glided into a round machine. Alani's heart was riddled with anxiety and she tried to breathe through the panic.

"We're okay. They have doctors here that are going to make sure everything is fine," she said, aloud. The space was so tight that Alani felt like she was suffocating. A voice came through an intercom.

"Alani, you're very lucky. I don't see anything to worry about on this side of the desk. No broken bones, no internal bleeding. A severe concussion, however, but considering, I'd say that's pretty good."

Alani sighed in relief. "And the baby?"

"Once we pull you out, Dr. McEwen is waiting to examine you."

Alani felt relief. If she was fine, her baby would be too, right? They pulled her out and allowed her to sit up. She was sore, achy, beaten, but nothing was broken. She insisted on standing to see for herself.

"Take it easy. Lie down and we'll take you up to fetal medicine. Your doctor is waiting for you."

Alani climbed onto the hospital bed and a male nurse came to rise the bars on the side and then proceeded to deliver her upstairs.

She smiled, when she saw her doctor.

"Alani, I hate to see you under these circumstances. Let's get you onto the bed and take a look at that little nugget in there, eh?" the woman said.

Her bedside manner was so gentle and so unalarming that she made Alani calm instantly. If there was something wrong, her doctor would be more urgent, right?

Alani laid back and closed her eyes, as the doctor lifted her shirt. She felt the cold gel against her belly and then felt the pressure from the scope. It rolled across her stomach, but something was different. Every other time there had been a steady hum that filled the room. Where was that hum? Why was it absent? She felt her doctor press harder, harder than she ever had before. Still no sound and Alani knew. Alani knew before the woman even fixed her lips to move.

"Alani, I'm sorry, but there's no heartbeat."

Alani lifted weak eyes to the doctor's. "I'm sorry, what?" she asked. There had to be a mistake. She had just felt him kicking less than an hour ago. She had just felt...

Her eyes filled. "There has to be a mistake. Check again," she whispered.

"Alani..."

"Check again!" Alani demanded. Such despair clouded the room, as the doctor rolled the scope over her belly, again. She pointed to the screen. "There's the fetus."

Alani recoiled at the term. Fetus. It was too scientific. So technical. It was words of detachment.

"There's no pulse, Alani. I'm so sorry. We need to get him out of you."

Alani was drowning. She was standing on dry land, but somehow invisible water was rising above her head as everything around her muted.

"All of our O.R.'s are booked right now, but I'd really like to get the fetus out immediately. How do you feel about pushing?"

"Push my dead baby out?" Alani whispered in disbelief.

"It's important to deliver as quickly as possible."

Alani nodded, but she felt no strength. The staff in the room sprang into action, preparing the bed she laid on and her for delivery. It was like she was dreaming, they all moved in slow motion, as they put an IV in her.

"Would you like an epidural?"

Alani shook her head. No. She wanted to feel every moment of this because it was all she would have to remember this baby by. The pain of this night. They induced her labor, starting her on Pitocin and breaking her water. She felt like a science experiment from all the poking and prodding. An hour passed by before the contractions intensified and she dilated.

"Okay, you're at 10. I need you to push. It's time."

"I can't," Alani whispered. "I can't do this." The defeat in her voice caused her doctor to look up. Alani was tortured by the sounds of babies crying outside her door, of mothers screaming as they gave birth, of families celebrating. The miracle of life was all around her. This was the labor and delivery floor. Why was there no cheering outside her room? No cigars being passed around by friends of the father? No eager eyes peeking through the glass window, attempting to get the first peek at a new baby? Inside her room, it was like the morgue. It didn't seem fair. Alani had cursed this pregnancy the entire way, hating it, resenting it, wishing it had never happened. It wasn't until she discovered she had lost her baby did she realize how selfish she had been. She felt responsible for this. Her words, her wishes, had been granted in the worst way; and as she lay, sweaty and in pain, she desperately wanted to take it all back. There was power in the tongue and hers had placed a curse on her child. A part of her didn't want to push because she would have to face the fact that her baby, Ethic's baby, their love in human form was gone. She hadn't wanted it until this very moment. She hadn't realized how much it had meant until now and it was too late to do anything but mourn.

"I'm sorry but you have to," the doctor urged.

"I can't!" Alani screamed.

"You can."

The baritone was sturdy, strong, and Alani lifted weak eyes toward the door. Her breath caught in her throat, as she sat up on her elbows, legs open, hospital gown clinging to her tired body. Woe was all over her. It was the first time she had seen him in months. She hadn't wanted to. She had been so full of hate that she wondered if it had infected her womb and poisoned their son. She shook her head. She wanted to speak but couldn't form words, as sobs replaced them. Ethic crossed the room and removed his jacket, placing it on the empty chair next to the bed.

"Is this the father?" Dr. McEwen asked, looking up at Alani, in confusion.

Alani was silent, and as her eyes filled with fresh tears, she searched for a reaction in Ethic. He was the father and she had selfishly hidden his child from him. Alani knew her reasons for keeping him away were valid, but now with a dead child rotting in her womb, she felt venal. At least she had gotten a chance to know this baby. She had felt him, she had talked to him, and heard a heartbeat. She had seven, beautiful months to mother this child, to bond with it while it grew inside her, and she hadn't shared any of that with Ethic. She knew that the greatest hurt in the room would be his because she saw hope in his eyes. He was anticipating a healthy delivery, she could see the anxiety of an expectant father dancing through him. She couldn't tell him that this baby was dead. She didn't even want to believe it herself.

"I am," Ethic whispered, never taking his eyes off Alani. "Am I?"

She nodded and opened her mouth to fill in the blanks for him, but only her cries slipped out. His chest swelled, as he took in a deep breath, overwhelmed by the revelation. She was beautiful. The roundness of her face, her distended belly, her messy hair, even her swollen nose, it was a vision. She was lovely, she was a woman who was giving birth to his child.

"I'm very sorry for your loss."

The words were odd in the delivery room. You didn't hear those words when babies were born. They didn't belong there. It was the only thing that jarred his attention from Alani. He set incensed eyes on the doctor, his brow bent in confusion. *Who the fuck is she talking to?*

"The trauma she sustained today was significant. There is no heartbeat."

Alani covered her mouth, as she gasped. She would never get used to hearing it and she saw Ethic waver as his jaw clenched and his temple throbbed. He turned from her and placed both hands on top of his head. He took a step toward the door, his shoulders rounding over, as if he wanted to double over in pain, but he recovered, never folding. He cleared his throat and lowered his hands, as he turned around, his face convulsing as he held it in. His lips trembled, as he opened them to speak, before deciding to trap his bottom lip between his teeth. No words. He couldn't find them. This news was testing him, threatening to tear him apart. The revelation had knocked the air from his lungs and it took all his will not to bitch up. He nodded, as he swiped a hand over his face, slowing at his bearded chin before falling in despair at his side. He was lost, but like a road map leading to sanity, he looked to Alani for help...for clarity. The doctor had to be wrong, but as he stared at her, through her, he knew it was true and a spark of resentment flashed within him. She was the most beautiful, ugly sight to behold.

He was holding back, she knew it. He was containing anger, sadness, probably a bit of hate as he sniffed away his emotion and swiped another strong hand over his mouth. He squared his shoulders, took a deep breath, and then walked back over to Alani's side. He sat her up in the bed, climbing behind her, sitting her between his legs. She melted into his chest, as he wrapped his hands around her body. Finally, someone to hold her up, to place the heaviness on…help. Ethic was the best type of help. Her chest caved in, as she cried. He placed his hands on her bulging, lifeless belly. She had envisioned his hands there so many times. She had felt guilty for wanting his lips to kiss her belly and to rub her feet at night, so guilty that it made her hate herself for being so weak for him.

"You've got to push," he whispered in her ear, his words breaking, as he stared at his strong, black hands against her brown skin. The contrast of the colors were beautiful. Her belly was beautiful, but it was lifeless and for Alani to live she had to release the dead. He kissed her shoulder and Alani's eyes closed as she locked the feeling into her memory. She knew she would need it for later. Somehow, she knew his touch would be scarce after this day and she wanted to remember how it felt. They had been writing a love story since the day they met, and it was full of pain. She knew this secret she had kept would end it once and for all.

"I can't," she sobbed, as her sweaty hair stuck to her face and she continued to squeeze her eyes closed.

"Not by yourself, but I'm right here. You're strong, Lenika."

"I'm not," she groaned, as she shook her head against his chest. She was too weak to lift her head. If she was giving birth to a baby she could take home, perhaps she would have been able to muster up some strength, but she was in no rush to face reality.

"But I am and I'm here now. I've got you," Ethic reassured. It was the thing that made Ethic so different from other men. When he said something, he meant it, and when he meant something, his actions reinforced his words. This man, who was supposed to be her man, was solid. He was dependable. He was consistent. He had left a void in her life that would remain empty for all her days because there was no upgrade after him.

"I just want to keep him inside. When I push him out, they're going to take him from me," she cried.

"Him?" Ethic's voice was filled with a mixture of sadness and discovery. He had another son, one he would never get the chance to know, and Alani knew it was her fault. "No one is going to take him until you're ready. That's my word, but I need you to push. Okay?"

Alani nodded and opened her eyes. She pursed her lips and blew out a sharp breath, mentally preparing herself for the upcoming contraction.

"Okay, it's important that we get the baby delivered. He can't stay inside you much longer. You ready? Give me a big push in one..."

Alani's belly quaked, as she cried. Ethic put his lips to her ear. "I want to meet my son. You got to be strong for me. Take my hands."

"Two..." the doctor counted.

Ethic held out his hands and she gripped them, as she felt her insides tighten as the next contraction began. Her mouth fell open, her fingertips curled as her nails dug into Ethic's hands.

"Three!"

"Grrrr," Alani growled, as she clenched her teeth and pushed. Ethic kissed the top of her head.

"You're doing so good, baby," Ethic whispered. He was choking on resentment. She could hear it, but he was so self-less that he put his feelings on hold so that he could help her navigate through this tragedy.

"Yes, you are," the doctor agreed. "I need you to do it again. One, two, three."

"Push, Lenika, push," Ethic whispered, as he held her body firmly, his chest acting as her support as she tried again. He felt her, giving her all, pouring every ounce of strength she had into delivering his son. He could feel her heart pounding; her parted thighs trembled, as two nurses held them open. Her hair was drenched in sweat, her face salted from tears, her voice raspy from the guttural screams erupting from her.

"It hurts!" she cried.

"I know!" Ethic whispered, passionately. "I know. I feel it too," he said, as he released one of her hands to place it on her forehead, pulling it backward, slightly, to kiss her temple. He wasn't talking about what she was feeling physically, he had no idea about the pain a woman endured during labor; but that other pain, the pain he knew that was crippling her…he felt that shit. "You're broken. I know, but you deserve to see his face. We've got to say goodbye to him, Lenika. You're his mother. I can do a lot, but I can't do this part for you. I can do everything after this. I can hold you while you cry, I can kiss him before we lay him to rest, but this is your part. So, push, baby. Push."

"Aghhhh!!!" Alani felt the pressure between her legs ease, as her baby passed through her and she collapsed against Ethic in exhaustion. Her body went limp in his arms.

"That's my girl," Ethic whispered, as he kissed her neck.

The doctor delivered the placenta and was still between her legs, stitching her up as Alani croaked, "Can I see him?"

The nurse cleaned the baby gently, as Ethic arose from the bed. His child was the only thing that could pull him from Alani in that moment. He was amazed at her strength, hypnotized at the miracle of a woman's body, but his son, his silent son, was somehow calling him.

There was a baby wailing, screaming, at the top of its lungs.

Ethic heard it. Why couldn't anyone else hear that shit? Why were they ignoring it?

The dread in his stomach wrenched, as the reticence in the room deafened him. He would cut out his own heart to give it to his son, if he could. He would lay down his life to hear just one cry. The nurse handed the baby to Ethic and his resolve detonated. The bluish hue of his son's face weakened him. Ethic couldn't see past the tears in his eyes. He held his son in one arm, tucked him under his rib like a football, and wiped a hand down his face with the other, all the while keeping his back to his Alani.

"Aww, man," he whispered. Ethic couldn't breathe. He was drowning from the tears he was holding back. He could feel the emotion rising in him and he was bobbing at the surface, trying to keep his head above water. He lifted his son to his lips and kissed his forehead, not caring that there was still traces of Alani's blood present. It was in that moment that Ethic understood why Alani could never forgive him, because he didn't think he would ever forgive her for this.

I could have protected her. If I had known, I would have protected you. He couldn't stop staring at his newborn child or was it 'newdead'? He wasn't born. He wasn't breathing. Dead. A baby. His baby. And she didn't tell him. She had coerced his daughter onto her team to help her tell this malicious lie. He felt anger. No, anger wasn't enough. It was rage mixed with an unfillable emptiness.

"Ethic?" Alani's voice was so small that she sounded childlike and he closed his eyes. He knew his hurt couldn't compare to hers. Women were created to give life. No woman should know what it felt like to have a tomb in her belly. Alani had birthed the dead, and after burying her first child he could only imagine the strife she felt. He tucked his anger, doing what men were expected to do - *"un-feel."* He turned to her, knowing he had to be the root that kept her planted in sanity because he had seen her go crazy and her version of crazy was dangerous. Losing their child in this way was enough to send her back to that place.

"He's beautiful like his mama."

Ethic handed her the baby and Alani bawled. She adjusted the receiving blanket around his face, so she could see him clearly. He looked like Ethic. His little, button nose and closed, slanted eyes sat on top of skin that should have been light because all babies were born light until their true color came in, but instead, he was blue. He was a member of Ethic's tribe. Alani instantly saw Bella and Eazy in her son. She laid him on her chest and lifted her eyes to the sky, sucking in a deep breath. How had she ever thought she would be able to give him away? This was their son…their love…evidence of what they shared right in her arms. She could have never let him go. The old adage *'be careful what you wish for'* rang true, because now Alani wasn't given the choice. A day that was supposed to be filled with joy had been substituted with agony.

"I'll give you some time," the doctor said, as she finished up and exited the room.

Ethic sat on the edge of the hospital bed. Alani leaned into him, as she rubbed their son's back, gently, patting him as if he could feel it, as if she could soothe him, as if she had just nursed and was awaiting a burp. Her lips quivered, as she placed a hand over the back of her son's head, pulling him to her shoulder and resting her head against his cheek. "I just felt him this morning. He was just kicking and then…" She stopped speaking, as thoughts of Cream filled her mind.

Ethic stood, reading her thoughts. The tender spots inside him, the soft side that he reserved for his children, went rigid. He flipped the switch that turned off his emotions and Alani felt the mood change in the room. The temperature even chilled and Alani felt a shiver meet her spine.

"I've got to go," he said.

"Ethic, please, don't," she wept, when he was halfway to the door. She knew where he was headed. An innocent baby had gone to heaven today, somebody had to pay the toll. "Just come back and name your son. He needs a name."

Ethic lingered but didn't face her. Malice clung to him, destroying the spirit of the man she knew. She could see it eating away at him and she was sure some of it was aimed at her.

"I pressed pause on a nigga I should have erased. I let him breathe when I knew what needed to be done," Ethic said, his tone incensed with an eerie calm. It was the type of calm that overcast the skies before a violent storm would roll in. Alani stared at his tense back, the muscles of his strong shoulders were tight, as he bent over to grip the edge of the sink that sat near the door. Sparks of anger ignited in him, as he swept the medical supplies on the counter to the floor. Alani jumped, but she was afraid to speak. Ethic had hesitated to take Cream away from her, but now she was burying her son...their son...but she knew in this moment it was fuck her. This was *his* son. She knew how much fatherhood meant to him. "I hesitated because I know what you see when you look at me. You see a killer. You see a monster and I didn't want to be that to you...not again. I wanted to prove that I could be something else, somebody that was worthy of you, so I let him live." He turned and walked over to Alani, leaning over her and gripping her chin, forcing her to look at him. Her eyes were full of sadness and a twinge of fear, her hands still holding their baby, securely, as Ethic glanced down at him. "This is all I am. All I know how to be. A protector. The list ain't long, but I'll murder any nigga for the ones that I love," he said. His grip was firm, but his thumb slid across her cheek, wiping away the tear that was making its way down. He was a phenomenon of a man. Harsh, yet gentle. Terrifying, yet soothing to her soul. Maybe it was the reason why she loved and hated him equally.

"For Bella?" she whispered. He didn't respond, but she could see the irises of his eyes flicker. She was his daughter, blood-born,

Ethic would rip a man's heart out of his chest for her. "For Eazy?" she continued. His first son, the carrier of his bloodline, the purest version of himself. Ethic would tear down cities for that boy. "Morgan?" Alani named, her tears unstoppable. He lowered his head, as he thought of what he had already done for her. Alani nodded too because seeing this force, this hurricane, building within him, she knew she was witnessing the same rage that had sent him to her house the night he had killed her family.

"And me." She didn't ask this time because she didn't need to question it. She knew. She had always known. Ethic would kill for her. "And him." she looked down at their son. Ethic's soul was tormented. It was sinful to love someone as much as he loved Alani. He lowered his lips to his son's head and kissed him once more, the chill of death sent a shiver down Ethic's spine. Life wasn't fair. Where were the red cheeks, the thrush-covered tongue, the incessant cries that would have him sleep deprived for months? The shitty diapers that they would flip a coin over to decide who would change him? No one knew loss greater than Ethic, but as he felt Alani shudder beneath him, he thought, *she knows.* He turned, pinched the bridge of his nose, and headed for the door. Alani felt doom cloud the room, as his heavy steps carried him away, taking her strength with him. He was walking out, and she wasn't sure if he would come back.

"You owe me!" she yelled to his back, snot running out her nose and pooling in the valley above her lips. Alani lost it, as the words she had held back for months flew out her mouth. "You owe me, and I don't want you to leave. I don't want you to kill for me. I want you to *not* kill for me, Ethic. You're wrong. I don't think you're a monster. I think you're a beautiful, loving, loyal man, and I've fought myself for months because I love you. I'm ashamed that I love you, even after what you did. You made a horrible mistake, but you're not a monster. I want you to be around for your kids. I don't want you to go after Cream because I know what he's capable of. He is a monster and I don't know if you'll come back because you paused for me. You hesitated. He won't. I want you to be here for your kids, Ethic. I want you to be here for...for..."

"For what?" Ethic asked.

"For me!" she shouted. "You buried my daughter. You put the dirt on her casket. I couldn't let her go and you stopped everything you were doing to bury her. Now, I need you to stay because I can't let him go either and I need you to help me. My babies are dead, and if something happens to you, who is going to help me live? Who is going to teach me how to breathe again?"

Ethic stood there, splintered. He had wanted her forgiveness. He had prayed to a God he didn't even know if he believed in, he had been so desperate. But as he stood in front of her, he knew that what they shared was filled with too much pain to ever survive. They would bleed each other dry, while loving one another to death. Somebody had to end the cycle of hurt. He had hurt her, she had damn near killed him, and still, he wanted her. Still, he craved her, like she was made of good dope and he was an addict. Most men were pulled in by good pussy, and women used that as their weapons to keep men rooted. Alani had pulled Ethic in with her spirit, attracting him to her alter like she was godly. Perhaps, that had been the sin that made them so tragic. Ethic worshipped her, and God's jealousy had sabotaged them from the start. He didn't know, but standing there watching her hold his son in her arms, knowing that there were months that he could have spent kissing her belly, feeling him flourish inside her, made Ethic enraged. He couldn't turn his gangster off. It wasn't something he imitated or a role he played. Ethic was simply cut from the cloth that made him crave blood after a loss this tragic.

He was more Malcolm than Martin. He couldn't be who she wanted. He couldn't save her because he couldn't save himself. "You got to breathe for yourself, Lenika," he said.

Ethic may as well have plucked her heart from her chest and crushed it between his strong hands. He was too good of a man to ever hurt her on purpose, but she knew him well enough to notice his passive aggression. She hadn't missed the fact that he no longer called her Alani, almost like he refused to, like he had decided that they really were just strangers passing each other by and it hurt. "You know me, Ethic," she cried.

"You kept the fact that I had a child growing inside you away from me. You convinced my daughter to lie to my face every day. I could have had months. I could have loved him for months. If I had known he would still be here," Ethic's voice cracked, but he quickly gathered himself. "I killed your daughter." He saw her recoil. Hearing him say it aloud injured her, but he had to state the obvious. He had to lift the veil that they had been viewing each other through. They had built one another up so high in their heads that they were neglecting to see reality. They were poisonous to one another. When their paths had intersected, the devil had marked an X at the spot. Something demonic was intertwined in their connection. He knew she wouldn't understand, he was aware that it would hurt, but one of them had to let go. "We don't know each other at all."

When Ethic walked out, Alani wanted to break, but there were no pieces left of herself to dismantle. The shards of her life were already at her feet. They had been walked all over. Life had been cruel to her. She stared at her precious son. He was the only evidence she had that proved she had known love - once upon a time. She lifted him to her face and kissed him once more, and then laid him on her chest.

"You are love, my little one. Too much love for this ugly world," she whispered. She couldn't stop kissing his face. What she wouldn't do to be able to see the corner of his mouth turn up in a smile the way her daughter's had done all those years ago when she had been born. "Your big sister is going to be right by your side." She caught the sob that came to her, trapping it in her throat. "God, please take care of my babies." Her thoughts drifted to Ethic. "Please, take care of him too and give me the strength to walk away."

R.I.P
Love Ezra Okafor

TO BE CONTINUED...IN ETHIC 3
COMING DECEMBER 1ST, 2018